SEASIDE

Embrace

Seaside Summers
Love in Bloom Series

Melissa Foster

ISBN-13: 978-1-941480-28-1
ISBN-10: 1941480284

SEASIDE EMBRACE

Cover Design: Natasha Brown

WORLD LITERARY PRESS
PRINTED IN THE UNITED STATES OF AMERICA

A Note from Melissa

Hunter Lacroux has got quite an edge to him. I knew he needed a strong, passionate woman who could not only stand up to him, but also stand by his side in good times and bad, and Jana Garner is his perfect match. I hope you enjoy their super-sexy love story as much as I enjoyed writing it!

The best way to keep up to date with new releases, sales, and exclusive content is to sign up for my newsletter. www.MelissaFoster.com/Newsletter

ABOUT THE LOVE IN BLOOM BIG-FAMILY ROMANCE COLLECTION

Seaside Summers is just one of the series in the Love in Bloom big-family romance collection. Characters from each series make appearances in future books, so you never miss an engagement, wedding, or birth. If this is your first Love in Bloom novel, you have many more loving, loyal heroes and sexy, sassy heroines waiting for you!

Download a free Love in Bloom series checklist here: www.MelissaFoster.com/SO

Get **free** first-in-series ebooks and see my current sales here: www.MelissaFoster.com/LIBFree

Visit the Love in Bloom Reader Goodies page for downloadable checklists, family trees, and more! www.MelissaFoster.com/RG

Be sure to check out my online bookstore for pre-orders, early releases, bundles, and exclusive discounts on ebooks, print, and audiobooks. Ebooks can be sent to the e-reader of your choice and audiobooks can be listened to on the free and easy-to-use BookFunnel app. Shop my store: shop.melissafoster.com

THE SCENT OF patchouli and sex hung in the air as Jana Garner slid silently from the sheets in the unfamiliar room. A thin glow from the streetlights seeped between the heavy curtains, cutting a path across Hunter Lacroux's bare ass. God, he had a perfect ass: firm and squeezable at once. The kind of butt that Jana knew would defy gravity and still be pure perfection well into his graying years. She couldn't help but admire his powerful physique one last time. Something to draw upon later when she would surely berate herself for hooking up yet again with the unfairly irresistible pigheaded man.

One beautifully sculpted arm arched across his forehead, and the other stretched across the pillow on which she'd slept, revealing the tattoo of the four essential life elements wrapping around his bicep. She'd asked him about it once, and he'd said he was an *earthy* guy. She didn't linger on his tattoo for long. His broad chest was too tantalizing, and it led to ripped abs. Abs that, even when he was sleeping, were perfectly defined and lickable. *And oh so delicious.* Her gaze drifted lower, to hips that held the secrets of perfect thrusts, and—*lucky for her*—never seemed to tire. The sheets were bunched across his danger zone, which was an ideal location for them, because there were two things about Hunter Lacroux that drove Jana wild: his wickedly dark eyes that made her forget all the reasons why she should never touch him and that trouser snake of his that brought such immense pleasure, it kept her coming back for more.

Hunter was the one man on the planet she should stay away from and the only one she seemed unable to deny. She tiptoed around the bed and picked up her miniskirt and top, searching for her bra and panties and wondering how she'd ended up here again. She'd been out with her sister, Harper, her friend Sky, and Sky's fiancée, Sawyer, at a bar in Provincetown, when Sky's brothers Hunter and Grayson and their friend Clark had shown up. She vaguely remembered getting into a heated debate with Hunter. *Don't we always?* Hunter knew Jana had been training under her brother Brock, a local boxing champ, for almost three years, and he'd been intent on giving her shit about women infiltrating a *man's* sport.

Asshole.

The next thing she knew they were several shots of tequila to the wind and stumbling along Commercial Street to…? She looked around the room. *This place*, wherever that was. It looked like a motel bedroom, but in reality, knowing Hunter, it could have been a friend's house where they'd crashed for the night.

Tequila. It was always her undoing. She should know better than to do shots of it anytime—but especially when *he* was around. She momentarily wondered why her sister hadn't dragged her ass away from him. Harper knew she had fallen into bed with him before and had sworn off him. Damn her.

She glanced at her reflection in the mirror above the dresser. Her long blond hair was knotted and tangled, and her eyes were bloodshot. She definitely had that recently fucked look. *I really need to stop doing this.* Her eyes dropped to the reflection of Hunter. *Especially with you.*

If she were honest with herself, she'd admit that she needed to stop blaming Harper, too, and take some responsibility for her actions. She was twenty-five, for goodness' sake, not sixteen.

She stole another glance at Hunter, remembering the way he'd fisted his hands in her hair, tugging until her scalp stung, and nearly growled her name as he found his release. The man was an animal in the sack, better than any man she'd ever been with. She didn't do relationships, not after a string of horrible breakups and hurt feelings. She'd sampled enough men over the years to be certain of two things. Men as talented in bed as Hunter were hard to come by—*although*, she mused, *easy to come with*—and if she were looking to settle into a monogamous relationship, which she definitely wasn't, it wouldn't be with a player like him.

She pulled on her clothes and sank down to her knees, looking under the furniture for her panties. *Where the hell were they?* She checked the bathroom and remembered the feel of the cold marble against her bare ass.

Nope. Panties wouldn't be in there.

She tiptoed back into the bedroom, grabbed her purse from the chair and picked up her flip-flops. She glossed over his jeans lying by the foot of the bed and his T-shirt by the door in one last search for her lingerie. Her eyes danced over the chair in the corner, the dresser, the...*Ohmygod.*

Her stomach dipped as she plucked her bra from the top of the lampshade in the corner of the room, where he must have tossed it last night. He was definitely an aggressive and fun lover. Two admirable traits—if they weren't attached to bullheaded Hunter. She didn't know what it was about him that pissed her off, but every time they were together they clashed like oil and water, then tangled in the sheets like starving castaways fed for the first time in years.

One last sweep of the room confirmed that her panties were a lost cause. It wasn't the first time she'd left panties behind—and it probably wouldn't be the last.

She opened the door as quietly as she could and stepped into the brightly lit hallway, tiptoeing out the front door. The sign out front read, WE RENT ROOMS BY THE HOUR! GRAB A DATE AND COME ON IN!

Holy crap. That was a new low, even for her. She ducked her head and continued on her thankfully short walk of shame to her car, where she found a piece of paper shoved in the crack of the door. She recognized Harper's perfectly scripted writing.

J, I tried to dissuade you. Call me later, you big ho! Xox, H

Jana climbed into her car and closed her eyes, letting her head fall back against the headrest. She probably should have thought about the busy day she had today before she'd picked up the first shot last night. She had boxing practice at seven with Brock, and she'd agreed to help out this week at Undercover, her brother Colton's bar. She started the car, and a quick glance at the clock told her she had four hours until she was supposed to meet Brock, which meant she might be able to catch two hours of shut-eye if she was lucky.

Her cell phone vibrated with a text. Caller ID revealed the name DO NOT RESPOND! She cringed, remembering that she'd programmed that in after the last time she'd slept with Hunter. She opened and read the text anyway. *You snuck out again? Seriously? At least when I do that I remember my underwear.*

The smiley face at the end of the text told her that she'd now officially hooked up with Hunter too many times. He was getting comfortable, and that was the last thing she needed.

HUNTER PULLED UP in front of Grunter's Ironworks at ten after eight and parked his younger brother's truck. He and Grayson had been in the metalworking business together for years, and he still never tired of seeing the Grunter's Ironworks emblem on the building.

He climbed from the truck and checked his phone one last time. He hadn't expected Jana to respond to his text, but that didn't stop his gut from knotting at the thought of the saucy little blonde ignoring his message. She was a spitfire of annoyance and sensuality that was hard to ignore. He shoved his phone into his front pocket, chuckling to himself about the little package he'd left for her on his way in to work, and headed into his shop.

Clark Shelton was sitting at his desk with his back to the door, talking on the phone. Hunter and Grayson had grown up with Clark, and they'd hired him to run their business after college. Hunter headed to the back of the shop to begin work on a sculpture he was designing for a local competition. He'd been trying to conceptualize the project for a week, and nothing felt right. But the competition was too big to walk away from. The winner would not only have their work featured in a community beautification project, but would also be awarded a major art contract with a national children's foundation.

The beautification project, and the competition, were funded by Parker Collins, an actress who was building a summer home in Wellfleet. The project was her way of appeasing local residents who were dismayed over the size of her sprawling summer home. The project included creating massive gardens and a gazebo for outdoor concerts across from the harbor. Hunter was designing a sculpture for the competition, and Grayson was working on designs for the gazebo.

Grayson was leaning over the drafting table. He lifted serious eyes to Hunter.

"Jana get home okay last night?"

"I assume so. Why?"

"You *assume* so?" Grayson smirked. "She left before you woke up again, didn't she?"

Hunter scoffed. "Why do you care?"

"Maybe because she's like a sister to Sawyer, our sister's fiancé, remember? I don't want you to fuck up their relationship."

"Let me worry about that, *little* brother. Trust me, she was all in. It's not like I took her against her will." Hell, she'd been all over him, tearing at his clothes before they'd even made it into the rented room.

"A'right, but if you hurt her, you know Sawyer will go crazy on your ass, and I'm not protecting you." Grayson laughed. He and Hunter were both over six feet tall, with athletic physiques, but unlike their other brothers, Pete and Matt, they'd spent their lives out *alpha*ing each other. While their brothers seemed to morph into responsible adults the day they became teenagers, Hunter and Grayson had accepted that role in their professional lives, but their personal lives were a different story altogether.

"Yeah, I'll remember that." He laughed at the idea of Grayson protecting him, but he knew his brother was right. Not only had Sky become close with both Jana and her sister, Harper, but she brought them to almost all their get-togethers, too. It seemed like Jana was always around, and she was the last person he should be hooking up with, considering he usually banged a woman a few times at most, then closed that door. But flames ignited every time he and Jana were in the same room, and she had some kind of crazy hold over him that he'd been unable to escape.

Grayson lowered his gaze to the designs again. "I drew up the plans for the detail around the arches." While neither Grayson nor Hunter was interested in settling down in their personal lives, when it came to their business, they had a whole different attitude. They'd worked hard to build a reputable business that they could be proud of. Their love of their craft showed in their exceptional designs, and that kept them in high demand.

"Cool." Hunter came around the table to check out the designs. The competition required only designs and a small scale model of the gazebo, while the sculptures were expected to be full-size and ready for display by the competition date, which was a little more than five weeks away.

They had gone back and forth about the finite details for the gazebo, initially thinking about using a seashell theme, then moving to more of an overall oceanic theme, until finally they'd agreed on something more naturalistic. When Hunter had presented the idea of tangled vines interspersed with fish and shells, as well as clusters of berries and leaves, Grayson had loved it.

"You any closer on the sculpture?" Grayson asked.

"I'm working on something, but it still doesn't feel right. I figured I'd fabricate some of the pieces and see if I start to feel good about it."

He needed to get on the ball, but for some reason his creativity was at a standstill. Hunter was a perfectionist. This carried over to his clients to the nth degree. He sometimes spent hours laboring over the slightest angles or twists of metal.

The fact that Hunter did not go to the same lengths for a relationship wasn't lost on him.

CHAPTER TWO

BY SEVEN THIRTY Jana's arms felt like wet noodles. She'd arrived at Cape Boxing right on time, and like always, Brock was waiting for her. Her eldest brother was never late to anything, and when he'd agreed to coach Jana, he'd drilled it into her head that she'd be treated like all his other clients. That usually wasn't a problem, but lately these early-morning workouts were hindered by her all-too-often late nights with Hunter. He was definitely a distraction she didn't need. Not while her schedule was already so full with boxing *and* dancing. She loved boxing as much as she loved dancing, but ever since her boss at Cape Dance, the studio where she'd taught for the last two years, left town to open another studio, leaving her to handle all the administrative and marketing work as well as teaching, she'd felt as though she were racing just to keep up with her responsibilities.

"Jana? You sort of spaced out for a minute." Brock slapped the heavy bag with his palm. "Focus."

"Right. Sorry." Focusing was more difficult this morning, when every move made her thighs ache, bringing Hunter, and their latest hookup, to the forefront of her mind.

"Lack of focus leads to—"

"I know. I know. Openings for my opponent," she said. Brock was known as "the Beast" for his status as a local boxing champion, and Jana appreciated the time and attention he gave to coaching her. She'd spent a lot of time in fight clubs. Their mother used to drag her and her siblings to Brock's practices and sparring matches. Harper and Colton had never been enamored of the sport, but Jana had been awestruck from the moment she'd walked into the club until the very second they'd left.

For years she'd fought the urge to train, putting her energy into her dance and theater work, where girls were supposed to be involved, at least according to her parents. But the very essence of the sport spoke to her, from the smell of sweat and conviction that permeated every boxing club to the boxers' grunting and visceral sounds. Having made her mark as a dancer and an actor, she felt as though she'd fulfilled her parents' need for her to be a stereotypical girl, and she'd finally given in to her love of boxing and began training. She related to the look of determination that not only filled a fighter's eyes, but took over their body, plumping up their veins and ripening their muscles. But it was more than the scents and energy of the sport that drew her in. It was the sense of control and power that came along with it. Boxing instilled a different type of confidence than dance had always given her. Dancing made her feel beautiful and feminine, graceful in ways that nothing else ever could. Boxing was all about strength and escaping fear. She had to climb out of her head when she fought, and climbing out of her head was always a good thing.

She focused on the bag as she nailed it with one hard strike after another. She needed a good workout today just to get Hunter off her mind. She hadn't been able to sleep after she'd arrived home in the wee hours of the morning. Every time she closed her eyes she saw the sensual look in Hunter's dark eyes, felt the strength of his hands as they moved over her skin. When she'd showered, she'd seen the abrasions on her inner thighs from the scruff on his jaw and had to wear her long exercise pants to cover the evidence of their tryst. She punched the bag harder, faster, trying to escape the shiver racing down her spine with the thought. But just like the last time they'd hooked up, she knew it was going to take a lot more than a few punches to outrun the memory of those delicious hours spent in Hunter's arms.

"I see Tequila Girl made it in." Sawyer grinned as he joined them by the heavy bag. Sawyer had been the East Coast Boxing Federation cruiserweight titleholder and ranked number three in the Northeast Boxing Association. He'd retired after his doctor told him that one more blow to the head could lead to permanent damage.

"Tequila Girl?" Brock crossed his arms over his broad chest and cocked a brow.

"You're my brother." She grunted as she punched the bag. "Not my babysitter."

"Did Hunter get you home okay?" Sawyer asked.

Jana scowled at him. She'd known him so long that he was like an older brother. The last thing she needed was another lecture from either him or Brock about self-confidence, treating her body like a temple, and the rest of the garbage they deemed important.

"Hunter? Why would Hunter have to get you home?" Brock asked.

"I got myself home." She put more effort into each punch. "Thank." *Punch.* "You." *Punch, punch.* "Very much."

She stepped out from beneath their overbearing presence and moved to the speed bag.

"I'll leave y'all to your workout," Sawyer said.

Jana turned with a narrow-eyed gaze. "Gee, thanks, Sawyer."

He shrugged. "Hey, he's my fiancée's brother. I've got nothing but good things to say about him." He nodded at Brock. "But *he* might have a different opinion."

He and Brock high-fived as Sawyer headed over to the ring.

"Before you give me crap, I'm a big girl, Brock. I can handle myself." And according to the look on Hunter's face last night, she handled herself very well.

"I have no doubt you can, but Hunter? You know he's gone out with half the girls who hang out at Undercover."

"So?" She began punching the speed bag again.

"So? Jana, hasn't anything I've said to you over the years sunk in? Why would you hook up with a guy who's been around that much?"

She turned to face him and wiped the sweat from her brow. "Brock, look who you're talking to."

He winced and held up a hand. "Let's not go there, please. You know how I feel about your choices."

"What? It's not like you're a prude or anything." She wasn't embarrassed that she didn't do relationships. Why should she be? Most guys didn't care about relationships. Why should women be looked at sideways for doing the same?

"No, but you are my little sister." He took a step back, as if just the thought of her having sex repulsed him.

"Good. That's exactly what I was going for. Stay out of my personal life. 'Kay?"

"Point taken. Just be careful. Hunter's a nice guy, but…"

"Don't worry, Brock. I know exactly what he is. Arrogant. Annoying. Bullheaded." Tension riddled her body just thinking about their debate over boxing. She turned back to the bag and said, "Obnoxiously loud with his opinions," and then spent the rest of her training period purposely *not* thinking about Hunter.

After practice, she showered and dressed in the locker room, feeling bad about snapping at Brock. He was a great brother. Macho, protective, funny. How could she fault him for caring?

On her way out she stopped by the front desk and found him working on the computer.

"Hey." She peered at the computer screen. "Working on schedules?"

"Mm-hm." Brock glanced at her outfit. "You look cute."

"Thanks. I'm trying to get a good price on advertising for the studio. I figured a cute outfit couldn't hurt, and besides, I'm waitressing for Colton tonight. This outfit earns great tips." She twirled in her short skirt, which luckily covered her inner thighs. "Hoping for huge tips to help offset the new boxing gloves I want."

That earned her one of his heart-melting, brotherly smiles, which made her feel better. She didn't want him to think she was slutty, even if she believed in enjoying life to the fullest.

"Cool," he said. Then his eyes turned serious, and she knew she was in for one of his lectures. "Look, Jana. What happened with you and Spencer, that was ages ago. It's time to get over it and treat yourself like you deserve to be treated."

Just hearing her last boyfriend's name made her feel guilty and angry. He'd wanted marriage, and she hadn't been anywhere near wanting to settle down. She'd tried to break up with him for weeks, and he wouldn't take no for an answer. She'd done the only thing she knew would finally end his efforts once and for all—she'd made sure he'd found her with his best friend. Hurting him hadn't been her intent, but after a string of broken promises by men before him, she'd been at her wit's end. Hurting him had been an unavoidable outcome, but his revenge had been humiliating, and from that day forward, she swore she'd never put herself in that position again. She pushed those thoughts away, unable to deal with them right now.

No, she was never going to change her ways. She'd only hurt someone else, and that wasn't something she ever wanted to do again.

"I know you care, Brock. I get it, and I appreciate your concern, but there's nothing between Hunter and me. It was a onetime thing."

He shrugged. "Even if there was, you're right. It's not my place to get involved. But I swear, Jana, if he hurts you, I'll lay him out flat on his ass and I won't feel bad about it. Got it?"

Thank God he didn't know about the other times they'd hooked up. He'd probably have already killed him.

HUNTER WORKED INTO the evening, surrounded by sounds of torches hissing, the forge and the blowers creating an underlying hum, mallets clanging, metal twisting, and machines cutting. The potent aroma of smoldering metal centered him. He loved the hard hands-on work, but it was the creative aspect that came from somewhere deep inside his soul that made him feel as though he was adding something of value to the world. He and Grayson both enjoyed designing, and they both excelled at getting the details on paper. But while Grayson was known for creating larger, solid pieces like hibachis and furniture, Hunter was all about finite intricacies and the melding together of delicate lines and bold statements.

He was busy working through a few ideas on the whiteboard when Clark entered the shop.

"I thought you took off hours ago?" Hunter had assumed Clark had left when Grayson had, although he'd noticed that Clark had been staying later at the shop over the last few weeks.

"Nah. Not tonight. I thought we could go out and grab a beer."

"Sure. Let me just get this thought down on the board." Clark and Hunter had been each other's wingmen until Clark had begun dating Nina, whom he'd eventually married, and now they had a one-year-old son, Billy. They rarely went out anymore.

"Give me ten minutes?" Hunter asked.

Clark pointed a thumb over his shoulder. "I'll head over to Undercover and grab us a table."

Hunter had been hanging out at Undercover long before Jana's brother Colton bought the place. As he stepped from his truck in the parking lot, he caught sight of Jana's red VW Bug, and his thoughts turned to last night. He couldn't stop the smile tugging at his lips, or the twitch in his pants at the memory of Jana riding him hard and fast. She was the sexiest woman he'd ever been with, the way she owned her sexuality. She was confident and aggressive and somehow still excruciatingly feminine. And that opinionated mouth of hers was immensely talented. He might just have to give her another shot.

The bar was dimly lit and, like most nights, every table was full. Hunter made his way around the dance floor, eyeing a group of women who were clearly checking him out. He flashed a grin, nodded, earning himself a round of giggles and flirtatious smiles.

"Hunter!"

He turned at the sound of Clark's voice, and his eyes locked on the hot blonde serving his buddy's drink. He'd know that body anywhere. She looked damn fine in a black miniskirt and peach-colored top that clung to her lush curves like a second skin. Jana wasn't very tall, maybe five three or four, but those enticing dancer's legs of hers looked long and lean, and Hunter couldn't help but remember them wrapped around his waist as he'd taken her over the edge for a third time last night.

"Hey there, handsome."

He shook his head to clear his mind and turned at the familiar, *yet not*, voice. He couldn't place the smiling brunette's name.

"I haven't heard from you in weeks."

Laura? Lisa? Yes! Lisa! "Lisa, hi. Sorry about that. We had a good time, but uh…work's been busy." Hunter didn't often go out with women more than once, and this particular woman had seemed clingy. A definite turnoff. His eyes drifted back to Jana just as she turned, and their gazes collided. Hunter's pulse sped up like he'd just downed a can of Red Bull.

"Mine, too," Lisa said. "I'm not busy tonight. Are you?" She touched his arm, bringing his attention back to her.

"Uh…" He watched Jana roll her eyes as she walked away from the table. "Yeah, actually. I'm here with a buddy. Sorry." Without giving her time to say more, he headed across the room.

"Sorry I took so long," he said as he slid onto the chair across from Clark.

"No big deal. I ordered a pitcher when I saw you come in."

"Thanks." Hunter saw Jana heading back their way, carrying a tray with their pitcher. A guy reached out to stop her as she walked by. She smiled at him, said something Hunter couldn't hear, and then she laughed. Hunter didn't know why that made his gut feel funky, but it definitely did.

He shifted his eyes away when she brought the pitcher to the table.

"Hunter," she said not unkindly, but with no hint that he'd been buried balls deep inside her last night.

"Helping Colton out again?" he asked.

She glanced at the guy who had stopped her moments ago and smiled when he noticed her looking over. "Yeah," she said absentmindedly. She reached into the apron around her waist and took out an order pad, returning her attention to Hunter and Clark. "Can I get you guys something to eat?"

"I had a pretty memorable meal last night," Hunter said, enjoying the flush rising on her cheeks. "It might be hard to top that."

Her eyes narrowed. "Hm. I'm always up for a challenge. Maybe you should try the filet mignon. I hear it's pretty juicy tonight." She settled a hand on her hip and smirked as her eyes moved over his chest, down his stomach, lingered on his groin for a beat, then moved slowly back up to his face again. "Although, it might be too much for you."

Clark stifled a laugh, covering it with a cough.

"Bring it on. In fact, bring me two. I'm ravenous." He crossed his arms and leaned back in the chair.

"Hope your eyes aren't bigger than your appetite." She turned to Clark and said in an overtly sensual tone, "A handsome guy like you must have a hearty appetite, too."

Clark raked his eyes over Jana's breasts, sending an unfamiliar streak of jealousy through Hunter. "You have no idea. I could eat all night."

She leaned one palm on the table, glancing quickly at Hunter before setting a hot stare on Clark. "I bet you could. I'll bring you the same, then?"

Hunter's blood boiled. Even if they were only hooking up, she shouldn't be flirting with his buddy. His *married* buddy.

When she walked away, Clark shook his head and laughed. "Christ, man. That chick wanted it bad. I'd like to—"

"Dude!" Hunter didn't want to hear what Clark wanted to do to Jana. Hell, he didn't want to think about anyone with her. "You're *married*."

"Yeah, about that..." Clark took a drink of his beer and shifted his eyes away. His face turned solemn as he sighed. "Nina and I..." He looked at Hunter and his voice went soft. "We're separating. I actually wanted to ask you if you'd mind if I stayed at your place for a while. Not long. Just until I figure out where I'm going to rent."

"Rent? What about Billy? Why are you separating?" Hunter had been the best man at their wedding. He'd been the first person outside the family to hold Billy after he was born. He'd never seen this coming.

"Man, you have no idea what it's like." Clark rubbed the back of his neck.

Hunter focused all of his attention on his friend and felt like he was *seeing* him for the first time in a very long time. His sandy hair was longer than usual. Worry lines mapped his forehead, and he looked like he hadn't shaved—or slept—in a few days. He'd noticed his friend had looked more tired after Billy was born. Had he just gotten used to seeing him look exhausted?

"Of course you can stay at my place, but what happened?"

"All I do anymore is go to work, go home, and take care of Billy." Clark's tone was heavy, exasperated.

"Yeah, it's called being a parent." Hunter took a drink of his beer, wondering what was really going on.

"Right, but I'm also a man. I have needs. Nina stays home all day with him, and when I see her, she's tired. Half the time she hasn't even showered, and she's..." He shook his head. "She's so wrapped up in Billy that she never even notices me anymore. She barely even looks at me, and we never talk. Hell, Hunter, we haven't had sex in months, man. It sucks."

"Months?" Hunter couldn't imagine going without sex for two weeks, much less a month. But still...

"Months, and even then, it's like she's always listening for Billy." He sucked back more beer, then leaned forward across the table. "Remember back in high school, how you had to do it fast so you didn't get caught?"

Hunter nodded.

"It's like that. Only getting caught is ten times worse, because it means walking the halls with Billy while he's crying his little heart out. I love him, man. You know I do. But..." His eyes skirted over the bar. "I miss this. I miss being a man. Making out and wondering where it will lead. The thrill of the chase."

"You're married, Clark. *Married.*" He wasn't sure how to handle this. On the one hand, having Clark to hang out with again would be awesome, but Clark was being selfish, and the idea of him busting up his family didn't sit right with Hunter.

"Yeah. Mistake of a lifetime." He held Hunter's steady gaze. "Don't ever get married. That's all I can say."

"You can't mean that. What about Nina? She loves you. She relies on you."

"She doesn't even notice me, except to pay the bills and take care of our son." He took another swig of his drink. "Look, I don't know what's going to happen. Maybe we can work it out, maybe not. But I need this, man. I need your support. I need to be out, talk some shit with pretty women."

Talk some shit with pretty women, well, that was the script of Hunter's life, but Clark was married, and there was a big difference between being single and being married—even if they weren't living in the same house.

But Clark had always been there for Hunter. When Hunter's father was in rehab for falling into the bottle after Hunter's mother died, Clark was there to talk him through his pain. When Sky fell apart around the same time and Hunter nearly went crazy with worry, it was Clark who helped him realize that being there for Sky *was* doing something. *Of course* he would be there for Clark, and he'd go one further. He'd make him see the error of his ways before he got too far away from the life he knew his confused friend desperately wanted, even if he was out of sorts right now.

"Yeah, I get it." He stretched a hand across the table and fist bumped in confirmation.

"Bros before hos, man. Bros before hos."

Jana returned to the table with their food. "Don't let me down now, boys. Show me that you're not all talk and no action."

The last thing he'd let Clark do was *take action* on any woman other than Nina. *Flirting?* Maybe. *Touching?* No fucking way.

And definitely not with Jana.

CHAPTER THREE

JANA WAS DOING all she could to hold it together. She hadn't expected to see Hunter, and she definitely hadn't expected to flirt with his friend, but what else could she do? She practically lost her mind every time Hunter was near. After finding her panties stuffed in an envelope on her windshield at the gym with a note that said, *I don't like to hold on to evidence,* what was she supposed to think? She'd thought he was just as done with her as she was with him. She'd even called Harper to get her take on it. After all, Harper was far more reasonable when it came to men. After giving Jana an earful for sleeping with Hunter again, she'd judged his note as an outsider, with no emotions involved, and she'd come up with the same interpretation. No evidence equated to no further interest.

Apparently they'd both deciphered it wrong.

And why didn't her body get the message about being *over* him? Her pulse had been racing from the moment she'd seen the brunette approach him when he'd first arrived. Not only that, but he and his friend had moved to the bar half an hour ago, and they'd been flirting with every woman who walked by. She should be oblivious, not annoyingly hoping for something more.

"You okay, sis?" Colton gently touched her shoulder as he moved behind her to grab a bottle of liquor from the shelf. He was a year older than Jana and quieter than either Harper or Brock, more thoughtful and less opinionated. He and Jana had always been close. She was the first family member he'd trusted when he came out, and he was the first one she'd trusted with her decision to never have another boyfriend.

"Yeah. I just need to hit the ladies' room." She whipped around the corner to the narrow hallway and was glad to find the restroom empty. She ran her hands under cold water, fixed her hair, and then leaned against the sink and gave herself a pep talk. Hunter Lacroux was just messing with her head tonight. The same way she was messing with his. They were too alike, and that was what was making her head spin.

She needed to move past him once and for all.

She drew her shoulders back, lifted her chin, then headed back out the bathroom door—and ran directly into Hunter's incredibly hard chest. His large hands landed on her arms, sending a shock of electricity straight to her toes.

"Whoa. Slow down, beautiful." He gazed down at her with those smoldering dark eyes of his, and her pulse went crazy again. "Why are you in such a hurry?"

"Some of us are working, not flirting." *Take that.*

"Really?" He squeezed her arms a little tighter. "It sure seemed like you were flirting with Clark." He leaned in closer, his scruff brushed against her cheek as he said in a low, gravelly voice, "Did you get the silk panties I was kind enough to return?"

Why did hearing such a big, strong man say the word *pant-ies* turn her on?

She pulled her shoulders back and leaned away from the massive dose of masculinity that was slowly stealing her will to remain distant.

"I did. Thank you. The last thing I want is for you to have anything to hold over my head."

His hand slid to her lower back, and he pressed his hips forward, holding her against his impressive erection. She stifled an embarrassing whimper of desire.

"Baby, I want to do a lot of things with you, but the only things I'm interested in holding over your head are your wrists. Bound in silk. While I bury my face between those glorious thighs of yours." He ran his tongue over the shell of her ear and whispered, "And I promise you, when that happens, you'll be thanking me—and begging for more."

She had no idea how she managed to remain upright, much less speak, but she pulled a lie right out of thin air and said with a feigned air of confidence, "Been there. Done that."

"Yeah?" he snapped gruffly. "Well, not with me."

She scoffed, even though the image of Hunter, naked and holding her bound wrists above her head, was making it hard for her to remember exactly why she shouldn't partake in him just one more time. But some thread of rationality told her that if she didn't end this now, she'd never gain control over the rampant lust between them, and she actually *liked* Hunter as a friend, despite his arrogance. She didn't need to put him in an uncomfortable situation with her brother, or with Sky and

Sawyer. And, if she were honest with herself, she didn't want to lose his friendship, either.

She clung to those thoughts and managed, "Like *that's* anything special?"

He stepped impossibly closer, trapping her against the wall with his powerful thighs. "Have you already forgotten how good it feels when we're together?"

God, no. Not one blessed second of it.

"Women line up to be with me. I'm successful, in great shape, and"—he reached behind her and gripped her ass, then slid one hand beneath her skirt and brushed his fingers between her legs—"pretty damn good at knowing what you like."

She pushed from his grip, teetering on the edge of sanity. "Don't forget *obstinate as the day is long*." She took a step away, intending to get back to work…just as soon as her body cooled down and her legs worked again.

Hunter lifted his eyes, and she followed his gaze to a couple standing at the edge of the hallway kissing. He lowered his voice and said, "You expect me to believe you don't want me?" Wrapping his hand gently around her arm, he tugged her in close again. "Because I happen to think you do."

God, why did his confidence turn her on so much? "You know, even if I did want to get laid—"

"Which you do," he reminded her.

"Jesus." He was too much. "See? *That* assumption is why I don't want a relationship with any man. Least of all you!" She spun on her heel, and he pulled her against him again.

"Don't fool yourself, Jana. You're just like me. You don't

want a relationship. But you want me."

"Dream on," she said with a smirk. "You wouldn't know how to romance a girl if your life depended on it."

"Is that what you think?" His eyes bored into her.

She held his stare, hating herself for getting even more turned on by the tightening of his jaw and the determination in his eyes. Knowing he wanted her *that* badly made her stomach flip and dip like a schoolgirl's. His pecs brushed against her erect nipples—*stupid nipples*. And damn it to hell, she loved that, too.

She'd let Hunter get to her again, and when he lowered his lips to hers—the arrogant bastard—she got lost in the deliciousness of his savory mouth, and *forgetting* Hunter Lacroux went out the door. He didn't just kiss her. He claimed her with powerful strokes of his tongue as it slid over hers, laying claim to every inch of her mouth. When his hands encircled her, holding them so close she could barely breathe, he breathed air into her lungs, never breaking their connection. And when his knee slid between her thighs and he backed her up against the wall, she was powerless to deny herself the pleasures she knew he'd give. Her hands glided up his back, over the hard muscle, then down over the curve of his perfect ass, as his lips left hers and he kissed the corner of her mouth. With one final press of his hips to hers, he cupped her face between his hands and she had no choice but to look into his hungry eyes.

His lips were pink from the intensity of their kiss, and she knew hers were probably worse. She could feel the abrasions from his whiskers.

"Don't fool yourself, pretty girl. There's nothing I *can't* do."

HUNTER NEVER BACKED down from a challenge, and Jana Garner was looking up at him with a combination of lust and anger in her eyes—the biggest challenge of all. She felt so good in his arms, and every single thing she said made his insides simmer. It pissed him off to hear her say she didn't want him when he knew he was her sexual match in every way. Even if they didn't want a relationship, what harm was there in hooking up again? Why was she fighting the obvious chemistry between them?

"Neither one of us wants a relationship. I'll give you that. But you kiss me like you want me." He brushed his thumb over her cheek, trying not to think about how soft her skin was against his rough hands. "You might not want to admit it, pretty girl, but one day you won't be able to keep from telling me just how much you want me."

She opened her mouth to speak and he pressed his finger over her lips, gently shushing her.

"Every word out of your mouth either sets my body on fire or pisses me off. How about we play it safe and you keep whatever it is to yourself?" He paused, giving her body time to stop trembling and for the lust to wash away from those beautiful eyes of hers. She had to get back to work. What felt like an hour had in fact been only a matter of minutes, but he didn't want to keep her from doing her job.

Okay, maybe he did. He wanted to lift her into his arms and carry her to a bed—any bed—and have his way with her until she was screaming his name in the throes of passion, like she had last night. But since that couldn't happen, and he had a friend waiting at the bar whom he had to babysit, he lifted her hand to his lips and pressed a kiss to the back of her fingers, then said, "Until next time."

As he passed the kissing couple and reentered the bar, he drew his shoulders back, the *Prove Jana Wrong Plan* already forming in his mind.

CHAPTER FOUR

JANA HAD CONVINCED herself that Hunter's goal last night had solely been to mess with her head, but when she'd come out to her car in the morning to go to the dance studio, she'd found a handful of tiger lilies that looked like they'd been picked from the side of the road beneath her windshield wiper with a card from Hunter. She was pretty sure he'd gotten a free card in the mail with those return address labels that were mass-marketed right before the holidays, because it had a picture of a cute white puppy wearing a Santa hat—and it was only June. Inside, he'd written, *How's this for romance? Hunter.*

At the time she'd laughed it off as him messing with her again, but now, as she had discussed it with Harper over lunch during her break from work, she had to wonder why he'd go to such lengths.

"Want to know what I think?" Harper asked. They were sitting on the Wellfleet Pier eating lobster rolls from Mac's Seafood and watching a family with three young boys fish a few feet away. Well, that and checking out the hot guys docking the boat at the end of the pier.

"Sure." Jana picked at her lobster roll.

"I think when you go to the bonfire tonight you should ask

him. Right there in front of everyone you should bring it up. Call him out on it." Harper tucked her long blond hair behind her ear and straightened her red plastic sunglasses. Jana couldn't see her expression behind the lenses, but she knew her older sister well enough to picture her blue eyes, alert with surety and confidence.

"Call him out on it?" She shook her head at her sister's ridiculous suggestion. "This is Hunter we're talking about, right? Big guy, speaks his mind no matter what? Sky's brother? Can you imagine what type of comeback he'd have and what Sawyer would do if he knew Hunter was messing with my head?" She laughed, but inside her stomach knotted at the thought. "And Brock? He told me that if Hunter hurt me he'd kill him."

Harper rolled her eyes. "Brock is not going to hurt anyone. You know that. Besides, Hunter's not hurting you. He's playing with you. Just like you play with him."

Jana finished her lunch and pushed to her feet to throw out her trash. Nothing was as relaxing as sitting on the pier with the gentle breeze blowing in off the bay, but she had a class to teach, and she didn't want to respond to Harper's comment about her *playing* with Hunter.

She shifted her eyes to the hot guys who had docked their boat, hoping for a distraction from Hunter, but they didn't do anything for her. Not even a tingle of excitement. Not to mention that they were openly ogling Harper, who probably didn't realize her short summer dress was rising with the breeze.

"Harp, you're giving those hotties an eyeful."

"Ohmygod." Harper jumped to her feet, holding down her wayward dress. She turned away from the guys and laughed. "There are benefits to working by the pier, aren't there?" Harper was a screenplay writer, and last summer she'd been hired to write a racy sitcom for cable. She mainly worked from home or coffee shops.

"Heck, yeah. Hot guys at every turn, the beach, the theater, and our friends." Jana sighed. "I just wish my life weren't so crazy. I feel so scattered these days. Working for Marco is a bear. He was supposed to bring in clients, but since he moved to Plymouth, it's all on my shoulders."

"I thought that was temporary," Harper said.

"Yeah, me too." Jana had taught dance for Marco Luger, the owner of Cape Dance, for the past two years. When she'd first begun working for him, he'd handled the business end while she taught, but now that he was busy opening the other studio, Jana was overloaded. When she'd happily accepted the extra work, it was with the understanding that it would be for only a month or so while he got the other studio up and running. Months later, she was not only still doing the work, but when she'd requested a raise, he'd claimed he couldn't afford it.

"You've got to ask him for a raise again if he's going to keep relying on you to grow the business. You know that, Jana. Usually you're so aggressive. Why are you so careful with him?"

"Harp, how many dance studios are there on the lower Cape?"

Harper shrugged. "I don't know. Two? Three?"

"Exactly. And I *love* teaching everything. I want to teach

hip-hop to teenagers, ballet to sweet little girls with big dreams, and, well, everything to adults. No other dance studio does it all."

"Maybe you need to compromise. Give up some of what you want for what you can get."

"You're always so practical. I don't want to give up any-thing. I love it too much, and besides, I'll lose those skills if I don't use them." She needed to change the subject, because they'd just argue about how Jana should try to focus her efforts on one thing at a time. It was a sore subject for Jana, especially since, for the first time in years, she'd had to forgo the theater work she loved so much. But until Marco came back or hired someone else, she couldn't spare the time.

"I'm having breakfast at Seaside with Sky the day after to-morrow. Are you going?" Through Sawyer, Jana and Harper had become good friends with Sky and all of her friends in the Seaside community.

"I'm not sure," Harper said. "I have a lot of revisions to do tonight, which is why I'm missing the bonfire, so it'll depend on how much I get done."

Jana walked her back to her car. "What do you really think I should do about Hunter? I mean, why does he care if I think he's romantic or not? He's more of a player than I am."

Harper lifted her sunglasses and Jana saw the seriousness in her eyes. "Jana, I don't know. I mean, you two are like oil and water one minute and insatiable with each other the next. You're at a whole different sexual level than I am when it comes to guys."

"Gee, thanks, sis," she said with a sarcastic lilt to her voice.

"I don't mean that in a bad way. I mean, you have more experience than me. You enjoy yourself more. You're freer. I'm not a prude or anything, but you have no qualms about any of it, and I…I'm slower to the finish line, I guess."

"That's okay." Jana sighed. "I'll figure it out."

Harper hugged her, then climbed into her car. "You always do."

Jana wasn't so sure about that. "Have a great time writing! Make it hot and sexy. Think of *me* as your character."

Harper waved and blew her a kiss as she drove away.

The dance studio was located around the corner from the harbor. Jana walked along the road thinking about Harper's suggestion. There was no way she'd call Hunter out in front of everyone, because she might not like his answer. That thought bothered her. She really did like him as a friend, and as a lover. It was just putting the two together that got messy for them, because it couldn't lead anywhere.

She gazed at the upper deck of the Pearl Restaurant, where couples were sitting beneath colorful umbrellas. They looked happy, the men and women leaning in close. Jana hadn't had a real boyfriend since Spencer, and that was five years ago. Relationships petrified her. They made her feel claustrophobic. But it was scenes like these that made her heart flutter longingly and a little voice whisper in the back of her mind about *one day*…followed by the urge to run in the opposite direction.

She shifted her gaze to the gallery next door and noticed a man carrying a large metal sculpture of a fish. It was nearly as long as he was. The artist, a handsome man in his midthirties who sometimes sat out front of the gallery while he worked, followed him out. The smile on the artist's face told of his joy of finding a home for a piece of his artwork, and she wondered if Hunter felt that way when he sold one of his pieces.

As she neared the studio entrance, she realized how strange of a thought that was, because when it came to Hunter, she usually didn't think much beyond his looks, his danger zone, and the pigheaded opinions that came out of his big mouth.

Oh, that mouth.

No, she wasn't going to stroll down Hunter Road today. She needed to concentrate on her impending meeting with the *Cape Cod Times* to solidify marketing space, and then she had three more classes to teach.

Her cell phone vibrated. She pulled it out of her purse, and her pulse quickened at the sight of DO NOT RESPOND! on the screen. She stared at the screen for a long time, debating whether she should open it. Who was she kidding? She swiped the screen, unable to resist reading Hunter's text.

Pick you up at 7 to watch the sunset before the bonfire. Be ready.

She had to read it twice to believe it. What the hell was he up to, telling her what to do? She wasn't about to be told to be ready for any man.

She typed a quick reply—*No, thanks*—and pressed send, irritated with him for assuming she would want to go anywhere with him. Seconds later her phone vibrated with another text.

Is that any way to treat a romantic invitation?

Lord, really? Was he that competitive? She responded with,

What do you really want?

Her phone rang seconds later, stopping her in her tracks. She accepted the call and put the phone to her ear. Before she could say a word, Hunter's deep voice flooded her ear.

"The truth."

She sighed. "What?"

"You asked what I wanted. I want you to admit that you want to be with me."

"Hunter—"

"I'm not going to be baited into a fight. Just say you want me, and you'll feel much better."

He said it so confidently that despite her annoyance, it made her smile. "Oh, will I? Well, for your information, I don't want you." If she were Pinocchio, her nose would have instantly grown.

"Now that we've established that you're a sucky liar, I'll be at your place at seven. I don't like to wait, so be ready."

"Oh, that's *super* romantic," she said flatly. "Listen, I—"

"Seven, pretty girl. See you then." He ended the call, leaving her slack-jawed, annoyed, and slightly turned on.

CHAPTER FIVE

HUNTER SHOVED HIS phone in his pocket and stalked up front to find Clark. They'd stayed up half the night talking about Clark's troubled marriage, and Hunter was even more determined to get his buddy to work things out with Nina. She was a beautiful woman with a big heart, and he knew from what he'd witnessed, and from the things Clark had said last night, that she was an incredible mother. Their trouble seemed to boil down to Clark feeling undesirable and stripped of his manhood, and Hunter had no experience with that. But he was willing to try to figure it out. Right now, though, as he leaned against Clark's desk and crossed his arms over his chest, he needed his buddy's help. Clark was married. He'd once romanced his wife into marrying him. Maybe talking about that would remind him how much he loved her.

"Romance one-oh-one. Give it to me."

Confusion washed over Clark's face. "What?"

"Romance. You know, flowers and all that bullshit. Tell me what I need to know." He was determined to get the words *I want you* out of Jana, and to do that, apparently he needed to know how to be romantic.

Clark laughed so hard his chair tipped back. "You think I

can teach you how to be romantic so you can bone that chick from the bar? Man, move on to the next girl. What the hell do I know about romance?"

"You're married. You got a woman to marry you, Clark. There had to be romance involved." Didn't there? From what Sky said, everything Sawyer did was romantic. Maybe he was asking the wrong guy.

"I don't know. I guess I did some things." Clark sounded mildly annoyed. "I brought her flowers a few times. Made reservations for dinner, shit like that."

Thinking of the flowers he'd picked from his yard earlier that morning, he said, "That's romantic? Any jackass can do that."

"But that's what romance is. It's doing stuff like that because you're thinking about her and you want to see her smile, not doing crazy shit like taking her to Paris to show off." Clark turned in his chair and typed something into the computer. He spun the monitor so Hunter could see the wikiHow page How to Be Romantic. "Here, study this."

Hunter skimmed the headers: *Be Thoughtful, Be Creative, Keep Things Fresh, Keep Growing Together.*

A picture of a gift was beneath *Be Thoughtful.* He thought of her panties and chuckled, then thought of the flowers. *Done.*

There was a picture of a dude playing a guitar and a woman hanging over his shoulder smiling. *Yeah, that totally doesn't equate to getting sex. Moving on...*The next picture featured books with a note tucked between them, sporting lipstick marks. *Jana has an incredible mouth. Now we're getting somewhere.* She could put those luscious lips anywhere she'd like on him, but putting them on paper would be a waste. *Next…*

The next picture showed a couple texting. *Done.* And a picture of a dude cleaning out a car. *Not happening.*

Be Creative looked more interesting, with a picture of a couple lying in bed. The woman wore a red bra and panties as she rubbed the guy's back. He was smiling—*and probably hard.* Well, Jana hadn't rubbed his back, but she'd rubbed other things. *Done.*

More pictures of couples followed: reading together, drinking wine, holding balloons. *Balloons?* He skimmed over the next few images under *Keeping Things Fresh*: holding hands, shaving…He reached up and touched his whiskers. *Really? Shaving?*

He heard the front door open, and Grayson's voice filled the lobby. "What the hell are you reading?"

Grayson's face was freshly shaved, his thick hair neatly brushed.

"You shaved," Hunter said.

"I also manscaped. Wanna see?" He pulled out the front of his pants. "Got a date tonight."

"You shave for dates?" How did he not realize that before now?

"Sometimes. You think women like razor burn on their thighs?" Grayson shook his head like Hunter was an idiot. Maybe he was. He'd never once shaved his face for a date. Manscaping, sure, but his face?

Grayson pointed to a picture on the computer under the header *Keep Growing Together.* The picture showed a man lying on his back with his feet up in the air doing some crazy acrobatic shit with the woman. Her ass balanced on his feet as she hung upside down, legs in a cheerleading pose he'd seen girls do way back when, hands flying out behind her...while they kissed.

What. The. Fuck?

Grayson read the caption aloud. "Do activities that raise your adrenaline." His eyes rose to the title of the article. "Seriously, dude? What *are* you two doing?"

Clark held his hands up in surrender. "It's all him, man, not me. I just got out of this shit."

Grayson's eyes narrowed. "Yeah, about that. You and I have to talk. You can't leave your wife and kid, Clark."

"Agreed," Hunter said emphatically, just as he had last night about a billion times.

Clark opened his mouth to respond and Hunter said, "Don't even try," as Grayson chimed in with, "Get over it."

"Whatever. Neither of you are married," Clark responded. "So don't give me shit. Things are different once you get hitched and have a kid."

"Yeah, it's called owning up to your responsibilities," Hunter said. "Why do you think I don't have a girlfriend?"

"Because you don't shave," Grayson said with a laugh.

"Because you're a male slut," Clark added.

"Because I don't want that responsibility. You think I want to be the person a woman relies on to listen to her and talk about girl stuff? Really, the thought of listening to drama turns my stomach, and sleeping with the same chick year after year? Man..." He shook his head, although he couldn't remember the last time he'd had a woman beneath him besides Jana. Holy shit. Had they been hooking up for that long?

Grayson pointed to the picture on the monitor of the acrobatic, upside-down kiss. "If you're doing shit like this, I'm not sure you ever have to worry about getting married. Besides, if you're trying to learn how to be romantic, you really *do* need a lesson. Romance comes from the heart, not from an article."

"How the hell do you know?" Hunter asked.

"Jesus. Did we even grow up in the same house? Everything Dad ever did for Mom was romantic. Coming home at night on time was romantic. Helping with us when we drove her crazy all day was romantic. Hell, Hunt. Working in the goddamn hardware store from sunup to sundown was romantic. He did that for her, and for us. To make ends meet and to make sure we all had what we needed and that Mom was happy. Even I could see that." Grayson stopped at the door to the shop and set a serious stare on Hunter. "And sleeping with the same chick year after year? Look at Pete and Jenna. Sky and Sawyer. They're happy as hell. You might not want that, but I'm beginning to think we're the ones missing out."

"No way," Hunter mumbled as he watched the door swing closed behind Grayson.

"I hate to agree with him, but you have no clue what you're talking about, Hunter." Clark turned the monitor back toward him and laughed at the picture. "Although that is some kinky shit."

"Wait, why do you say I have no clue? You're the one who left your wife."

"Yeah, because we *never* have sex. Hell, we never even talk."

The anger in his voice was palpable. "But I still *love* her. I still *want* her."

"Then call her, dumbass. Talk to her. Do those things on that stupid article." Hunter hoped to hell his friend would do the right thing. Even if *he* didn't want to sleep with one woman forever, he knew Clark, and the broken guy in front of him wasn't the stand-up, loyal-to-the-end buddy he knew and respected.

Clark just shook his head like Hunter didn't understand, and the crazy part was, he sort of did. He thought it all came back to not really wanting one woman forever. He'd never tell Clark that, but despite what Grayson had said, Hunter had to question the whole monogamy thing.

Hunter patted Clark's shoulder and said, "At least think about it, okay? She loves you, Clark. She texted you a hundred times last night. That's love."

"That's 'can you drop off diapers tomorrow,' because Billy has a cold and she doesn't want to take him out." Clark sighed. "And yeah, I dropped them off this morning."

"Good man," Hunter said as he pushed from the desk to return to the shop.

"Hunt?" Clark called after him.

"Yeah?"

"Thanks for letting me crash at your place. I know this is a messed-up situation, and I know you don't want me to leave Nina, but I need to figure this out my way."

Hunter nodded before pushing through the doors and getting back to work, thinking about what he'd read on wikiHow and about Clark bringing diapers to Nina. That was *thoughtful*, wasn't it? Even if she'd asked him to bring them? Surely leaving flowers for Jana counted, too. But he had a feeling that romance went beyond flowers and diapers. He just had to figure out what else there was—and why he cared.

By six thirty that evening he'd decided that he'd wasted too much time trying to figure out how to be romantic. It probably didn't matter if he was romantic or not. He and Jana had great sexual chemistry, and he was sure she'd remember just how incredible it was and admit she wanted to do it again. All it would take was a few kisses, and she'd be saying, *I want you*, in her sleep.

He showered and dressed in cargo shorts and a tank top, pulled on a hoodie, and climbed into his truck. Taking one last glance at himself in the rearview mirror, he studied the scruff on his jaw.

"Goddamn it." He pushed from the cab and headed back inside. He took the stairs two at a time and stalked into his master bathroom. Every muscle tightened against what he was about to do. His head told him he was a fool, but something inside him urged him on. He was making an effort for a woman, and that made his skin feel too tight. He tugged at the front of his tank top, trying to shake off the uncomfortable feeling. Lathering up his scruffy cheeks, he palmed the razor, trying to ignore the nervous feeling clawing at his gut. As he shaved the whiskers from his jaw, and his clean-shaven face was revealed, he questioned himself again. And a foreign feeling rose within him.

He felt good making an effort for Jana. But the aftershave was only to ease the burn. At least that's what he told himself.

She probably wouldn't even notice. Jana wasn't like most women, getting all dramatic over stupid things.

Feeling slightly emasculated without his scruff, he changed into jeans and forwent the truck, grabbing his motorcycle keys instead on the way out the door.

JANA HELD THE phone to her ear, listening to Sky tell her who was coming to the bonfire. They'd moved tonight's gathering from Cahoon Hollow Beach to Pete and Jenna's home on the bay, where they'd have to use the large hibachi Grayson made. Open bonfires weren't allowed on bay beaches.

"Sounds great. I can't wait to see sweet little Bea and the rest of the girls and their babies." Pete and Jenna had had a baby girl this past winter, and they'd named her after Pete's mother, who had passed away unexpectedly a few years earlier. Their friends Amy and Bella had given birth last summer to their daughters, Hannah and Summer.

"We'll get to see the baby boys tomorrow at breakfast." Sky's excitement made Jana smile. "Jessica and Jamie are coming down late tonight from Boston, and Leanna said she and Kurt are making arrangements to stay at the cottage for the rest of the summer. She's just finishing up a big jam order tonight." Leanna owned Luscious Leanna's Sweet Treats, and she made her jam out of a converted cottage on their bayside property. She and Kurt stayed at that house most of the year; then, like the other Seaside cottage owners, they stayed at Seaside during the summers.

"Dustin and Sloan are adorable. I can't wait to see them again," Jana said, thinking about how cute Jessica and Leanna's boys were. They'd been spring babies, and there had been a big party to celebrate their births.

"Want us to swing by and get you tonight for the bonfire?" Sky asked.

Sky knew that something had happened between Jana and Hunter before Sky had met Jana through Sawyer, but Jana didn't think she knew they'd hooked up several times since. Even though they'd left the bar together the other night, Sky had probably assumed Hunter had just been making sure she got home okay. Hunter was always making sure their friends were okay. In Sky's eyes, it wouldn't look like anything more if Hunter gave Jana a ride to the bonfire, so she told Sky the truth.

"Um, no thanks. Hunter's giving me a ride over."

"Cool. We'll see you there, then. Tell Hunt I said to behave."

Jana laughed, like that was even a possibility? They ended the call, and she looked over her outfit one last time. Skinny jeans and a batik top should send the not-interested vibe, right? She wasn't wearing a miniskirt or anything that allowed easy access. She'd even French braided her hair, because she knew that Hunter loved tangling his hands in it as much as she enjoyed him doing it, and if it was tied back, there was no chance of *that* happening. Jana was well aware that each of these little changes were merely crutches to keep her under control as well as him, but a girl had to do what a girl had to do.

Since when have I needed crutches? As she slipped on her flip-flops, a knock at the door sent her heart into panic mode. That was new, too. Lord. Hunter *had* gotten under her skin. She needed to find a way to get him out. *Fast.*

Squaring her shoulders, she told herself she could resist Hunter Lacroux. She'd had him, and as magnificent as he was, what they had was a revolving bedroom door. Even though she didn't want more than that, she knew it was better to bolt that door closed now than to enjoy it time and time again.

Even if every time was better than the last?

She pushed that thought aside and opened the door.

Holy mother of all things sinful. Hunter stood in a pair of low-slung dark jeans stretched tight over his thick thighs. His black hoodie was open in the front, revealing a tank top that clung to his muscular pecs. But it was his face that had her licking her lips, hungry for a taste of him despite her steely resolve to remain distant. His chiseled jaw was on full display, clean-shaven, surrounding full, kissable lips and making him even more drop-dead gorgeous than usual. Top off his cleaner image with the black bike helmet under his arm, and he was the perfect contrast of badass and gentleman.

Jana's cognitive processes stalled.

When he leaned in and pressed a kiss to her cheek, the scent of Tommy Hilfiger mixed with his own potent scent was intoxicating and enticing.

"Hey, pretty girl."

His sexy smile and gravelly tone sent heat straight through

her core. "Hey," she managed, trying to kick her brain into working order as he raked his eyes down her body.

"Damn, you look hot."

His eyes darkened as he set his helmet beside the door and slid a hand around her waist, tugging her in close. Her resolve disappeared as he took her in a hard, hungry kiss. There was nothing romantic or polite about it. It was a kiss of white-hot desire and it made her head spin. He was hard as steel, and as he cupped her ass and held on tight, she gave in to the desire that had been simmering since last night at the bar and pushed his hoodie off his shoulders, clawing for skin. In one swift move he shook off the jacket and kicked the door shut. His eyes were dark and possessive as he reclaimed her body against his.

"Jana."

Her name was drenched with need, igniting new flames inside her. He made her feel wanted and sexy, and in the space of a second she was racing through the virtual revolving bedroom door. Their legs bumped and tangled as they kissed and tore at each other's clothes, moving toward the couch. Her shirt went first—and he didn't even bother to unhook her bra. He ripped it from her body, tearing the clasp off and sending it flying across the room.

"You're gorgeous." He lowered his mouth to her breast, sending prickles of lust to her core.

He teased and taunted the taut peak with his teeth as he worked her jeans down her hips. She kicked them off and tumbled backward onto the couch wearing only her panties as he came down over her. Slanting his mouth over hers again, he shattered any remaining thoughts. Her entire body ached with need as he ground his hard length against her wet center, creating friction that drove her quickly toward the edge of insanity. She needed this. She needed *him* pounding into her, making it impossible to think of anything else but him. Hunter knew just how to touch her, to sooth the chaos from her mind.

She fumbled with the button on his jeans, and he grabbed her wrist and drew back, challenging her with his eyes.

"Say it, pretty girl."

Damn you. She struggled against his grip, and he grinned. It was a wicked, cocky grin, and when he lifted her arms above her head, he sent new desires searing through her. He had to know what he was doing to her, that all she could picture was the image he'd left her with, of her bound wrists as he took her. *Bastard.*

"Not a chance in hell." She arched her hips against his, knowing he couldn't resist her any more than she could resist him.

He lowered his cheek to hers and pressed the unfamiliar smooth skin to hers. He'd never been clean-shaven in all the times they'd hooked up, and boy, did she like the feel of it. She loved the scratch of his whiskers, the tantalizing burn it brought as he pleasured her, but this? This ratcheted up the hotness, and her curiosity, even more. What would he feel like now, with those soft cheeks rubbing against her inner thighs?

"You know you want me," he growled in her ear.

"Shut up and put that mouth of yours to use," she said with just as much vehemence.

He tightened his grip on her wrists, tugging them higher while trapping her hips beneath his. "Don't play with me, Jana. You know you want me." He accentuated his words with another thrust of his cock, angling his hips this time so he brushed upward between her legs.

She ground her teeth together. "That's a lot of big talk. How about some action? Or maybe you're scared you won't hit the mark this time?"

"I always hit the fucking mark." He kneed her legs open wider and pressed against her, causing more delicious friction.

She curled her fingers, trying to get to him, wanting to feel him, but she'd be damned if she'd tell him so.

"Prove it."

He transferred her wrists to one of his big hands, holding them firmly against the back of the couch as he reached for his pants. "I'll prove it, all right."

Finally he was going to satisfy her and forget this silly nonsense he had in his head of needing to hear her admit how badly she wanted him. Wasn't it obvious by the way she was writhing beneath him, practically begging to be fucked?

He grumbled as he lifted his hips to strip off his jeans. She instantly missed the weight of him. He tugged and shifted, pulling her up with him by the wrists as he toed off his shoes and tried to get his jeans off.

She couldn't help but giggle at the sight of his big body and all those muscles as he stood at a funky angle and struggled to get his pants off one-handed.

"You can let go of my hands to take your pants off."

"Fuck." He let go and stripped himself bare.

Jana's breath left her lungs in a rush as his rigid length sprang free. She'd had him half a dozen times at least, and still, she was practically salivating at the sight of his gorgeous physique. He picked up his tank top and wound it around her wrists.

Her eyes shot up to his. "What are you doing?"

He silenced her with a heated gaze.

Her pulse kicked up as he tied the shirt, binding her wrists together.

"Wait!" Her eyes widened at the look of hunger in his eyes. She was panting now, a combination of wanton desire and a trickle of fear.

His devilish grin turned softer, as did his tone. "What is it, pretty girl?"

She trapped her lip between her teeth, unwilling to admit her lie. Just being bound like that made her insides ache and pulse with need. And, as she stared into his eyes, seeing all that heat, all that desire meant just for her, she was surprised that she saw something more this time—concern. She'd seen that look in his eyes dozens of times, but always aimed at his siblings and closest friends. And, she realized as he ran his finger down the length of her arm and touched his lips to hers in a kiss so tender it made her insides melt, that she trusted Hunter. She'd never allowed anyone to tie her up before, but she was ready to do this with him. To take this hookup to a new level. To surrender her pleasure to Hunter, giving him total control.

"Take me hard," she whispered against his lips.

CHAPTER SIX

IT WASN'T THE words Jana said that sent him into action—although he loved hearing his favorite request coming from that sexy mouth. It was the look in her eyes the moment before she'd said them, a look of trust that stirred something deep inside him. And made him realize, maybe for the first time ever, that the thundering in his chest was coming from his heart. His heart had never come into play with women before, and it took him a moment to process that and finally move past it and regain his momentum.

He snagged a condom from his jeans and rolled it on. Jana licked her lips, making him instantly harder. He sealed his mouth over hers, and she returned his efforts with firm thrusts of her tongue and sweet little moans of pleasure that tore through him. He moved down her body, teasing her nipples, squeezing them once before roughly gripping her panties in his fists and tearing them from her gorgeous hips. Jana wasn't shaved bare, like so many women these days. She had a narrow patch of blond curls between her legs, which held her sweet scent and made shivers race through him every time his mouth was on her. But that would come later—she'd asked for him to take her hard, and that's exactly what he intended to do.

He gripped her hips and lifted them slightly as he shifted her lower on the couch. "Keep your arms above your head."

Jana's eyes went wide at the force as he laid her flat and thrust in deep. Her lips curved up in a lascivious smile.

"Again." She curled her fingers around the edge of the couch.

Hunter might have just died and gone to heaven. He came down over her, needing to feel her beautiful mouth as he took her harder than he ever had before. Claiming her, possessing her. Filling her so completely he knew she'd feel reminders of him tomorrow, and he liked knowing she'd think of him being inside her.

"Hunter—"

He'd learned that her voice took on a higher pitch when she was about to come, and he liked knowing that about her, too. He lifted her hips, holding tightly to her ass and getting the angle just right to send her over the edge. He pistoned his hips, and she buried her face in his neck, moaning and crying out as her inner muscles pulsed with pleasure, tightening like a vise around his cock.

"That's it, pretty girl, let go." He continued the relentless pursuit of more—always more. He enjoyed pleasuring Jana, seeing her eyes slam shut, her jaw tighten, and knowing it was all for him. At least tonight.

That thought usually didn't bother him, but now his gut twisted with it. As she came down from her climax, he pulled nearly all the way out, leaving just the head inside her.

"Hunter," she said through clenched teeth, arching up,

trying to take more of him. "God…"

He bit back the urge to tell her that he hated thinking about her doing this with other guys. That was too weird. Too foreign. Too much. He wanted to fuck the feeling away. He thrust into her again and again, until all that was left was the feel of her tight channel around him and the thought of pleasuring Jana until she wouldn't be able to remember ever being with another man.

She was hot and willing and felt so good. That should be all that mattered. The here and now. He held on to that thought as he lifted her legs around his waist, slid a pillow beneath her hips, and took her over the edge one final time before finding his own explosive release.

They lay spent for a moment before he rid himself of the condom and gathered her trembling body closely as he unbound her hands. Her arms fell limp as he held her against him.

"I've got you," he whispered. "I've got you." He carried her into the bedroom, his heart making itself known again with fast thumps and a tightening in his chest.

"Wow," she whispered. "That was…incredible."

He sat on the bed and held her for a long time, brushing her hair from her cheeks, stroking her arms to ease the ache he was sure she felt. Cradling her naked body against him, he tried to make sense of the unfamiliar emotions washing through him. Gone was the urge to roll away from her and fall asleep, or to dress and leave. He wanted to sit right there, holding her until she had her strength back, until he was sure she was okay.

And that rattled him to his core.

"We're supposed to be at the bonfire," she said softly against his chest.

Part of him wanted to cling to that excuse, wash up and get the hell out of there, but a bigger part of him wanted to stay right there holding her. Which was exactly why he *needed* to force himself to move.

"We missed the sunset, but we can still make the bonfire," he said, reluctantly setting her beside him on the bed in the dark room. She looked sweet with the sexy afterglow pinking up her cheeks and the hazy look of a satiated lover lingering in her eyes. *Oh hell.* She had that trusting look in her eyes again, too.

With a groan he pushed to his feet. "I'm going to wash up."

He stalked into the bathroom and took a cold shower. When he came out with a towel wrapped around his waist, he expected to find Jana covered up and moving around, but she was still sitting on the edge of the bed, naked and tired. *Sweet and sexy.*

His heart did that *notice me* thing again.

"Come on, pretty girl." The tenderness in his voice was new, too. What the hell was she doing to him? "You need to get cleaned up so we can go." He pulled her upright.

She pressed her hands against his chest, and after smiling sleepily up at him, she rested her cheek against his skin and said, "You shaved."

His heart beat a little harder.

"And showered. Twice." He didn't mean to sound so rough, but she was talking all mushy-voiced with him, and that wasn't

Jana. Jana was snappy and fierce, not sensitive or the kind of girl who noticed things like whether he'd shaved. He liked that she noticed, but he hated the way it made his insides go soft.

He took her by the shoulders and turned her toward the bathroom, then smacked her ass. "Go on. Get in there or I'll climb in there with you and we'll never get out of here."

"Just like a man," she said with a little more energy as she sauntered toward the bathroom, looking devastatingly tempting. "Promise me sunsets and give me orgasms instead."

FORTY MINUTES LATER Jana and Hunter pulled up in front of Pete and Jenna's house. She'd hoped that the ride over would help clear her head, but the rumbling of the motorcycle between her legs only reminded her of Hunter making her feel all sorts of wonderful. When she was showering and dressing, she'd gone through a bevy of emotions, from curiosity—she was dying to know what other sexual tricks Hunter had up his sleeve—to feeling way too many positive emotions toward him. He'd been sweet and careful with her after they'd had sex. He'd never done that before. Usually they either parted ways without a word, or they fell asleep without touching and she snuck out, as she had the other morning.

She liked that softer side of him. She always knew he had a caring side. He was protective of Sky, and he always seemed to be asking after her, or touching base with one of his brothers, but she'd never seen him that way with any other woman. Not that she'd ever seen him with the same woman twice, and that didn't escape her mind either. They'd been together too many times already, hadn't they? Too many for both of them.

And then there was the anger that laced her every thought for giving in to her desires. Anger at herself for wilting beneath his heat and anger at *him* for kissing her in the first place, and for looking so hot that it was impossible for her to deny him. He'd even *shaved,* not to mention the cologne. She'd hoped the cool night air whisking across her skin on the ride over might quell her reaction to him, but as Hunter helped her from the bike, looking every bit as sinful as he did when he'd first arrived at her door, she felt renewed lust simmering inside her.

He lifted her helmet off her head and ran his finger over her hair. "I like your braid." He grabbed hold of her thick plait and gave it a little tug. "Should have thought of that earlier."

"God, you're such a—"

He smirked as he draped an arm over her shoulder. "Come on, pretty girl. Blink away that desire in your eyes, or they'll know you want me."

"*Ugh!* I don't want you," she said as they walked past the house and across the dune. She couldn't even fool herself. How would she fool anyone else? A breeze swept off the bay, and she shivered. He drew her closer, and as big and warm as he was, she tried to push away, because that's what they did, wasn't it? They didn't snuggle. But he held on tight, and God help her, she loved it.

"That's not what you were saying an hour ago. I seem to remember the words *more, harder,* and *yes* coming out of your luscious mouth several times."

"Shut up and take your arm off of me. I thought you didn't want people to see—" She let the sentence hang in the space between them.

"It's not *my* eyes they'll see want in."

She pried his hand off her shoulder and groaned. "You're infuriating. You think I don't see how much you want me in the way you look at me?" She stopped walking toward the group and stalked closer to him. "You think they won't be able to tell that we've just had sex?"

"Not by my eyes." He shifted his gaze casually to the group at the bottom of the dunes and waved.

"Well. They won't see it in mine, either." She stomped down the dunes and tried to force a smile, ignoring his chuckle behind her. She was *not* going to look at him. Not one single time. Not even a glance.

Their friends were gathered around a roaring fire. She drew in several calming breaths and finally managed a real smile when Sky jumped up and ran to greet her.

"You made it! I thought my brother hijacked you or something!" She embraced Jana, and when Sky walked toward Hunter, Jana made a point of not looking over. She kept her eyes locked on baby Bea, nestled in Pete's arms, fast asleep.

"Oh my goodness. She's so precious." Jana knelt beside him and admired the baby's tiny pink lips and long eyelashes.

"She's precious, all right," Pete said, his gaze shifting over her shoulder.

She assumed he was watching Hunter, but Jana wasn't

about to turn around and check. She felt Hunter approaching. Felt his presence as tangibly as the sand beneath her feet.

Hunter leaned down and took the sleeping baby from Pete's arms. "Let me hold my beautiful niece." He smirked at Jana and snuggled his freshly shaven cheek against the baby. Bea had a fluff of dark hair, like Pete and Jenna. The baby sighed as he held her within his heavily muscled arms. Jana had never seen anything sexier than that pigheaded, beautiful man holding the tiny baby. Jealousy tiptoed through her. She kind of wanted to be the baby, all snuggled in safe and warm against Hunter's chest. His smirk had been replaced with a genuine smile as he lowered his lips to Bea's forehead.

Her insides went soft at the sight, and she fell a little harder for Hunter.

"Sit down," Amy said, patting the blanket beside her. Tony, her husband, sat on her other side, with one arm draped over the back of her chair. "We forgot to bring extra chairs, but you and Hunter can use Hannah's blanket. She's in the playpen fast asleep." Amy pointed to two playpens behind Tony. "Summer's asleep in the blue one."

"Thanks." Jana sank down to the blanket, determined not to keep staring at Hunter as he reached one hand into the cooler beside Grayson and somehow managed to grip two bottles, while still holding Bea with one arm.

"So, did you figure out the whole romance thing?" Grayson asked.

Jana's eyes leaped to Hunter. *Romance thing?*

The annoyed look in Hunter's narrowing eyes told her that

Grayson had just slipped up.

As if he'd heard Jana's thoughts, Sawyer asked, "Romance thing?"

Hunter sat down beside Jana, still cradling Bea, and handed one of the drinks to her. When she didn't take it, he arched a brow and smirked, as if to say, *Take it, or they'll know something's up.*

She reluctantly took the drink, trying not to let her heart swell at the scent of the baby and Hunter mixing together.

"Clark's having trouble with his wife," Hunter explained. "I was trying to find ways for him to help their relationship."

Sure you were.

"Romance will usually do it." Sky leaned her head on Sawyer's shoulder. "That's how Sawyer won me over."

"I think everything Tony does is romantic." Amy reached for her husband's hand.

A wisp of her blond hair blew onto Amy's cheek, and Tony tucked it behind her ear, then leaned over and kissed her. "What was it that you said last night? Seeing me changing Hannah's diaper was like watching mommy porn?"

The girls laughed and Caden, Bella's husband, said, "Bella tells me that listening to me sing to Summer is better than listening to Adam Levine or Luke Bryan."

"Bella?" Jenna said. "You lie to your man like that?"

"Hey!" Bella leaned in to Caden's side. "Neither of those guys could look as hot as my hubby does with Summer. They couldn't hold a candle to him anyway. You've never seen my man wearing nothing but his holster and police boots."

"And she never will," Pete said as he pulled Jenna onto his lap.

Jana glanced at Hunter, who looked hot as sin no matter what he wore, and even more handsome holding a baby. It had been almost a year since they'd first hooked up, and in the months since Sawyer and Sky came together, she and Hunter had continued hooking up—*and* arguing like cats and dogs.

Was that why she always snuck away while he was sleeping? To avoid a morning argument? To ensure he knew they'd shared nothing more than a night of fun? She had no idea what the reason was, but she knew it irritated Hunter. Mostly because he claimed that escaping was his modus operandi, and Jana thought that made doing it even sweeter. She loved having the upper hand.

"Tell them the truth, Hunter," Grayson urged. "He and Clark were looking up *how to be romantic*." He laughed, and Jana felt her jaw drop open at his unknowing reveal of Hunter's truth.

Hunter shrugged and sucked back his drink, like it was no big deal.

Now, as she thought of Hunter searching *how to be romantic* after she'd thrust the challenge on him, she felt a little bad for always sneaking off.

She shouldn't keep watching him, but she was unable to look away as the others rattled on about romance and online information. She shouldn't feel like she wanted to reach out and touch him and tell him that looking up *how to be romantic* might just be the most romantic thing she'd ever heard in her entire life. But it was, and as her hand touched his arm and the words fell from her lips, she discovered that a moment of silence mingled with a single look could hold a million meanings. Tangled up with surprise and disbelief, she saw gratitude in Hunter's gaze. Genuine, heartfelt appreciation, and that made her body warm for a whole new reason. She liked that reason a lot. In fact, as a smile spread across her lips, she realized—or maybe *accepted*—that she liked Hunter a whole lot, too.

CHAPTER SEVEN

THE NEXT MORNING Hunter set out for an early run, hoping to shed the tension nesting in his shoulders and outrun the emotions spiraling inside him. He tried to make heads or tails of what he'd felt last night when he was with Jana, but by the time he'd finished his run, he was no less confused.

Running had never done it for him, but he'd hoped this time might be different. If nothing else, at least it woke him up after a lousy night's sleep.

He went into the shop early. Just the sight of their warehouse and shop brought a modicum of relief. He and Grayson had bought the property a few years earlier at auction. The purchase had also included a building that was right off of Route 6, the main highway through the lower Cape. They'd planned to make that building into a showroom, but they were so busy from the moment they got started that they sold their work as quickly as they could make it. With the help of Pete and their good friend Blue Ryder, both skilled craftsmen, they'd renovated the barn into an office and workshop. They'd replaced the old wooden floors with concrete, built a brick forge, installed proper ventilation systems, and brought in power. The custom shelving and machinery hubs brought a sense of organization to their creative chaos. The showroom idea had gone by the wayside, and the building remained empty.

Hunter didn't trust himself to work with the forge until he had his mind and body under control. The forge was the hearth used for heating metal. Safety had to come first, and in his line of work, that meant being in total control at all times. He definitely did not feel in control of his emotions. He'd been trying to figure out why Jana wouldn't admit she wanted him when she so obviously did. It shouldn't matter one way or the other, but she was sending him mixed signals, and it was pissing him off.

He was still coming up with a theme for the sculpture for the community beautification competition and was trying not to stress as days were passing by without a firm direction. He laid out the pieces he'd fabricated the other day and decided it wasn't so bad, even if he wasn't feeling bonded to it yet. Maybe if he worked on it for one more day, it'd speak to him. He hadn't been blocked creatively in so long that on top of everything else, it annoyed the hell out of him.

He decided to fabricate curls of wrought iron that could be used to accentuate just about any design. The scroll bender machine allowed him to focus on the task at hand without the danger of burning himself or anything else around him. He laid out the pieces of iron he intended to curl and set out the sections, the parts of the machine he'd drop into place to allow for a larger curl around the first. Once the parts were laid out he began curling the iron. Whether he was heating metal, hammering it into place, installing rivets, twisting, curling, or designing on paper made no difference to Hunter. It all made his adrenaline rush. He loved taking an idea and bringing it to life. *Life* was a palpable element in all of Hunter's designs.

Every piece of art he created, whether architectural or for show, got the same attention to detail. He preferred to bring textures and naturalistic elements into all of his creations. His favorites were elements that symbolized growth and stability, or fluidity and change.

"I'm here," Clark called to him when he arrived.

"Gray's going to be late," Hunter hollered back, remembering his brother mentioning it last night.

He knew Clark had planned to meet one of their buddies for dinner last night, and when Hunter had arrived home, Clark was on the phone in the guest bedroom. He assumed—*hoped*—he'd been talking to Nina.

Clark brought a to-go cup of Dunkin' Donuts coffee back to Hunter.

"Thanks, man."

"You were gone when I got up this morning. I thought you'd need it. Have fun at the bonfire?" Clark's eyes still appeared tired, but if he was tired from talking to his wife all night, maybe that was a good thing.

"Yeah. It's always good to catch up with everyone. And it was great to see Bea. She's really cute." After holding Bea last night, seeing her sweet face, and smelling her baby scent, he'd thought about how innocent babies were. How they relied on the adults around them to love them and keep them safe. As he looked at his friend now, he couldn't fathom how Clark could leave his son. If Hunter had a child, he couldn't imagine leaving it while he went to work, much less moving out.

"I heard you on the phone when I got in last night. Things better with Nina?" Hope filled his chest as a smile spread across Clark's face. And, he noticed, Clark had shaved today. That had to be a good sign. Shit, he'd never noticed stuff like that before. Jana must really be getting to him.

"Nah. Robert and I hit the Beachcomber last night. Met this hot blonde and—"

Hunter ground his teeth together. "Tell me you didn't mess with her."

"No, I didn't *mess* with her. We talked, man. That's it." Clark shoved his hands in his jeans pockets, his shit-eating grin still in place, which further angered Hunter.

Everything pissed him off lately, but after hanging out with his friends last night, feeling the love of each couple, seeing the evidence of their love in the babies' faces, he was even more upset over Clark's separation.

"At one o'clock in the morning?" It came out as an accusation, and Hunter didn't try to soften the message.

Clark's smile went flat. His brows drew into an angry slash. "Yeah, what's it to you? We talked. We didn't fool around. I never touched her. We talked about shit."

"What kind of shit?" Hunter crossed his arms, unwilling to ease up.

"I don't know. Billy. Marriage. Life." Clark paced, and Hunter knew he'd gotten to him.

"With some chick you met at a bar? You shared the details of your marriage with her? Clark—"

"What?" The venom in his voice rivaled the disgust moving through Hunter.

Hunter knew he was on the verge of saying things he would regret. He took a step back, trying to regain control.

"Don't you think you should be putting your time into your relationship with Nina? The mother of your child?" As he said the words, he pictured Clark out at a bar, sidling up to a random pretty woman, while Nina sat at home with Billy, probably crying her eyes out over their separation.

"Christ, Hunt," Clark said. "I thought you were on my side in this."

"I am on your side. But I've got to be honest, Clark. I'm on Billy's side, too. Have you thought about what Nina's doing while you're out drinking and picking up women?"

"I didn't pick her up." Clark began pacing again. He ran a hand through his hair and sighed. "Nina won't talk to me. She said I need to grow up. *Grow up!*" He scoffed, shook his head. "I work my ass off to keep her and Billy in a nice house, to put food on the table…"

"Listen, Clark, I don't claim to know much about relationships, but maybe Nina needs to feel like a woman as much as you need to feel like a man."

Clark stopped pacing.

"Think about it." Hunter leaned against the workbench. "I know it's been forever since you guys have had sex, but take that further. When's the last time you had *wild, crazy, uninhibited* sex with your wife?"

Clark shrugged. "I don't know. Before Billy, maybe?"

"Well, maybe you don't need to flirt with other women. Maybe you need to flirt with your wife. When was the last time you told her how beautiful she was? Hell, when was the last time you looked at her like you couldn't keep your hands off her?"

"She doesn't talk to me, Hunter. I'm sure I look at her like I'm trying to decide if I need to walk on eggshells or not."

"That's an even better reason to put forth more effort, man. You *married* a woman who used to make you hard when you heard her voice. Remember? You told me that she owned you. *Owned you*, Clark. She's the same woman, only now she's also the mother of your child."

"She's even more beautiful than the day I met her, but—"

"No. Stop. No 'buts.'" As he said it he knew just what Clark needed to do, and it surprised the hell out of him that he was the one who realized it first.

"Let me babysit Billy tonight while you go out with your wife. Call her up and ask her out on a date. Show her you want to try to remember the couple you once were. Flirt with her. Let her know you think she's beautiful." The more he thought about it, the more he wanted this to work. "I'll even do you one better. Take her to a B&B for the night. I'll stay overnight with Billy."

Clark scoffed again. "You? Babysit overnight? I can ask my mom or something. You don't need to do that."

"Do you want your mom knowing you're having trouble in

your marriage?" Hunter knew he wouldn't want that. Clark's mother was a primo meddler. "Let me do this for you. Go make plans to fuck your wife until she can't remember why she was mad at you in the first place. You'll both feel better."

"Really?"

Hunter nodded.

"Who knew that you had marriage advice in you?" Clark slapped him on the back and headed toward the front office. He stopped halfway to the door and turned back. "When you talk about me and my wife, it's not *fucking*. It's making love. There's a huge difference. When it comes to Nina it's all about love, man, nothing less. Thanks for reminding me."

Hunter smiled to himself, and he realized that he was no longer pissed. He zipped off a quick text to Jana, then set aside the rods he'd been working with and started up the forge.

AFTER TEACHING HER classes and organizing her thoughts for the next day's classes, Jana filled in at Undercover, finally arriving at the little cottage she rented at a few minutes after eight. She was tired from being out so late again last night, and as she retrieved her mail, her arm muscles burned, a gentle reminder of what she and Hunter had spent their time doing before the bonfire.

She rifled through the mail on her way across the seashell walk that led to the front door. She loved the cozy cottage. It wasn't in walking distance to any beaches or tourist attractions, and she liked living tucked away at the end of a dirt road. The cottage had only one bedroom, with a kitchen barely big enough for one, a living room–dining room combination, and one full bath, which was perfect for her. As much as Jana loved being with people, hanging out and listening to music, when she was home, she wanted privacy.

The owners of the house had a landscaper who maintained the yard, and she loved having her first cup of coffee sitting at the kitchen bar while the sun crept over the backyard. That first morning light gave the yard a magical feeling as it shined down on rosebushes, rhododendrons bursting with large blooms, and tall pitch pine trees surrounding the lush green lawn.

As she stepped onto the front porch, she thought of Hunter again, standing in her doorway with his helmet under one arm, looking like sex personified. She smiled, then quickly wiped the grin from her face as she remembered his earlier text. *Ready to admit it yet?*

No, she wasn't ready to admit anything to him. Why did he even want her to?

She shook her head as she unlocked the door, stopping cold when the memory of his cologne hit her. She couldn't remember him ever wearing cologne before, and it dawned on her that maybe he'd worn it for her.

No way.

She thought of his freshly shaved cheeks.

Maybe…

She realized she hadn't heard from him since that text early this morning, which confirmed in her mind what she'd been thinking all day. Last night when she'd seen him with Bea, she'd seen him through girly goggles, those invisible lenses that make men appear like something they weren't simply because of the presence of a baby, or puppy, or kitten.

She set her things by the front door and sank down on the couch with a sigh, glad to be off her feet. She toed off her shoes and tucked her feet beside her, still thinking about last night. She'd let Hunter bind her wrists, and she'd loved knowing he was in complete control of her pleasure and her safety. Why had it been so easy to trust him? She should probably feel embarrassed by what they'd done, or worry that he might tell someone like Grayson or Sawyer, when he was out with the guys. Oh, she hated that idea, but she couldn't hold on to the worry, and she realized that she had a strong sense of trust when it came to Hunter. She tried to dissect where that trust came from. Was it a false sense of security that she needed to let go of? She hadn't trusted a man in years—if ever—other than her brothers and father, but that was a different type of trust.

She tried to slough off the worry. Of course she trusted Hunter. He was *Hunter*, the guy who always tried to make sure his family and friends were happy. The guy who had dropped everything for Sky too many times to count. The guy who made beautiful art and looked at her like he wanted to devour her.

Ugh. That was what was wrong with the equation. *He was Hunter:* The guy who looked at lots of women like he wanted to devour them—and made good on that desire.

As she leaned back and closed her eyes, she wondered why that should matter. Hadn't she done the same thing with men? Well, maybe not lately, since she and Hunter began hooking up more regularly, but she was definitely the girl who didn't go home alone if she didn't feel like going home alone.

Why was she thinking about what he did with other women anyway? It wasn't like she was looking for a boyfriend. If she were, she would walk away from him in a hot second, because he was *not* boyfriend material. But she was only looking to have fun, so…She didn't see a need to walk away just yet. Not when everything he did when they were alone made her feel more alive than any man ever had. Not when every kiss set off a five-alarm fire inside her and every touch made her crave the next. And especially not after the way he'd carried her into the bedroom and held her until she'd stopped trembling last night.

She'd been trying not to think about those tender moments, because she didn't believe they meant anything, but every few hours the feel of his arms around her crept back in. The look of compassion that had washed through his eyes returned.

She had to stop thinking about those seconds—and that's really what they were. *Seconds.* Flashes of something she'd probably imagined.

She fixed herself a salad and ate it while flipping through a gossip magazine. She was looking forward to taking a long hot bath to soothe her aching muscles and relax her into what would hopefully be a long night's sleep. She was having breakfast with Sky and their friends at Seaside, and she was excited to have some girl time. Sometimes her days flew by so quickly she barely had time to think.

At nine she filled a glass with wine and ran a hot bubble bath. She stripped out of her clothes, then thought better of the one glass of wine, wrapped a towel around herself, and grabbed the bottle, bringing it with her into the bathroom. She slid into the divine warmth and closed her eyes.

The ache in her shoulders was just beginning to diminish when her cell phone vibrated from within her jeans on the floor by the tub. She ignored it, determined to relax. A few minutes later it vibrated again. She gulped down her wine, and when her phone vibrated a third time, she gave up and reached for it.

Despite herself, a smile tugged at her lips when she saw DO NOT RESPOND! on the screen. She wondered what Mr. You Know You Want Me would say if he saw that. She read the first text. *What are you doing?* Then the second. *Missing me?* And finally, the third. *Guess what I'm doing?*

She wiped her hands on the towel, wondering why he was suddenly texting her, and sent off a quick reply. *You're texting me.*

She set the phone down and closed her eyes again, hoping that was a bland enough response to warrant a little peace. When her phone began vibrating like it was on speed, she couldn't help but satisfy her curiosity.

She opened the first message, and while she was trying to figure out whose adorable little boy was in the selfie with Hunter, several more pictures came through. She scrolled through pictures of Hunter and the green-eyed cutie. He sent a picture of the little boy sitting on his lap with an open book, and she tried to picture Hunter reading to the child. The next picture was of them both eating curly pasta. Next was a picture of the little boy in cute pajamas with bears on them, and finally, a picture of the little boy fast asleep, snuggled beside what was probably his favorite blanket.

Jana heard her voice saying, "Aw," before she realized she'd said it aloud. Another text came through.

I'm babysitting Clark's son so he can go out with his wife.

As good of a guy as he was, she couldn't imagine him giving up a few hours to babysit. But that was just like Hunter, doing something that made her think he could be more than a hookup if he ever wanted to be.

She responded honestly. *That's so sweet of you.*

Hunter's response came seconds later. *It's fun, actually. The little guy is great.*

Jana typed back, *How late are you babysitting?*

His response came quickly. *All night. Clark and Nina needed time to reconnect. Billy's down for the count.*

Jana tried to process Hunter giving up an entire night to babysit, and before she could respond, he texted again. *It was my idea.*

Jana stared at the text for a minute. His idea? Wow. Her phone rang, and she nearly dropped it in the tub. She answered his call, and true to Hunter's form, he spoke before she had a chance to even say hello.

"Now it's your turn," he said. "What are you doing?"

Her eyes dropped to the bubbles in the tub. "Taking a bath." *Oh God, why did I tell you that?* She closed her eyes, expecting a snappy comment in return.

"Sore from last night?" he asked with an empathetic tone.

Surprised, she said "No" too quickly, then softer, "Maybe a little. In a good way."

"I'm sorry. I didn't mean to hurt you." He sounded like he

meant it, which made her stomach flutter.

"You didn't. I'm not complaining." Her bravado felt funny while she was in the bath, naked.

"Is the bath helping?"

"Yes. The wine helps, too. Hold on." She set the phone down and refilled her glass. When she picked it up again, she said, "Sorry, I'm back."

He was silent.

"Hunter?"

"Yeah. I'm here." He let out a loud breath. "Just trying not to think about you in the bath. Naked."

"Funny. I'd think you'd be all over that thought."

"Maybe if I were in a position to come see you, yeah. I'm trying to delete the image of you naked from my mind right now. Don't talk for a second. Your voice gets me every time."

Good to know. Toying with Hunter was the perfect way to relax. "It does?" she said in the most seductive voice she could muster.

"Jana," he growled.

Oh, this is so fun! She was giddy despite herself and couldn't resist using her best Little Miss Innocent voice. "What, Hunter? You don't want to hear about how the bubbles are just starting to dissipate and I can see my nipples poking through the surface, and—"

"Fuuuck," he whispered.

Hearing the restraint in his tone turned her on. She'd never had phone sex before, but teasing Hunter was too much fun to stop.

"Now, that sounds like a good idea, but since you're there and I'm here…" She sank lower into the water. "The water's getting cooler, but I'm getting warmer."

"You're getting…" He said something she couldn't make out. Then she heard him moving around. "I'm taking the baby monitor into the guest room."

"Look at you, all responsible like a big boy."

"I'll show you a *big boy*," he growled.

Jana's body shuddered with that promise. She heard a door close and then Hunter breathing harder.

"Tell me what you're doing, Hunter." She slammed her eyes shut and mouthed, *Oh my God!* to the empty bathroom, unable to believe she was actually doing this.

"I'm getting comfortable, taking off my jeans." She heard the sound of what she assumed was his clothes landing on hardwood. Then he came back on the line.

"Okay, pretty girl." Confidence controlled his deep, lust-filled voice. "I want to see you."

"What?" Her eyes flew open wide. "No."

"Come on. Let's FaceTime. It's just you and me. Billy's asleep. Let me see that pretty face of yours."

"No. No way." Her body prickled with excitement at the enticing thought of crossing another line with Hunter.

"You won't let me see those gorgeous blue eyes of yours while we get naughty?"

She didn't answer, because a big part of her wanted to watch him touch himself, too. The idea had her panting. Her nipples were on fire they were so hungry for his touch.

"Have you done this before?" he asked.

She contemplated lying, but "No" slipped out before she could stop it.

He was quiet for a long moment before saying, just above a whisper, "Neither have I."

He was silent again, and she knew he was being honest.

"I've never wanted to pleasure a woman without being in the room before, but the thought of making you come with just my words and your hands? Jana, that's so fucking hot."

She felt her cheeks heat up, and she was so caught up in thinking about watching him touch himself that she couldn't respond.

"You still there, pretty girl?"

"Mm-hm."

"I trust you, Jana. Do you trust me?"

"Yes," she whispered, unsure if she'd said anything at all.

"Good, because you can. One of the things I like most about you is that you're not afraid to enjoy your sexuality."

She closed her eyes, feeling nervous and excited at once.

"You're not afraid to tell me what you like," he said in a heady voice, "or to take what you want from me. Most women aren't like that. Did you know that?"

"No," she whispered.

"You're different. I think that's why we keep coming back to each other. Because we're the same in that way, Jana. With you, I can be myself. I can take, demand, push the limits, and I know you'll tell me to back off if I come on too hard. You will, pretty girl, won't you?"

"Yes." Her body was trembling now, not from the tepid water, but from the anticipation of doing something so naughty with Hunter. The scintillating sound of his voice had always turned her inside out, but right now it had her on pins and needles.

"Good. I always want you to feel like you can tell me what you want. What you need."

The air left her lungs in a nervous rush. She slid one hand beneath the water and touched the slick heat between her legs, trying to ease her needy ache.

"Jana?"

"Mm." Eyes closed, her finger moved over her swollen sex.

"Tell me you want me, baby." His voice was thick with need, and she knew he wanted, maybe even needed, to hear it, but she wasn't about to give in.

"Never." The word came out heated, accompanied by a smirk.

"Fuck, Jana. Really?"

"Really." She smiled, eyes still closed.

"You're going to be the death of me."

"Not tonight, I hope."

He laughed, a deep, sexy laugh that made her want him even more.

"I want to see you, pretty girl."

The hand between her legs stilled. Her eyes blinked open. She could say no. Deny him what he wanted. But that would be denying herself what she wanted, too.

CHAPTER EIGHT

HUNTER'S HANDS WERE shaking. He had no idea what had possessed him to turn up the heat with Jana, but hell if he wasn't hard as stone and ready to play. The baby was fast asleep, he had the baby monitor, and the doors were locked. So it wasn't worry over Billy that was causing his hands to tremble. He was nervous about what they were about to do. He'd never jerked off in front of a woman before, but with Jana, he couldn't imagine anything more erotic.

"I want to see you, too." Her voice sounded thin and shaky, and he knew she was nervous, too.

"I'm going to end this call and FaceTime you. Don't go anywhere." He ended the call, ran into the guest bathroom, where he'd seen a bottle of lotion, and tossed it on the bed while the FaceTime call connected faster than he thought possible. The idea that Jana might back out in the thirty seconds it took to call made his heart race.

Her face appeared on his screen, and he could see the porcelain tub behind her shoulders, water at the crest of her collarbone, and the rosy blush on her cheeks, which was beyond sexy. She smiled, then immediately trapped her lower lip between her teeth. He wanted to climb through the phone and kiss her luscious lips. She was so fucking brave it blew him away.

"Hey, pretty girl." He was shirtless, wearing only his black boxer briefs. He held the phone where he knew she couldn't see lower than his chest. His heart was racing so fast he worried she'd be able to tell.

"Hey."

"Nervous?"

She nodded.

"Me too. You look so damn sweet. Not at all like the mouthy blonde I'm used to."

Her brows drew together, but the edges of her lips curved up. "Well, you don't have that arrogant tilt to your smile, either. You sure this is okay while you're babysitting?"

He held up the baby monitor so she could see it. "The magic of electronics. I'd never do anything to endanger Billy."

She blinked several times. "I know you wouldn't." Her voice was breathy, and he wished he could feel it on his skin.

"Can you set up the phone so I can see you? Free your hands?"

She pressed her lips together and her eyes darted around the tub. "Yeah, but it's getting cold in here. Hold on." She set the phone against something, giving him a clear shot of the upper half of her body as she leaned forward, and he heard water running. "I'm adding warm water; hold on." She went up on her hands and knees, and he thought he might come at the view of her up on all fours.

"Holy hell, you're fucking incredible, pretty girl." He palmed his cock through his briefs, then quickly took them off and set them on the chair by the bed in case Billy woke up.

"Stop. You're embarrassing me," she said as she turned off the warm water and settled back into the tub.

He set the phone up on the bedside table so she could see his face.

"Lower, please," she said.

His eyes shot to hers. "You are a naughty, naughty vixen, Jana Garner. And I like you way more than I should right now." He hesitated before moving the phone. He was torn. He wanted to watch her face while she touched herself, but getting a view of her whole body *and* face would be ideal.

"Set the phone farther away, so I can see all of you."

"You first," she snapped. Her confidence had returned, and it sent fire through his veins.

"Christ." He shifted on the bed so he was farther from the bedside table, and she had a clear shot of him from mid-thighs up. He gripped the base of his cock and squeezed, trying to quell the dull ache at the base of his spine.

"Wow, the angle makes you look huge!" She laughed.

"I am huge, and you know it."

"Well, let's not get into *that* debate." She laughed again as she moved her phone into position.

"Christ," he grumbled. Now he wanted to climb through the phone so he could remind her just how huge he really was. Again and again and again.

"I can't believe we're going to do this. If you tell anyone about this—*ever*—I swear I'll castrate you!"

"You know I never kiss and tell. Besides, you think I want other guys picturing you naked in a bathtub?" As he said the words, possessiveness that was usually reserved for those closest to him flared in his chest, taking him by surprise. Before he could stop himself, he said, "Tell me you won't do this with anyone else." Fuck. That came out more demanding than he meant it to.

"What? Do you think that after doing this with you, I'll suddenly want to do it with everyone?" She rolled her eyes. "Hunter," she said softly. "I never would."

She rested her head back against the tub and closed her eyes. She was so trusting, it made his possessive urges spread like wildfire. When she opened her eyes and turned to face the phone, her shoulders dropped the tiniest bit, like she had been mentally preparing herself for what they were about to do.

"Close your eyes again," he said quietly.

"Why?" Confusion riddled her brow.

"Because you looked so sexy. Just for a second."

"But I want to see you."

"Jesus, woman. Stop arguing for thirty seconds and close your eyes." He wished the lights were out and there were candles, which was weird as shit, because that's another thing he never did. Light candles for a woman. But for some reason, he wanted that for Jana.

When she finally closed her eyes, he took a moment to get his fill of her. Her full, heavy breasts were clearly visible beneath the soapy water. He loved to hold them, taste them, tease them. His eyes traveled lower to one bent knee, and lower still, to where her hand lay over her left hip.

When he spoke, his voice was thick with desire, and soft. "Imagine a dark room, candles set up around the tub."

"Mm. I like that."

"You're lying against my chest. My thighs press against your hips. My cock is hard against your back as I reach around and cup your breasts. Touch your breasts for me, pretty girl."

She cupped her breasts.

"That's it. Now brush those beautiful nipples with your thumbs."

She did, and her lips parted with a sigh, a barely audible moan escaping.

"That's my girl. Jesus, you're so sexy." He put lotion on his palm and fisted his cock, pumping slowly as he watched her.

"Now move your hand down your stomach…That's it, slowly, as if it were mine. What do you want me to do to you, pretty girl?"

"Touch me," she panted out.

"Touch yourself where you want me to touch you." She slid her fingers between her legs, and her neck craned back as she moaned. Then she lifted her head and glared into the phone with a seductive, dark stare.

Her lips curved up as she watched him stroking himself. She licked her lips, swallowed hard, and then her lips parted again. The hungry look in her eyes nearly took him over the edge.

"I like this game," she said in a throaty voice that was sexy as fuck.

"Put your fingers inside yourself, as if they were my cock. Tell me how it feels." He watched as her other knee broke the surface, and her legs fell open. Her knee blocked his view in the tub, and her eyes were glued to his hand as he pumped his hard length. "Talk to me, pretty girl. How does it feel? I can't see. You have to tell me."

"I'm…too busy watching you."

"Squeeze your nipple while you finger-fuck yourself."

She did and cried out, arching up. Her eyes closed as her head lolled back. Hunter grabbed his balls with his free hand.

"Let me see you, baby. Look at me." He was so close to coming he had to squeeze the base of his cock again to regain control.

She opened her eyes, and he could tell she was almost there, too. Her gaze was hazy, her eyes fluttering open and closed.

"Feels…so…good."

"You do feel good, baby. You're so tight, so slick with need. Make yourself come, but I want to hear you say my name when you do, and I want to see those beautiful eyes so I can get lost in you, too."

He saw her arm moving faster, and he quickened each stroke on his rigid shaft.

"I'm gonna…." She brought her eyes to his. "Gonna come."

"Me too, baby. Squeeze your nipple again and let go, as if I were right there between your legs. Hard, fast—Oh shit! Jana—" Hot ribbons of come shot across his chest at the same time as she cried out his name. "Hunter! Oh God!"

Their eyes locked, and Hunter swore that in that split second everything changed. He didn't just see Jana in a bathtub, with the flush of her orgasm glistening on her cheeks. He saw *only* Jana. *His* Jana. He lay back, eyes still on her, feeling bound to a woman for the first time in his life. He smiled, hoping she felt it, too, but she was leaning forward, reaching, and she ended the call. And his heart did that *notice me* thing again, only this time it felt dark and heavy as sadness consumed him.

CHAPTER NINE

ALL MORNING JANA felt elated, liberated even, like she'd joined a new club. *The Virtual Sex Club*, she mused. She loved the way Hunter had looked at her last night, the way he'd made her feel sexy and sensual instead of dirty or cheap, and seeing him touch himself? Well, there were no words to describe the delight she'd taken in that little nugget of pleasure. She could have watched him all night long—*until she just couldn't.*

She'd turned off the phone in the same way she'd always snuck out after he fell asleep: without a word. Only this time she hadn't escaped a morning after. She'd escaped the emotions she'd thought she'd locked away years ago, which were responding to everything they'd shared and threatened to reveal themselves because of the way he'd looked at her in those last few seconds.

Now, as she parked her car in front of the laundry building in the Seaside cottage community to meet Sky and the girls for breakfast, her nerves came alive.

She angled the rearview mirror and looked over her face. Would they be able to tell what she'd done? Did she look…sluttier? *Ugh!* The girls were definitely not sexually repressed, but what she'd done last night suddenly felt forbidden. Beyond naughty. And Hunter was Sky's brother, which made it feel even more like she was crossing a line. She really needed to either stop sleeping with Hunter, or…what? Admit to Sky she was having lots of great sex with Hunter but they weren't even dating?

Why did she think she could do this? It was one thing to hook up and then go on with her days like Hunter was any other guy, but he was Sky's *brother*! She needed to wipe the freshly fucked glow off her face. How did he do this to her with *virtual* sex? The man was a master at seduction.

A knock on her window made her jump. She cut the engine and smiled up at Bella, who was holding baby Summer on her hip and balancing a bowl of dry cereal in her hands. Summer had blond hair like her mama and big brown eyes. She reached her pudgy hands out to Jana as Jana stepped from the car, and as she took the sweet girl in her arms, all her worries melted away.

The power of babies seemed to have grown exponentially overnight.

"You're right on time," Bella said, pulling her into a gentle hug. "The guys just took off for a run, and Leanna brought her newest jam creation for us to try. Oh my gosh, you should see Sloan! He looks just like Leanna now. It's amazing how much babies can change in a few weeks, and Dustin? A Jamie mini-me with Jessica's eyes. Crazy cute, I'm telling you."

Jana couldn't get a word in edgewise, but she didn't care. She was in heaven with Summer pulling on her hair and giggling as she tickled her pudgy belly. They walked across the quad, which is what they called the grassy area between the cottages where they had bonfires and cookouts.

It was a sunny, breezy morning. Crows cawed in the pitch pine trees, and their girlfriends' chatting and giggling made Jana smile.

"Jana!" Leanna was the first to greet her. They hadn't seen each other in weeks, and Leanna looked as happy as always. Her dark hair was tousled, and when she drew back from the hug, she slapped her hand over her mouth. "Oh my goodness. I got Strawberry Spice jam all over you. I'm so sorry."

"I'm on it." Jenna pulled Leanna away and began wiping down Jana's shirt with a wet washcloth. "With babies around, I'm always prepared. I should have had a baby years ago. I could have saved lots of stains from Leanna's hugs."

"Thanks, Jenna, but it's really okay." Jana set Summer in her high chair and went around the table to kiss the others. "Hannah banana looks just like you, Amy." She kissed Hannah's cheek and Hannah held up a fistful of cut-up peaches. "No, thank you, sweet girl. You eat it."

Hannah shoved the food in her mouth with a giggle.

"Oh my goodness, look at you." Jana squeezed Jessica's shoulder. "Can I hold Dustin? Please?"

"Absolutely." Jessica lifted Dustin into Jana's arms.

"He's like a lump of doughy cuteness," Jana said as she touched her nose to his cheek. "And he smells so…babyish." She looked from Jessica to Dustin and back. "I hate to say this, Jess, but this baby is all Jamie, from his jet-black hair to that stubborn little chin. He has your eyes, but wow. I'm surprised you didn't name him Jamie II."

Jessica laughed. "Jamie is way too modest to ever do that. Besides, we wanted to honor his parents. Dustin Ray Reed. Thank goodness his mother's name was Rachel."

Jana kissed baby Bea's head. "You guys must be in heaven. There's so much baby love around this table I can barely stand it."

"Here, sit down." Jessica pulled out a chair for Jana. "You look so natural holding him."

Jana rolled her eyes. "I can barely hold my own chaotic life together. The last thing I need is someone else relying on me."

Bella poured a cup of coffee and set it in front of Jana; then Amy added cream and sugar.

"Thanks, you guys," Jana said. "Hey, where's Sky? She usually beats me here."

"She called a few minutes ago. She said she and Sawyer were up late." Jenna raised her brows in quick succession. "She's not going to make it. Oh! I almost forgot to tell you! Lizzie called her late last night from New York! Apparently she got this big offer to sell the rights to her *Naked Baker* program. She and Blue left yesterday to meet with the network and sign the deal." Blue and Lizzie were two of Sky's closest friends. They'd started dating last summer. Lizzie owned the florist shop beside Sky's tattoo shop in Provincetown, and she also put on a monetized webcast called the *Naked Baker*, where she disguised herself with a wig and dark glasses and baked wearing only an apron and high heels.

"That's incredible," Jessica said. "I actually love her show. I get all sorts of ideas and test them out on Jamie."

"I bet you do." Bella smirked. "Please don't share the details. I've known Jamie since we were babies. The last thing I need is to think about you guys and whipped cream."

Jessica laughed. "Icing, too. Lizzie brought a whole new level of enjoyment to baking. Here, Jana, let me feed Dustin and you can fill us in on your life. It'll be nice to hear about someone else's chaos for a change." Jessica lifted Dustin out of Jana's arms and kissed his cheek. Then she set him in the high chair beside her.

"Yes, do tell." Leanna leaned forward. "You know I adore chaos!"

"You are the definition of chaos, Leanna," Bella teased.

"And proud of it, thank you very much." Leanna smiled at Jana. "Maybe we can help you calm yours, though?"

Jana looked around the table at their eager, empathetic faces. They always made it easy to air out her thoughts. "It's nothing new. You guys know I love teaching dance, and you know my stupid boss has taken off to Plymouth and basically left me holding down the fort."

"Yeah, the bastard," Bella said. "I don't know what makes him think he can treat you that way."

"Because he *can*," Jana answered. "I'm tired of being so crazed all the time. I run from boxing, to dance, to Undercover whenever I help out Colton. I love everything I'm doing, but I wish I could figure out a way to manage it better. And I miss doing theater *so* much." She hadn't realized she felt so frazzled until the words left her mouth.

"So, you want help figuring out how to manage it?" Amy asked.

Jana shrugged. "Honestly? I'm not sure what I want. I miss theater, and until Marco left to open the other studio, I was able to manage my life just fine. But now...I don't know. Maybe I need some kind of change."

"What are the three or four things you like doing the most?" Leanna asked. "I mean, I had eight jobs in four years before I settled on my jam business. You can't be half as crazed as I was."

"What do I like to do? That's easy. Dance, act, box, and..." She wrinkled her nose, knowing the girls would laugh, and said, "Have sex."

Jenna and Bella threw their heads back in laughter, earning a loud wail from Bea. Amy and Jessica covered their mouths and giggled as Jenna tried to soothe Bea.

Leanna's eyes went serious. "Well, we can't let you become a boxing, pole-dancing call girl, now, can we?" Which only made the girls laugh harder.

Amy reached out and touched Jana's hand. "You are *not* going to pole dance or be a call girl. Jana, if you don't want your boss to keep taking advantage of you, then don't let him. Can't you teach dance somewhere else?"

"Not on the Cape. There are only a few studios, and they each only offer certain types of dance. I don't want to give up teaching different styles. I don't want to settle and miss out on teaching the classes I enjoy, so I'm staying, but what I really want...one day..." She focused on a spot on the table, trying to gather the courage to voice what she'd been thinking about recently.

"What?" Jenna pushed.

"What I really want is to open my own dance studio, but I can't seem to make the numbers, or the time, work." She nibbled her lower lip, waiting for them to tell her she was right. There was no way she could do it.

"Oh my God. You totally should do it," Leanna said with wide eyes. She kissed Sloan's forehead and said, "Why not do it?"

"What's involved? Why don't you have the time?" Amy asked. "We're really good at figuring things like this out. We helped Bella with her work-study program at the high school, and—"

"We were right there in the thick of it getting Leanna's business started," Bella said. "Well, we didn't know Jessica then, but Jess is incredibly organized. She rivals Jenna, so I know she can help, too."

"Help? Wait…" Jana saw the gears churning in their minds as they began talking among themselves.

"We can totally do this," Jenna said. "Ames, get your notebook and let's figure this out."

Amy dug around in her baby bag and pulled out a notebook and pen.

"Wait, you guys." Jana looked around the table in shock. "You don't even know the situation yet. I only have a few thousand tucked away, maybe four or five. And my time? Well that's a whole other story. I'm not a big boxer or anything, but Brock is training me, and I love it, and I help Colton when I can for extra money, and I have all this responsibility at Marco's studio. Time is one thing I don't have."

Amy waved a dismissive hand. "Goodness, sweetie. We've heard it all before. You want your own dance studio? We can make it happen. A little grassroots marketing goes a long way."

"You just gave me an idea. What about using the community center for the classes?" Jessica suggested.

Bella's eyes widened. "Yes! Perfect! But we'll need Theresa's approval." She turned to Jana and explained. "Blue renovated the laundry building over the winter, so now we have the laundry area separate from the storage, which was really like a big empty barn since we hardly store anything now that we all live down here and have other houses. He made the storage area smaller, and now we have a recreation area for the community. It's gorgeous, of course, because Blue made it with hardwood floors and everything."

"We renovated it so when it rains the babies don't have to be out under umbrellas," Leanna explained. "It's one thing to get together as adults under umbrellas in the rain, because, you know, we never mind that stuff."

"But with the babies," Amy said as she touched Hannah's cheek, "we don't want them to catch colds. So now we have this amazing space. It's definitely big enough for dance classes."

"Theresa's approval." Jenna narrowed her eyes at Bella. "We should have asked over the winter, when the threat of another one of Bella's pranks wasn't hovering."

"Sky told me about your pranks," Jana said. "They sound hilarious." Every summer Bella pulled a prank on Theresa, who was the property manager, and fairly straitlaced.

"Theresa and I came to an agreement at the end of last summer. No more pranks. I'm done," Bella insisted. She wiped Summer's mouth and said, "I think she'd love to help you out. She might have to charge a nominal fee because of the association rules or something, but we can ask her."

"No more pranks?" Amy shook her head. "I don't believe it. You'll have withdrawals."

Bella laughed. "I think Summer will keep my mind occupied enough to take care of that. Besides, we have a dance business to plan."

They spent the next hour planning and strategizing every aspect of Jana starting her own dance studio. Midway through their planning session, with Jana feeling like she'd just been scooped up by the most amazing team of planners she'd ever met, she called Brock and explained what she was thinking about doing and that for the first time ever she'd have to miss their training session. Brock started to give her a brief lecture on commitment, then, being the incredibly supportive big brother that he was, told her he was proud of her.

"I think we have a solid plan." Amy flipped through the pages of notes she'd taken and read off their to-do list. "Bella, you're going to help Jana design flyers. Leanna, you're going to start getting contacts together that you used for your business to help spread the word, like that woman at the *Cape Codder* newspaper and the other media outlets we talked about."

"Yup. I'm excited," Leanna said. "You should have seen how happy they were when I brought them each a case of Strawberry

Spice jam." Strawberry Spice was Leanna's newest flavor, and all the girls agreed it was the best yet.

Amy continued doling out assignments. "Jenna, you're on list duty. You get to make lists of places for Jana to hang up flyers. And Jessica and I will work with Jamie to develop a website with online registration forms, directions, class descriptions, which Jana will need to help us with." She set down the notebook and grinned. "I'm so excited I feel like I could burst!"

"You guys, my boss would have a fit if he saw flyers going up in town." Jana tried to quell the worry in her stomach, but everything was happening so fast.

"Listen, that's his issue, not yours. He's not even here to see what you do at *his* studio. Do you think he's going to worry about yours?" Jenna reminded her.

"Besides, competition is what makes a business thrive," Jessica said. "Do you think Jamie worried about what Google would think when he unveiled his search engine?"

"Well, no. I guess you're right." A lump formed in Jana's throat. "You guys...I'm so overwhelmed. You haven't known me that long, and you're willing to help me do all this stuff?"

"It's not about how long you've known someone," Jessica said. "Gosh, I knew Jamie was the man for me from almost the very second I threw my phone at him when I was renting the apartment above Theresa's house."

The girls all laughed.

Jessica laughed, too. "It *was* funny. I also knew instantly that you guys were as kindhearted as you seemed."

Bella smiled warmly and said to Jana, "You still see yourself as Sky's friend, but, Jana, we see you as *our* friend. We're happy to help. Now all we have to do is check with Theresa."

"I have an idea!" Leanna jumped to her feet, waking Sloan, who had dozed off in her arms. He began crying and she lifted him to her shoulder and patted his back. "It's okay, baby. Mommy's just excited," she said in a hushed tone. Once he settled down, she spoke softly. "How about if I make Theresa's favorite muffins and we bring them to her tomorrow morning? That should soften her up."

"Sounds good to me," Bella said.

"Wait, you guys. Everything is moving so fast." Jana's heart raced with the idea that this might be able to really happen. "I can't just stop working and start this. I have responsibilities to Marco, and putting out flyers, getting ready, buying supplies, that all takes time. There's so much to do."

Amy waved her hand again. "*Pfft.* Easy peasy. Give Jerko a month's notice, tell Brock you're going to need some time off from training, and focus on making your dream a reality."

"You make it sound so easy. What if I fail?" Her stomach sank. "There are so few dance instruction positions here that I'd probably end up having to drive to Hyannis, or farther, to find another job if it doesn't work out. I'm sure Marco wouldn't take me back after I leave him."

"You don't want to work with him anyway," Bella reminded her.

"I'm the queen of making quick life-altering decisions," Leanna said as she paced with Sloan, who was now sleeping again. "The way I make them is by not thinking them through."

"Oh my God," Jana said. "Harper would lock you in a room far, far away from me if she heard you say that."

Leanna laughed. "That's probably a good strategy on her part. But what I mean is, don't think about failure. Don't even let that enter your mind. Just decide that you're going to make it work. What's the worst thing that happens? You have to start over, or drive farther?" Leanna held Jana's gaze. "Besides, how will you ever know what you're capable of if you don't try? It's like with love. When you know it's right, why question it?"

"Yeah, well. I'm not very good in that department either." Jana glanced at the message light blinking on her phone. She must have been so caught up in the conversation that she'd missed a text from DO NOT RESPOND! She swiped the screen and opened the message.

I dreamed about you in that tub all night. It was a very long night.

Jana felt her entire body flush as she turned her phone over on the table. She had a feeling it was going to be a very long day, too, now that the image of Hunter lying naked on the bed, stroking his hard length, was in the forefront of her mind again.

She thought about that for a moment. She was already exploring uncharted territory with Hunter. Why not make her entire life a shambles and upend her career, too?

"Okay. You've convinced me. Let's do this."

CHAPTER TEN

HUNTER HAD BEEN in a crappy mood all day. It started last night when Jana had ended their FaceTime call without a word. After what they'd done, he'd assumed they'd talk or *something*. Then he'd texted her this morning, and she hadn't texted back. Had he pushed her too far? Crossed a line she was too embarrassed to come back from? Damn, he hoped not.

Last night he'd realized just how brave Jana really was. Boxing was nothing compared to the trust she'd shown in him, the way she'd completely given herself over to their sexy video call. But what he hadn't realized until after she'd failed to return his text this morning was that he'd opened himself up to her, too. He'd trusted her and given just as much of himself as she had.

He tried to work out his frustrations through metalwork, but even the pounding, twisting, shaping, and in the end, *mangling*, just left him even more annoyed. It didn't help that Clark and Nina were arguing again. They'd had a nice time last night, and when they'd returned this morning it had seemed like they were making amends, but by noon Clark had already taken three calls from Nina, and every one of them had ended in an argument.

What was it about women and arguments?

With one last look around the shop, he grabbed his hoodie from his office and stormed up front.

"Taking off?" Grayson asked as Hunter stalked past the drawing table.

"Yup."

"Want to grab a beer?" Grayson set down his pen and leaned back, crossing his ankle over his knee. He looked so relaxed it magnified how stressed Hunter felt.

"Not tonight."

"What's up?"

Jana's got me tied in knots. "Nothing I want to talk about."

Grayson leaned over the table. "Okay, but I'm around if you need an ear. Or a wingman."

"Thanks." Hunter blew through the front doors. Clark had already left for the evening to meet Robert for pizza, and he'd been in an equally bitchy mood by the time he'd left. Hunter wondered if women were worth all this shit. He had no idea how Jana had gotten under his skin, but he was bound and determined to get her out.

He texted her on the way to his truck. *Where are you?*

He waited for her to respond, and when she didn't, he started the engine and drove to her house. The empty driveway made his gut churn. He knew she wasn't boxing. She usually boxed in the morning. Was she out on a date? Was that why she'd ignored his texts?

Why do I even care?

He paced her front yard for a while, trying to figure out what he could do to forget her, but the harder he tried to push thoughts of her away, the more he wanted to see her. Even if it was only to give her shit for ignoring him.

Fuck. He called Undercover to see if she was filling in there. Colton answered on the third ring.

"Hey, Colt. It's Hunter. I, uh…" *Shit.* Now he was checking up on her? What the hell was he thinking? He wasn't thinking; that was the problem. He grasped for an excuse for the call. "Jana left a sweatshirt at the bonfire the other night. Is she working tonight? I thought I'd drop it off."

"No, man. She's teaching at the studio, I think. But you can drop it off here if you want. She picked up tomorrow's night shift."

How could he have forgotten to check the dance studio? "Maybe I will. Thanks." He ended the call and drove over to the dance studio. Jana's car was in the lot, along with a handful of others. He parked along the road and waited, not wanting to interrupt her class and unwilling to leave without talking to her.

He rested his head back and closed his eyes for a second, replaying the night before in his mind. Jana had looked so sweet lying in the tub, and of course, beyond beautiful. He'd felt his heart wake up as he'd watched her, talked to her, *seduced* her. He opened his eyes. Maybe *that* was the trouble. But didn't women want to be seduced? Certainly she could have ended the call if she hadn't wanted to go there.

He chewed on that thought until women began filing out the front doors of the studio, and by then guilt had settled into his gut. He didn't want Jana to feel used, or cheap, or whatever it was that she might be feeling.

Hunter waited until all the cars were gone before stepping

from his truck. His heart was beating so hard he couldn't think. Thankfully, he didn't need to think to end things with Jana. He simply had to tell her that whatever was going on between them needed to stop, because it was totally messing with his head.

And his fucking heart, but he'd never admit that.

He crossed the parking lot and pulled open the front doors. The sound of hip-hop music filled his ears. He followed the music across the hardwood floor to the entrance of the studio. If the sight of Jana wearing skintight black booty shorts that barely covered the curve of her ass and a sports bra wasn't enough to stop him cold, the way she was moving her body was.

He'd seen her dance at crowded bars, and he knew that she could move that slinky body of hers. But the way she swayed her hips in one direction while her shoulders moved in the other, accentuating each move with a thrust of her pelvis, made him instantly aroused. She faced the opposite wall, and as the music slowed, she pointed in front of her and moved her arm in a half circle, as if she were performing for an audience. Hunter took a step back, not wanting to be noticed as she strutted across the floor like she owned it. With his artist's eye, he studied the fluidity of her moves, the sleek lines of her body as she swiveled her hips, seeing more than her sexy movements, but her femininity and in contrast, her power. The delicate way her fingers lifted and stretched, the strong angle of her chin as she used it to emphasize certain moves. She sank to her knees. Her head fell back, eyes closed, and her body began to sway, like the ebb and flow of the ocean. Her long blond hair swept across the floor, and he couldn't help but think about tangling his hands in her thick mane as their bodies joined together.

The music sped up, snapping him out of his reverie. Jana did some sort of moonwalk, then moved into the type of fast-paced, jerky dancing he'd seen professional dancers do in music videos. She was in total control. Each move was clipped and determined, as if she were sending a silent message to the universe. *I am Jana. Hear me roar.* The rhythm ended in a loud crash, and she collapsed to the floor in a heap. Hunter's instincts took over and he ran to her.

"Are you okay?" He searched her eyes, taking stock of her heavy breathing, the sweat glistening from her skin as she blinked up at him, confused.

"Hunter?" Pushing to her feet, she snagged a towel from a table by the door and wiped her face. "What are you doing here?"

"I…" The anger that had driven him there had been replaced by desire, but her response reminded him of why he'd come, making him angry with himself for being turned on, and he snapped, "You didn't return my texts."

She wiped the back of her neck and walked toward the lobby. "So?"

"So?" *Do I mean that little to you? Is everything I've been feeling totally one-sided?* He didn't know if he was hurt or angry.

"I was busy."

He followed her into a crowded office, annoyed that she could write him off so easily. She pushed between a rack of dance outfits and a stack of mats and leaned across a desk in the center of the room, giving Hunter a great view of her ass.

"What did you need, anyway?" she asked, straining to reach farther.

He should take the hint. Walk away. Chalk it up to his emotions being as fucked up as his creativity lately. But as if his body had a mind of its own, his legs carried him forward and his hands went to her hips, dragging her body against him. He felt the demand breaching his lungs and gave in to it all—the emotions, the desires, the unfuckingbelievable hold she had over him. "What do I want?"

"Hunter." Her warning was tentative at best, and it made him smile despite his rattled brain.

His fingers dug harder into her hips as she straightened to her full height.

"Jana." He loved the way her name felt as it burst from his lips, full of want and need and so much more. Could she hear it, too?

"What do you want?" she whispered.

"I don't know, Jana. What do you want?" He spun her in his arms. His lips hovered over hers. He could feel her heart beating frantically against his. Did she feel it? Did she know how much of him she already owned?

"I…" She licked her lips, and he pulled her tighter against him, wanting to follow that swipe of her tongue with one of his own. "You came to see me, remember?"

"Yeah, I remember." He cupped her cheek and brushed his thumb over her lower lip. "The trouble is, I can't remember why I was so angry when I came to see you, because right now there's not a speck of anything close to anger inside me."

"No anger," she whispered.

"Not anymore." He nipped at her lower lip. "You're killing me, pretty girl. The way you moved out there. Last night on the phone. Your voice tears at my insides. When you deny me, it cuts like a knife." He wanted to kiss her so badly he couldn't take his eyes off of her mouth. "You've gotten so far under my skin, you're a part of me I can't escape."

Her cheeks flushed, and she trapped her lower lip between her teeth. Her fingers dug into his waist. He leaned forward and tugged her lip free with his teeth.

"Do you want me, too?" He felt his lips curve up, realizing what he'd asked and how naturally the question had come.

Her eyes flared with heat. She was trying to be strong. He could feel it in her body as she tensed against him, and he knew she wasn't going to give him the answer he wanted. Her stubbornness was definitely one of the things he liked most about her.

But he wanted—*needed*—to hear the words from her.

"I'll give you sunsets." He nudged her knees open and pressed his hard length against her. "If you tell me the truth. Tell me you want me, Jana."

She was panting now as he wrapped his hand around the nape of her neck, holding her in place.

"We don't"—she licked her lips again—"do sunsets." Her eyes fluttered closed, then opened again.

"Maybe we should." He could hardly believe what he was suggesting, but hell if he wasn't thinking that everything would be *better* with Jana by his side. The prolonged anticipation of kissing her, tasting her, was unbearable. "Tell me what I want to hear, pretty girl, and I'll give you what you want."

He couldn't wait another second. Not even long enough to hear her response. He traced her soft lips with his tongue, earning a sexy whimper from her. It was killing him not to strip her bare and bend her over the desk, but he no longer wanted to be her hookup. He didn't want to share her with anyone, and he had no desire to kiss another woman. He wanted more. With Jana. Only Jana.

Her fingers climbed the muscles on his back, digging into his skin as she sealed her lips over his in a demanding kiss. Hunter met her tongue, swipe for eager swipe as he rocked between her legs. He lifted her onto the desk, never breaking their connection, and she widened her legs for him. He couldn't resist touching her hip, squeezing her thigh. She arched against him, spurring him on, until he finally gave into his desires and slipped his fingers beneath her shorts, feeling the slick heat between her legs.

"Fuck, pretty girl. You *do* want me." He was never going to get her to say it, not if every time they were together he gave her what she wanted, and for some reason, hearing her say it suddenly mattered a hell of a lot.

She hooked one leg around his waist, opening herself up to him. It took all of his willpower, but he pulled away. The pit of his stomach clenched tight with need and a sense of loss as he withdrew his fingers from her shorts.

"Hunter—" She reached for the button on his jeans, but he gently grabbed her wrist and shook his head.

"When you're ready to tell me you want me, you know how to find me." He lowered her leg from around his hip, and it seemed neither one of them moved for a full minute before he turned to leave.

"Seriously?" she called after him. "You're *leaving?*"

He strolled toward the front door feeling like a dick for leaving her hot and bothered, but he was just as ready, and for the first time in his life, he wanted more than a good fuck, and he wanted that with her. "Yup."

"Hunter, what the hell?" She grabbed his arm, and he turned to face her.

He willed himself to act casual, which was torturous when there was nothing casual about what he wanted to have with her.

"We're not even dating, Hunter. Why do you need to hear anything at all?"

She crossed her arms, and the hurt in her eyes nearly took him to his knees, but he dug deep and remained strong, somehow knowing he needed to, for both their sakes.

"I have no idea," he said honestly, "but with you, I do."

As he walked out the door her voice trailed after him. "Then maybe you should figure out this romance shit first!"

Maybe I just did.

CHAPTER ELEVEN

JANA AWOKE TO someone banging on her front door at five thirty in the morning. She clutched her blanket, heart pounding, and tried to coax her sleepy brain into functioning.

The banging stopped and she grabbed her phone. She'd missed three calls from DO NOT RESPOND!

Goddamn it, Hunter. What now?

Without reading the texts she went to the front door and peeked outside. Sure enough, Hunter was standing there in a pair of low-slung jeans and a sweatshirt, with the hood pulled over his head. She yanked the door open.

"What are you doing here this early, and why do you look like a gangster?"

His eyes roved over her clingy tank top and panties. "Do you always answer the door nearly naked?"

"Only to strange men who knock before sunrise. What do you want, Hunter? To drive me insane again and leave me high and dry? Because that's not really romantic." She turned and walked toward the kitchen.

He grabbed her arm and spun her around. "I tried to text you, but you didn't respond."

"Most guys wait until morning to text, so..." Jesus, he

smelled like cologne again, and now that she was more awake, she realized he'd shaved, too. She reached up and touched his cheek without thinking. The muscles in his jaw tensed against her palm. "I like you clean-shaven almost as much as I like your scruffy bad-boy look."

The edge of his mouth tipped up as he stepped in closer, backing her against the wall. He slid his hand beneath her shirt and brushed her nipple with his thumb, stealing her thoughts. "Glad you approve."

Her heart nearly stopped. Oil and water had never felt so good.

"Go get some clothes on before I finish what we started last night." He removed his hand from beneath her shirt and stepped back, leaving her hot and bothered…*again.*

Her eyes dropped to the bulge in his pants, and she was too confused to even try to comprehend what game he was playing. "Clothes?"

"Yeah, you know, the things that cover up those beautiful breasts and sexy little panties?" He took her hand and pointed her in the direction of her bedroom, then gave her bottom a pat. "Go on or we'll miss the sunrise."

"Sunrise?" she mumbled as she walked toward her bedroom wondering what he had up his sleeve.

They drove to the beach in silence, save for the low hum of the truck engine. Hunter looked over at her every minute or so, but he didn't say a word, just rolled his eyes over her face like he, too, was trying to figure out what they were doing. He parked at Indian Neck Beach and came around to her side of the truck as she was getting out.

"I was going to open your door for you." He reached for her hand and she stared at it for a beat.

"Why? What's going on?" She let him take her hand and help her out, then watched as he pulled a cooler from behind the cab of the truck and tossed a blanket over his shoulder. *Wow. You came prepared and everything.*

"We're watching the sunrise. I hear it's romantic." He took her hand and led her to the dunes, where they toed off their shoes and walked barefoot across the cool sand. Hunter wasn't exactly being warm, but she could see he was trying to bridge the gap between them.

Jana liked the feel of his hands laced with hers, but this whole scenario confused the heck out of her. "Hunter, *why* are we watching the sunrise?"

As they crested the hill, ribbons of blues and purples spread across the horizon, reflecting off the water with slivers of light.

"Wow." She stood for a moment, soaking it in. "It's so beautiful."

Hunter looked up from where he was spreading a blanket on the sand. He knelt on the blanket and opened the cooler. "Almost as beautiful as you."

He patted the seat beside him. He sounded so sincere that she was having a hard time reconciling his efforts with the man she knew. Or rather, with the parts of the man she knew within the confines of their relationship. She knew Hunter said nice things to people all the time, but the two of them didn't compliment each other in that way. They told each other they were hot or sexy, but only during sex.

She sank to the blanket beside him, and Hunter handed her a to-go cup of coffee that he must have had in a carrier inside the cooler, and then he handed her a napkin and a paper plate.

"What is all this?" she asked, as he set a banana-nut muffin on the plate, then set one beside it for himself. "Hunter? You brought my favorite muffin?"

He held up his to-go cup and smiled. "Here's to romance, pretty girl."

"You did all of this because I dared you to learn how to be romantic?" Warmth spread through her with the realization. "No one has ever done something like this for me before."

"Maybe you didn't challenge them in the right way." He took a sip of his coffee and lifted it toward her, as if he were toasting.

"So, you did this because you want to hear me say that I want you." She shook her head. "You're unbelievable. I should be in bed, sleeping."

He was about to take a bite of his muffin, and he stopped, mouth open, hand in midair. "Seriously?"

Her life was chaotic enough without confusing what was going on between them as something more. She still wasn't sure exactly what all of this was supposed to mean, and she was afraid to put herself out there on this new level with Hunter. What if she gave in and told him the truth—that she wanted him more than she'd ever wanted anyone or anything in her life—but this was all a game to him? She hedged her bets and went with a middle-of-the-road response.

"You could work on your delivery."

He shook his head, then took a bite of his muffin. His brows knitted, and he nodded as he chewed. "My delivery."

"Yeah. You basically burst into my house and dragged me out here. A woman likes a man with finesse."

He cocked his head. "How would you know? You're not exactly a relationship expert."

"I've had boyfriends before. Besides, a woman knows these things."

She turned away, watching a seabird land by the water's edge and peck at something in the sand. Hunter took her drink and plate and set them aside. He wasted no time in straddling her waist and taking her down to her back, arms pinned beneath his hands. *This* she understood. *This* was Hunter.

"Hunter." She laughed.

"Finesse, huh?" With a wicked glint in his eyes, he lowered his mouth to her neck and nipped at the sensitive skin just above her collarbone. "Tell me about this *finesse*." He dragged his tongue along her neck, then sucked her skin into his mouth, making her entire body catch fire. "First you want romance. Now you want finesse?"

"Hunter." His name came out like a purr.

He sealed his lips over hers in a punishingly intense kiss, then abruptly pulled away, gazing intently into her eyes. "I'm not good at finesse." He lowered his mouth to hers, brushing over her lips, a whisper of a touch, and spoke just above a whisper. "But I'm trying to get romance right."

He was quiet for a long moment. Jana could barely process the emotions in his eyes. He wasn't just looking at her like he wanted her. He was looking at her like he wanted *only* her. Her mind reeled as he eased off of her and sat back down, like he hadn't just sent her world spinning.

They ate in silence, and when they were done, Hunter put away their plates and cups, then scooted closer to Jana. She had never been more aware of their nearness than she was right then. Their legs barely touched from hip to ankle, but it was enough to send goose bumps up her arms. Hunter leaned back on his palms, reaching one arm behind her, so she was tucked in the recess of his shoulder but hardly touching him.

They watched the sunrise with little more than a few words said about passing birds or the colors in the sky. But even the air felt different around them now. Hunter was clearly making an effort, but she wasn't sure he even knew why he was doing it or what it really meant. She liked this, though, sitting close, content without tearing each other's clothes off. When she felt his fingers gently cover hers, she smiled. *Finesse.*

The sun lifted into the sky, its reflection dancing off the water like diamonds. The perfect backdrop to a strange and wonderful morning. She closed her eyes and lifted her face toward the warmth of the sun.

She felt Hunter brush her hair from her shoulder.

"The morning sun looks good on you."

She opened her eyes at the tenderness in his voice and the sweetness of his words and met his gaze. The tense lines around his mouth had softened. Gone were the clenched jaw and the in-control stare, and all that was left was his beautiful face. She was pretty sure he would bark at her for calling him beautiful, but when he wasn't making her crazy, she noticed things like the dimple beneath his left eye, his angular nose, and the way his dark brows arched slightly in the middle. When those brows came together and his gaze turned sinful, he could slay her steely resolve in a single hot second. Now the soft look in his eyes, coupled with the gentle sounds of the bay and the efforts he'd taken to be romantic, slayed her heart instead of her libido.

"What time do you have to be at work?" he asked.

"Work?" *Ohmygod!* She jumped to her feet and began gathering the cooler and tugging at the blanket. "We have to go."

Hunter jumped up, took the cooler from her hands, and followed her as she hurried back over the dune toward the truck. "Why? Do you teach this early?"

"No. I have to meet Bella and the girls." She picked up their shoes and held them against her chest as she ran across the parking lot. "I'm sorry. I don't mean to cut our time short." She really *was* sorry. She wanted to know what might happen next between them, like if she were reading a book, maybe the couple would have shared a tender kiss or said something sweet.

"For what?" He unlocked the door and she climbed in.

She waited for him to settle into the driver's seat and start the truck before answering. "To talk to Theresa about using the rec center for my new dance studio. Hurry, please."

How could she have forgotten to watch the time? Bella had texted her last night to say that Theresa was going back to Boston at nine o'clock for the day. She needed to hurry.

"What new dance studio?" Luckily, the roads weren't busy that early in the morning.

"I'm thinking about quitting Marco's and opening my own studio."

He didn't say anything more until they were driving down her street and he'd pulled into the driveway. She jumped out as soon as the truck stopped.

"You're opening your own studio?" He stepped from the truck as she ran across the lawn carrying her shoes.

"I don't know!" She fumbled with her key, and he came up behind her and took it from her hand, calmly unlocking the door for her.

"Why didn't I know that?" He stood on the front step, clearly waiting for an answer.

"Because we have sex; we don't talk." She saw something that resembled disappointment, or hurt, wash over his face, and she realized she was running off again. She slowed her frantic mind long enough to say, "Thank you for an incredible morning." She dropped her shoes by the door, waiting for him to leave.

"Maybe we should," he said, remaining on the front porch.

"Should…?" She'd been answering so quickly she hadn't really processed the conversation.

"Talk."

"Talk?" She laughed, thinking that maybe he was just playing with her, despite the effort he'd gone to this morning. "Seriously, I've got to get ready." She started to close the door, and Hunter put his hand against it, keeping it open.

"I'm being serious. We should…" He looked around the living room, as if the answer he was seeking was there somewhere. "Have dinner or something."

"Dinner?"

"Yes. We should eat together."

She felt every second ticking away, still confused at where all this was coming from. "We eat in bed. We're good at that."

He crossed his arms and lowered his chin, and she finally understood just how serious he was. *Dead serious.*

"You *want* to have dinner with me? To *talk?*"

"Yes." His response was accompanied by a single curt nod.

"Okay." *Oh my God. Hunter.*

"Okay." A hint of a smile played on his lips. "Tonight."

"It would be nice to ask me instead of tell me."

He dropped his gaze, and when he lifted it, his smile reached his eyes, and her insides went soft.

"Jana, would you like to join me for dinner tonight?"

She couldn't help but smile at the restraint in his voice. "I can't. I'm working until ten. But tomorrow I get off at seven."

"I'll be here at seven forty-five, then. Tomorrow."

"Fine. But just for the record, you could have *asked* if seven forty-five was okay."

"You're a pain, pretty girl. A sexy, smart, scorching-hot pain." He leaned in and gave her a quick peck on the cheek before heading back to his truck.

Jana closed the door and leaned her back against it, wondering how many stars had to be misaligned for Hunter Lacroux to ask her out on a real date.

CHAPTER TWELVE

JANA'S NERVES WERE strung tighter than a ballet dancer's shoe ribbons. She sat between Bella and Leanna on Theresa's couch, trying desperately to stop thinking about her morning with Hunter and focus on her meeting with Theresa. Jana could see from the serious look in Theresa's eyes and the firm press of her lips that she took her job very seriously.

A plate of muffins and a jar of Leanna's jam sat on the coffee table between them. Jana wished she could be on the outside looking in like the rest of the girls, who were watching the babies and, she was sure, watching Theresa's house like hawks.

Theresa crossed her legs and flicked a speck of thread from her pleated shorts. "So, you want to hold dance classes in the rec center? What types of classes, how often, and how many students do you expect to have per class?"

Jana folded her hands in her lap, trying not to fidget as she took a moment to gather her thoughts. "Yes, I would. I don't think you'd allow me to install a ballet bar, so probably hip-hop, jazz, line dance, experimental or freestyle, and maybe ballroom, if people sign up, but that's rare around here." Excitement filled her chest at the thought of actually being able to make these types of decisions for her own studio. "I was even thinking that you guys"—she turned to Bella and Leanna—"might be interested in taking a Foxy Mamas dance class."

"Hold on." Theresa held up her palm and eyed Bella. "Is that some type of dirty dancing? Because I'm not sure we want to get involved with anything like that."

Jana couldn't suppress a laugh before it came out. "I'm sorry, no. Let me explain. It's a beginner freestyle dance class I came up with for new moms, to help them get back in touch with their bodies after having a child. I've found that a lot of new moms feel less attractive, even though they're more beautiful than ever, after giving birth. They spend so much time being mommy that they forget they're women, too."

"Boy, that's the truth," Bella said.

"Dance is a very personal experience," Jana explained. "Learning to move in ways that help new moms feel sexy again is what it's all about." She pushed to her feet and reached for Theresa's hand. "Here, let me show you."

"Oh goodness, no." Theresa shook her head. Bella had warned her before the meeting that Theresa was all business, from her polo shirt and smart layered haircut to her cool demeanor, but Jana wasn't deterred. She believed that all women had an inner sexuality they could channel, and when given the opportunity, most had fun with it.

"Don't be shy. I'm not going to embarrass you. I promise." She pulled her to her feet and Bella gasped. Jana ignored Bella's reaction. Maybe if Theresa got involved she'd be more apt to let her rent the space.

"Leanna, Bella, please join us," she urged. Leanna jumped to her feet, while Bella was more cautious, remaining seated.

"I'm a total klutz," Leanna said. "But I want to take your Foxy Mamas class. It would be great to get in touch with my inner woman rather than my mama side for a while."

"Really? That would be great." Jana looked at Theresa. "I mean, if we end up coming to terms about the space. And, Theresa, please don't feel pressure to approve this whole thing. So, what kind of dancing do you like?"

"I don't really dance anymore," Theresa said. "But when I was a young girl I had my fair share of suitors. I wasn't a bad dancer."

Jana tried to ignore Bella's raised brows. "Wonderful! Here, let me put on some music, and we can see how it goes." She navigated to Spotify on her phone, and within a few minutes Leanna and Bella were rocking out to Taylor Swift, while Theresa moved cautiously.

"That's great. Now try this." Jana showed her how to move her hips in a more fluid motion. She wasn't surprised to see that Theresa picked up the moves quite easily.

"Theresa! Wow, look at you. I can't even do that." Leanna jerked her hips from side to side.

Bella laughed. "Girlfriend, you need that Foxy Mamas class bad."

"I know, right?" Leanna touched Jana's shoulder. "Can you help me do what Theresa is doing?"

"Of course," Jana said. "Theresa, that's marvelous. You've got it." She gripped Leanna's hips and helped her move in a less jerky fashion.

"I feel sexier already," Leanna said. "Kurt is going to be so happy."

They danced for a few minutes, laughing and chatting about how silly they must look. Jana assured them that they looked beautiful.

Theresa looked at her watch and gasped. "Oh my. I have to leave for Boston. I'm sorry, girls, but I need to cut our meeting short."

"Theresa, thank you for considering this, and for taking the time to talk with me this morning. I truly appreciate it." Jana didn't think before she moved in for a hug. Theresa stiffened at first, then awkwardly patted Jana's back. "As I said, even if you don't want to approve the space for classes, I'm so thankful that you took the time to consider it, and I'd still be happy to help you learn to dance if you'd like."

"Oh, goodness." Theresa stepped out of the embrace. "Well, we'll have to review the association bylaws. Assuming there are no legal issues, then we'll have to take a vote of the owners, and if they don't have an issue with it, then as long as we set up rules about hours of operation, number of people on-site, and parking...oh, and insurance. We'll have to speak to our agent about that, and you should look into that, too, Jana. There seems to be much to consider, and I really do have to leave."

"That's okay," Bella said as she opened the front door. "Why don't you take off? In the meantime, Jana can look into insurance and put together the other information you'd like to see."

"So, this is really a possibility, then?" Jana asked.

"Well, let's not get too far ahead of ourselves. We'll need to read the bylaws, as I mentioned. If that's in order, then as long as we can come to an agreement with the rest of the items, you have proper insurance, and the majority of the owners agree…" Theresa smiled as she reached for her keys, glancing around the room one last time.

As soon as they were outside and Theresa drove away, Jana said, "Oh my God! We might really do this!"

Jenna, Amy, and Jessica came outside with the babies and joined them, squealing with joy. After a round of hugs, the girls began talking about the details Theresa had mentioned: insurance, majority vote, parking.

Jana leaned against the laundry building and closed her eyes.

"Oh my God," she whispered more to herself than anyone else. "I might really do this."

HUNTER SPENT THE day helping Grayson with an order for hibachis that had come in late last week. Once they finished fabricating parts for them, Hunter's thoughts returned to Jana. From the moment he'd seen her dancing, so graceful and confident alone in her studio, he'd known exactly what he wanted to create for the competition. After leaving her house last night, he'd come straight to the shop and tried to sketch his ideas, but his thoughts kept racing, then just as quickly, fraying, just out of reach. He'd finally given up and realized that what he wanted to create was too big, too alive, for drawings, and he'd heated up the forge and gone to work.

Now, as he headed out the back door toward the warehouse where they kept the scrap metal, it didn't take long for his mind to skip from images of Jana in her skintight dance shorts and barely there top to the hurt look in her eyes when he'd turned away from her in the studio, causing his chest to tighten. Those thoughts were chased by the surprise in her eyes this morning when he'd shown up at her door, and later, to the confused look on her face as she studied him. His feelings for her had taken a deeper, meaningful turn, and he had a feeling that she'd not only noticed, but was confused by them.

Despite the hot and cold signals Jana had tossed his way, she'd not only gotten under his skin, but she'd found her way into his heart. Not only had Hunter found his creative muse, but Jana had also inspired him in other, more important ways. He'd begun looking hard at the man he'd become, and while he was proud of his accomplishments, and his loyalty to family and friends ran deep, he also saw his faults. And where Jana was concerned, they didn't look like mere fissures. He was staring at the fucking Grand Canyon. He was bound and determined to be the man she deserved. If she wanted romance and finesse, then she was going to get it.

Sometime later, with a cart of metal, he headed back into the shop.

"What's all that?" Grayson asked as Hunter laid the metal out on the table.

Clark came through the doors to the shop and hollered back to them before Hunter could answer. "Do you mind if I take off?"

Hunter and Grayson exchanged a hopeful glance.

"Going to see Nina?" Grayson asked.

"Sort of." Clark joined them by the machinery. "When we went out the other night, it made me realize how much I missed her, and how much I missed Billy."

"That's great, man," Hunter said. He'd heard him on the phone late last night, and he'd been hoping they were patching things up.

"Yeah, I guess. It also made me realize how far we have to go. As a couple, I mean." Clark rubbed the back of his neck and looked away for a moment before saying, "Nina made an appointment with a therapist in Yarmouth, and she wants to talk to each of us separately first, before we do any couples counseling. So I'm taking Billy out for a few hours."

"That sounds like a great start." Hunter was relieved. It sounded like his friend was on the right path. He went into his office, where he'd stowed the pieces he'd made last night. He'd only begun forging the metal for the body, but he could already feel it coming to life. He laid the pieces carefully on another worktable.

"Have fun with Billy," he said to Clark.

Clark lifted his chin toward the table. "New project?"

"No. Just an idea for the competition."

"Cool," Clark said. "Can't wait to see it. I'll catch up with you tonight at your place, then."

"I'll be late," Hunter said, eager to spend a few extra hours working on the sculpture.

Grayson lifted his eyes from where he was crouched before a shelf, picking through iron rods.

"I will, too," Clark said. "Catch ya later."

Grayson rose to his feet. He ran a hand through his thick, dark hair and studied the pieces Hunter had already made. He lifted the piece of metal Hunter had been working with last night. The form hadn't taken shape yet, but it was close enough that he knew Grayson would recognize where he was going with it.

"A woman's stomach?" Gray cocked a brow. "Wow, and I thought you and Jana were just fuck buddies."

"Don't call her that." Hunter snagged the metal from his brother's hand. "It's just an idea I had."

"To build yourself a woman?" Grayson teased. "I'm pretty sure she won't do for you what a living, breathing woman will."

Hunter ignored him.

Grayson laughed. "Okay, seriously. Tell me what's going on, big bro. I thought you were ending things with Jana, and then you show up at the bonfire with her after searching 'how to be romantic' online."

Hunter ran his hands over the smooth, cold metal and set it on the table as he chose the next piece. "It's a dancer, from the thighs up. I see her with her head back, and I'm thinking about thin twisted strips for her hair, hanging down. No eyes, just lashes, nose, and mouth." He pictured Jana in the studio, her head back, eyes closed, as she swayed to the music.

"Wow, dude. You've got it bad." Grayson smiled and patted him on the shoulder.

"It's a piece of art." He wasn't fooling anyone, least of all himself.

"She's getting to you."

Hunter leaned against the table. He crossed his arms and shook his head. "Shit. She already has."

Grayson laughed again.

"Seriously, Gray? What's so fucking funny?"

"You. You have this look of pain on your face, like you can't stand the idea of any woman getting to you, but then your voice is all dreamy like a girl's."

Hunter cocked an arm to punch Grayson, and Grayson sidestepped, laughing louder.

"Bastard." Hunter chased him around the table and grabbed him around the neck, wrestling him into a headlock. "Shut the fuck up."

Grayson continued laughing. Hunter ground his teeth together, trying to stifle his own laugh. Grayson elbowed him in the ribs and spun away with his arms up in surrender.

"Okay, okay. I'll shut up," Grayson said, barely stifling his laughter. "But she's definitely gotten to you. What's so bad about that?"

Hunter grabbed his leather apron and gloves and put them on. "Nothing is bad about it. I just don't need to be given shit about dating her."

Grayson's eyes widened. "Wait, so now you're *dating* Jana? As in, going out in public together on a real date, not just to meet with friends and leave together for the night?"

Hunter slid him an annoyed look and put on his safety

goggles. "Yes. We're going to dinner tomorrow. On a real date. My first one in, what? A decade?" He picked up a piece of metal with tongs and headed for the forge.

"You know, she's actually perfect for you." Grayson followed him over.

"Yeah? Why's that? Because she's smart as shit, sexy as hell, and a big pain in the ass sometimes?" Even as he said the words, he smiled. He loved when she was a pain in the ass. That's what made her *Jana*.

"Those things, sure. But she calls you on your shit every time we're out, just like you call her on hers. You two are like male and female versions of each other. You're both stubborn as hell."

Hunter turned the metal over as it reddened above the hot coals. "We're both sexy as hell, too," he teased.

Grayson grabbed a hammer and handed it to Hunter as Hunter rested the red-hot metal on an anvil. "So where are you taking her?"

"I was thinking about going to Undercover, because I know she loves to dance and she's comfortable there." He'd already nixed the idea of Undercover, because he wanted Jana all to himself, but he wanted to get Grayson's take on the idea. He began hammering the metal into shape.

"You mean you want to stake your claim where she works."

His brother knew him so well.

"Is that a dick move?" Hunter asked, already knowing the answer.

"Depends. Are you seriously going to date her? Do you even

know if you want to? Because I'm pretty sure she'll know exactly what you're doing if you take her there."

Hunter smiled. "Yeah, I definitely want to date her. And claim her. But I'm not taking her to Undercover. I just wanted you to weigh in on the idea to see if I was off base."

"Trust yourself, Hunter. Even if you haven't dated in a long time, you know how to treat a woman right. It's who you are, man. You and me both. We know what to do; we just choose not to. We fight it."

"I'm pretty sure I'm done fighting it." He turned the metal over and hammered it flat, then set it aside and picked up another piece with the tongs. "Well, we'll see. I'm taking her to the Wicked Oyster."

"Wow, you're pulling out all the stops. That place should be called Wicked Expensive."

"She's worth it." The answer came without thought and, he realized, laced with pride. He was taking Jana Garner out on a date, and that made him feel good all over. "By the way. Shaving? Turns out she totally digs it." *And it turns out that I like making her smile rather than seethe.*

CHAPTER THIRTEEN

JANA STOOD AT her kitchen counter the next evening with her cell phone pressed to her ear while she looked over the notes she'd been jotting down since her meeting with Theresa.

"I am so sorry I missed the breakfast when all this went down," Sky said. "Bella said you had her get the answers you needed for the insurance company, so what happens next?"

Jana glanced at the notebook. "I'm compiling a list of things I'll need for the studio, and Amy called earlier. She needed the class descriptions and details about what should be on the registration forms. Jamie hooked me up with sites where I could get templates for the other legal waivers I'll need, too. She said Jamie has the framework for the website almost done, even though we haven't nailed down the location. Those girls, and Jamie, are incredible. They move at lightning speed. How could Jamie possibly do it that fast? All he did was ask me what I wanted on it, and I showed him a few examples."

"Jamie's incredibly smart and talented. Think about it. He invented One Click, Google's rival search engine. Who does that? The man's a genius. A website for him is probably as easy as me tattooing a straight line." Last year Sky had opened her own tattoo parlor, Inky Skies, in Provincetown.

"I guess you're right." She flipped the page and saw where she'd scribbled, *Give notice to Marco?* and underlined it about fifty times. "If this really comes through, I'm not looking forward to giving my notice to Marco. He'll shit a brick."

"Good. He deserves it." Sky said. "I don't understand why you put up with his crap anyway."

"Because unless I want to wait tables my whole life, I have to play the game until I figure something else out."

Jana closed the notebook as a knock sounded at the door, making her instantly on edge. "I've got to go."

"Why so fast?"

"I have a date. I'll call you soon. I don't want to keep him waiting." She blew a kiss into the phone and ended the call before Sky could ask any more questions. Sky would probably get excited if she knew she was going out on a real date with Hunter, and she didn't want to give her false hope for something more, even though she couldn't deny that she'd toyed with the meaning of the date all afternoon.

Hunter had texted her once midmorning to tell her to dress up, and when she'd asked why, he'd replied, *Do you have to question everything?* She thought of that now as she glanced down at the dress she'd chosen. A midthigh, coral tank dress with a sheer strip along the waist and a lace overlay. Four inches of jagged-edged lace gave it a sexy hemline. She'd taken extra time to weave together a headband made of white flowers from the garden out back. She wore several shell necklaces of varying lengths and colors and a few silver bracelets on her wrist. Her sandals were flat, and she'd worn a piece of jewelry that wrapped around her middle toe and connected with beaded jewels up the center of her foot to an anklet. She felt sexy and cute, perfectly dressed for a night out. But when Hunter knocked again, her nerves came alive, making her acutely aware of exactly how different tonight was going to be.

She inhaled deeply, hoping to calm her racing heart, and finally opened the door.

Hunter's eyes widened, and he made no attempt to hide his visual inspection as his eyes moved to her painted lips, lingering for a moment before moving to her breasts, then hovering again at the flash of skin at her waist. His eyes trailed down her legs, all the way to her toes. When he finally met her gaze again, she saw his Adam's apple move as he swallowed, as if it were hard for him to find his voice, which made her feel sexy, and even more nervous.

"Hi," she said as he reached for her hand.

"Hi. You look…" He laced his fingers with hers, and with his other hand he lifted a lock of her hair, which she'd worn loose and tousled. The appreciation in his eyes was all the proof she needed that she'd made the right choice for everything.

"Incredibly sexy," he finally said. "And those flowers in your hair? Jesus…" He lifted her hand to his lips and pressed a kiss to her knuckles.

The sweetness of that kiss made her cheeks flush.

"You look really handsome, too." Hunter in jeans was enough to make her head spin, but Hunter in a pair of dark slacks, loafers, and a black button-down shirt could melt her panties right off.

He slid a hand around her waist and leaned in for a kiss. It wasn't anything like the hungry kisses they usually shared. This kiss was tender and soft and held the promise of more. And by more, she didn't think it was a promise of anything sexual. No, this kiss, coupled with the way he was holding her hand and keeping his body a safe distance from hers, told her that this was a promise of something important. Her emotions whirled around her, delighting and scaring her at once.

Jana was so nervous on the way to the restaurant that she had to use the old calming technique she hadn't used since she taught her very first dance class when she was nineteen. She closed her eyes and imagined the song "Let Me Down Easy" by Billy Currington. It was her go-to song for calming down when she was nervous, and now, as she sang the lyrics in her head, lyrics that were clearly not about dance but about love, she opened her eyes and stole a glance at Hunter, who reached for her hand and gave it a gentle squeeze, careening her nerves to life again.

Twenty minutes later they were seated at a corner table at the Wicked Oyster restaurant.

"You didn't have to take me someplace so expensive, Hunter. I would have been happy at Mac's or PJ's." The Wicked Oyster was probably the most expensive restaurant in Wellfleet.

Hunter was seated across from her, and before responding, he got up and moved to the seat beside her, making her feel even more special, and nervous again. He reached for her hand and laced their fingers together.

"I wanted to take you someplace we could talk. I know you love to dance, so I thought we could hit someplace else afterward. Your choice. This way I have you all to myself, without distractions, at least for a little while."

This type of attention was so different from what she was used to with Hunter that for a moment she couldn't respond. Luckily, the waitress came over to take their drink order. Her eyes lingered a moment too long on Hunter, whose eyes never left Jana. The waitress appeared to be in her late twenties, with creamy white skin that made her blue eyes pop and shoulder-length black hair. She was breathtakingly beautiful.

Hunter ordered their drinks, glancing only momentarily at the waitress.

When she walked away, Jana said, "She was gorgeous."

"I didn't notice." Hunter opened the menu and handed it to Jana.

Jana had the urge to roll her eyes and call him on laying it on too thick, but she bit her tongue, realizing that she'd looked at the waitress longer than he had. Everything about Hunter was different tonight. His shoulders weren't raised with tension, and his facial features weren't tight.

He was still holding her hand, and as he lifted his eyes, he caught her staring and smiled. "What?"

She lowered her eyes, suddenly feeling nervous again.

"What is it? You were looking at me funny."

"It's just...I don't know what to make of this." Honesty came easy with Hunter, even if she felt funny admitting the truth to him.

His brows knitted. "Our date?"

"Our date. You. This. Being here with you." She leaned closer and lowered her voice. "You're different tonight. Like, totally different."

Worry snuck into his eyes. "I'm trying not to be my typical asshole self."

"Oh my God, Hunter. You're not an asshole." Is that what he thought she thought of him?

"Yeah, I can be." He tried to pull his hand from hers, but she held on tight.

"Maybe we both can, but I don't think of you as one." She crooked her finger, and he leaned in closer, eyes on their hands. "To be honest, I like the person you are." She waited for him to lift his eyes, then said, "A lot."

That earned her a heart-melting smile.

"I like this, too," she assured him. "But you don't have to be someone else to try to impress me." Did that sound self-centered? Like he thought he had to impress her? She quickly added, "Not that I think you're trying to—"

He lifted his finger to her lips, gently silencing her. "I'm glad about all of that, but I like this. It feels good to treat you like the beautiful woman you are."

His eyes dropped for a moment, and when he met her gaze again, the wicked glint that she knew oh so well was back. "It feels almost as good as when we're not on a proper date and I get to ravage you."

He leaned back, and she tried to remember how to breathe.

THEY SHARED AN appetizer of steamed mussels and enjoyed their dinners and a few glasses of wine. Hunter had wanted to kiss Jana at least a hundred times as they talked, but he fought the urge, wanting this date to be different from what they usually did. But while conversation came easily with Jana, he caught himself getting lost in her smile, or the joy in her eyes as she talked about a musical she was in two summers earlier, before they'd even met.

"I wish I could have seen you perform." He imagined her up onstage and knew that she'd outshine everyone. If she could act and sing half as well as she danced, she'd blow anyone away.

Hunter paid the bill, and they headed outside into the cool night air.

"Did you know that this restaurant used to be located on Billingsgate Island?" Billingsgate Island was an island off of Cape Cod. A storm had divided the island in half in 1855, and the island had continued to erode away in the following years, until it was lost to coastal erosion in the late 1930s and early 1940s. He settled his hand on her lower back as they walked across the parking lot.

"No, but that's fascinating."

"This and many of the houses from Billingsgate were floated across the harbor to Wellfleet on rafts. Can you imagine how different everything must have looked back then? How different it was without the Internet, without cell phones, without everything at our fingertips?"

"Without midnight FaceTime sex?"

They both laughed. The lower Cape was less technology driven, but Wellfleet in particular was a sleepy little town that relied more on family outings than online entertainment. It was one of the things Hunter enjoyed most about the area. Although, as he gazed into Jana's eyes, he had to admit that he loved his iPhone now more than ever.

"I for one am very glad for technology." He couldn't help pulling her in tight against his side as they came to the truck.

"Thank you for dinner, Hunter. This was so nice." Jana put her hand on her stomach. "I'm so full, though. I don't think I can go dancing."

Hunter wasn't ready for the night to end, but he wondered if she was blowing him off. Maybe while he was falling for her one sentence at a time, she was wishing she were somewhere else. The thought killed him.

"Do you want me to take you home?" He tried to hide his disappointment by sounding casual, but he couldn't deny the tension in his voice.

"No." She wrinkled her brow. "Oh, wait. Do you *want* to take me home? Because if you do, then—"

He lowered his lips to hers and kissed her with all the adoration he'd been holding back over dinner. The kiss started so differently from the firestorm they usually battled. It was a kiss of confirmation, of their two worlds colliding. He couldn't resist deepening the kiss. She went up on her toes, hands fisted in his shirt. As he drew away to catch his breath, she tried to get nearer.

He'd promised himself that he was not, under any circumstances, going to land in bed with Jana tonight. After talking with Grayson, he realized that he already felt possessive of Jana in ways that made it feel like she was his even though she clearly wasn't. And by the time he'd picked her up for their date, he'd realized not only how much he wanted to make her *his*—but how badly he wanted to be *hers*. The thought should have made him run, but he'd had the opposite reaction. He wanted to try harder, to make her feel so special that she couldn't possibly want any other man.

Once he'd made up his mind, letting go of the tension he wore like armor had been surprisingly easy. Like he'd just been waiting for the okay from his stubborn brain to strip away the shield and bring Jana into his world.

Now he battled the desires coursing through him, the urge to take her home and show her how much he wanted her.

"Jana." He touched his forehead to hers, trying to regain control. "The last thing I want is for our date to end."

"Me either."

Her words shot straight to his heart, reminding him that taking her home was not his endgame. He had bigger hopes.

"How about a walk?" he suggested.

She nodded, and he reached for her hand, then thought better of it and tucked an arm around her waist, wanting to feel her close to him. He might not take her to bed, but being near Jana was becoming not only familiar, but something he craved.

CHAPTER FOURTEEN

"DO YOU LIKE to read?" Jana asked as they followed Main Street toward town, passing Herridge Books, which was closing for the evening. The town was reminiscent of days gone by, from the old-fashioned storefronts to the books residents read—paperback or hardback, not e-readers. The world of e-readers and smartphones belonged more to tourists than residents.

"Yes. How about you?"

"I do. I don't have much time to read these days, but I love a good science fiction or fantasy novel."

Hunter laughed. "No way."

"Way. *Big* way, actually. I love them. Harper makes fun of me for it, because I'm a total closet Trekky, and don't even get me started on *Doctor Who*."

"Jana Garner, I think you just made me like you a little more." Hunter had been a *Doctor Who* fan forever, but he'd never met a woman who liked it.

She leaned her head against him as they walked, and she felt so good, so right, Hunter was sure she belonged there.

They talked about their favorite episodes and how they both kept their love of science fiction quiet, for fear of being teased. He loved discovering that they had much more in common than just great sexual chemistry.

They passed the Wellfleet Market and the consignment shop, where a family was gathered out front eating ice cream cones.

"Tell me about this studio you want to open. I had no idea you were even contemplating doing something like that."

"I wouldn't say that I was contemplating it." She pulled him toward the street. "Want to get ice cream?"

He laughed as she hurried across the street with a bounce in her step. "I thought you were too full to dance."

"I was, but I can never pass up ice cream, especially not here, where they have my favorite flavor, Chunk O' Funk." They followed the stone path around to the back of the A Nice Cream Shop, where the line to order was at least ten couples deep.

"We don't have to wait." Jana looked up at Hunter, and he wondered how, in just a handful of days, she'd gone from the hot chick he wanted to fuck to the only woman he wanted to be with.

He shrugged. "I've got time to wait if you do."

"Really?" She scrunched her nose, looking impossibly cute.

"You're my only plan for tonight." He leaned in for a quick kiss. "But only if you tell me about this dance studio you want to open."

"It's still a little unbelievable to me. I'm trying to come to grips with it all, so it's hard to talk about." She hooked her finger in the front of his pants, and he could see the excitement in her eyes, tempered by worry.

"Do you want to try? Or would you rather not share it yet?"

Her forehead wrinkled, and her face grew serious. He hated the idea of being locked out of something so important to her, but he wouldn't push if she wasn't ready.

"It's okay, pretty girl. Tell me about your current job. Why do you want to quit? Is that something you're comfortable talking about?"

She explained about her boss leaving town on what was supposed to be a short-term basis but had turned into months, and how she was forced into taking over the job of a full-time manager. Irritation tightened his chest at the thought of Jana being taken advantage of.

The line moved quickly as she explained. After getting their cones, Hunter pulled her in close again as they walked back toward Main Street eating their ice cream.

"Have you talked to your boss about hiring someone new to handle some of the work you're doing?"

She ran her tongue around her ice cream and peered up at him from behind a lock of hair that had fallen in front of her eyes. Holy hell. Did she want to take him to his knees right there and then? There was absolutely nothing sexier than Jana eating ice cream.

She licked her lips and nodded.

He was wrong. Jana licking ice cream from her lips was neck and neck with her tongue sliding over the mound of ice cream. He couldn't tear his eyes away.

"You're killing me." He tightened his jaw and forced himself to look away before his arousal became any more noticeable.

"Warn me next time not to get you ice cream unless we're alone."

"Why?" she asked with feigned innocence.

He leaned down and spoke directly into her ear. "Because if you're going to use your tongue like that, I can't be held responsible for what I do with mine."

She mouthed a silent, *Oh*.

They finished their cones as they continued down Main Street and turned by the library, heading toward the harbor.

"Let me get this straight. Your douche bag boss won't give you a raise or hire someone else." He wanted to have a little talk with Marco.

"Nope." They turned the corner and the pier came into view. "So when I told Bella and the girls about it the other day, they asked what I really wanted, and 'open my own studio' just sort of came out. And you know the girls. They're so confident and so eager to help everyone." She shrugged. "Before I knew it, we were strategizing about renting the recreation center at Seaside for my classes. We met with Theresa yesterday, and I guess she's checking into things and the ball is rolling. Everything is happening so fast."

He tipped up her chin so he could see her eyes. He saw a hint of fear there, like a baby bird standing on the edge of a nest for the first time. Certain she can fly, but *what if*…Seeing that doubt in her eyes startled him. Jana put on such a strong front that Hunter felt like he'd peeled back another layer of her, revealing a little more of the *real* Jana.

"Do you want that? Your own studio, that space?" he finally

asked.

It took her a long time to answer, and in the quiet, he studied her for hints as to what she was thinking and felt himself getting lost in her instead. She looked younger, softer tonight, with the flowers in her hair and a dress that on anyone else would look too fancy, but on Jana looked, well, *perfectly Jana.*

JANA FELT HUNTER studying her, but not in the way she was used to, when he was thinking about all the dirty things he wanted to do with her. He was looking at her like he truly wanted to hear what she had to say. Like he really cared.

"I think I do," she answered quietly. "The more I thought about it, the more excited I became. But really? What do I know about running a business?"

"You're running a business now." Hunter took her hand and they walked around the bend, passing the Pearl, the Bookstore Restaurant, and the playground.

"I guess."

"You said you're not only teaching, but handling the billing, the marketing, and the administration. You're already there, Jana." Hunter led her to the middle of the grassy field between the tennis courts and a row of cottages and looked out over the harbor.

"When I was eleven or twelve, my family used to come here every so often. We'd get ice cream, walk along the beach. I never knew why my parents took us here, of all places, when we lived in Brewster, but I eventually found out that this was one of my mom's favorite spots. It was where my parents met." Hunter's gaze turned serious, and her heart ached for his loss.

"You must miss her very much."

"I do." He nodded, and his voice softened. "But I know she's still in here." He covered his heart with his hand. He blinked several times, and when he changed the subject, she knew he didn't want to talk about his feelings. "My father had a knack for teaching each of us what we wanted to learn. He bought Matt every book under the sun, about all sorts of topics that I'd never find fun, but for whatever reason, Matt loved them."

"He must still."

Hunter smiled. "Yeah. He loves teaching at Princeton. And you know my dad taught Pete to refinish boats, and he taught Grayson and me how to forge metal. My mom was never really happy about him teaching us something that was so dangerous, but after a few years, that changed. She saw how much we loved it, we proved we were responsible, and she saw how close Grayson, Dad, and I were from working together. And, eventually, she was okay with it."

"You're lucky he was so interested in spending time with you guys. My parents are living proof of generational gaps. They supported Brock's fighting, but other than that, they think we should all have nine-to-five jobs, and Harper and I should be married with two point five children. I have no idea how none of their four children ended up in conventional jobs."

Hunter tucked her hair behind her ear and lightly stroked

her cheek. Coupled with the tender look in his eyes, it was such an intimate gesture that it made her shiver.

"My father taught us that some people aren't meant to follow other people's dreams. That's what I'm getting at. One evening when we came here, my brothers and sister and I were running around, and I saw my mom and dad standing right here in this spot. They were standing close, like this." He stepped in so close their thighs brushed.

"I remember thinking about how I never wanted to forget seeing them like that. The next day I started my first real metal sculpture. It was the first time I felt inspired by something. Instead of just welding and forging to create something cool, I felt driven by an image. It was a sculpture of them, standing right here. It took me months to complete it. I could only use the forge when my father was around, and he worked a lot, because he owns the hardware store, as you know."

She had a hard time imagining Hunter waiting for anything. He *took*; he didn't *wait*.

"Anyway, after I made that sculpture, I knew exactly what I wanted to do with my life. I also knew, because my mother was quite practical and believed in telling things as they were, that my chances of making a career as an artist were slim, but I wanted it more than I wanted anything else in the world."

"That's how I feel about dance. I love everything about it. I get lost in it, Hunter. I've never really felt that way about anything else except boxing and..." She stopped before saying *you*. Quickly turning away, she brought her fist to her mouth. *Holy crap. I do lose myself in you.* She wasn't ready for this. She trusted Hunter, but she didn't trust this quick turnaround he was making. Her life was a crazy mess right now, and she didn't trust herself enough to see things clearly and make smart decisions.

"And?" He stepped around so he was in her line of sight.

He was so handsome, and the intense look in his eyes, the *tell me everything* look, combined with the tenderness of his request, made her stomach dip.

"And…" She couldn't let the emotions swelling inside her change anything between them. She was vulnerable, because of everything going on at work. That had to be what was causing her rampant emotions. "Having my own studio would be like a dream come true."

"Then nothing should stand in your way. Not Marco, not self-doubt. Nothing."

The way he said it, like he believed in her, like she deserved to make her dreams come true, comforted her and made her feel stronger. When he slid his hand to the nape of her neck and smiled, she felt herself welcoming this new thing blossoming between them, despite her resolve not to let it sway her emotions.

Jana went up on her toes, holding tightly to his waist as his eyes darkened and her heart turned over in her chest. "I like this side of you."

Their mouths came together in a series of slow, shivery kisses.

"I like this side of you, too," he said with a knee-weakening smile.

She was sure she was walking on air the whole way back to the truck. The distance they covered felt shorter, the travel time to her house quicker than ever before. She couldn't wait to wrap her arms around this new Hunter and explore whatever was happening between them.

They laughed on the way up the walk to her front door. When she stepped up on the porch, he spun her around so they were almost eye to eye. Her arms wound around his neck, and he gathered her hair in one hand and gave a gentle tug, sending shocks of lust through her.

"Thank you for tonight." He placed his other hand on her lower back, pressing her against him. It was all she could do to watch the emotions passing through his eyes. They were easy to decipher. *I want you.*

He kissed the tip of her nose, her cheek, her forehead, and finally—*finally*—his mouth found hers. She lost herself in the feel of his tongue searching, stroking, claiming her mouth. His hold on her hair tightened, heightening her arousal and pulling a moan of desire from her lungs. He swallowed it down. She wanted him to swallow her down. She wanted to feel this new Hunter as he sank into her.

"Can I see you again?" he asked against her lips, before kissing her again, lighter this time, quicker, leaving her hungry for more.

"You're leaving?" Her emotions skidded to a halt. She didn't understand. They didn't *leave* each other. They claimed and fucked and satisfied, and tonight she thought everything was changing. Getting even better. This would be the second time he was leaving her, when all she wanted was more of him.

He searched her eyes, and she wondered if he saw the desperation she felt. Was he messing with her again? Had it all been a stupid game to him? This was exactly why she needed to stop this nonsense. She never should have dared him to be romantic, even if she really, really liked him this way.

"Tonight changed me, Jana," he said just above a whisper, sending all those crazy thoughts sailing away. Just like that. "You opened a door inside me, or something. Whatever it is, I want to play it out, see what comes of it. If I go inside with you and do all the things that I want to do to you…" He held her against his hot, hard body. "You might confuse what we do tonight for what we've always done."

"I…I don't understand, Hunter. We've already slept together. Now it'll just be that much better."

The muscles in his jaw bunched, and his eyes narrowed. When he spoke, it was with all the white-hot demanding heat she was used to.

"The next time we come together, it won't be *just* anything. At least not for me, and I hope not for you."

He crushed his mouth to hers, kissing her like she was used to, like he wanted to tear off her clothes right that second and sink into her. Spirals of ecstasy tore through her core. When their lips parted they both gasped for air.

"The next time we come together," he said with a heated stare, "it'll be *everything*."

Panic chased the ecstasy away as she grasped for words. "Hunter, I…I'm not sure…I'm not sure we're ready for *everything.*"

"You let me worry about what I'm ready for, and prepare yourself, because I'm going to romance the hell out of you, and you're going to love it."

It wasn't until after he drove away that she realized he hadn't asked her to admit she wanted him.

CHAPTER FIFTEEN

HUNTER HAD BEEN working on the sculpture for the competition since seven o'clock that morning. He was acutely aware of the days he'd lost before he'd found his muse, and now, with just thirty days left until the competition, the pressure was on. Grayson was out meeting with a supplier this morning, and by the time Clark arrived, it was after ten. Clark had gone to see Nina last night, and when Hunter had come home to an empty house, he'd assumed Clark had stayed with her. But he'd heard him come in around three in the morning and knew that couldn't be a good sign. He didn't mind cutting Clark slack while he was having a hard time, but the guy could have let him know he'd be late to work this morning.

He went up front to talk to him, and the sight of Clark's disheveled clothes and messy hair worried him—until he got a look at his buddy's puffy, bloodshot eyes. He recognized the look of a hangover when he saw it.

"Trouble with Nina last night?" He couldn't temper his irritation. It was one thing to cut him slack for having trouble with his marriage, but he wasn't going to turn the other way at Clark throwing his life into a bottle. He'd watched his father disappear down that liquid trail, and it had been a long, painful road back.

"Nah. She was fine. Sorry I'm late." Clark sat heavily and rested his head on his palm.

"Have a few too many last night?" He crossed his arms, and when Clark lifted his eyes and met his gaze, Hunter leveled him with a serious stare. "Were you with Robert?" Robert was single and liked to party, but he was responsible. Hunter had a hard time believing that Robert would stay out until three on a work night and get flipping drunk.

"At first. He took off around ten." Clark's phone rang, and he pulled it from his pocket, glanced at the name, and sent the call to voicemail. "Shit."

"What's going on, Clark? I know I'm your friend, but seriously, dude. I don't want any part of you cheating on Nina."

Clark pressed his index finger and thumb to the bridge of his nose. "I'm not cheating on her."

Hunter lifted his chin in the direction of Clark's phone. "Who called? The same chick who's been keeping you up at night all week?"

"There's nothing going on." He scrubbed his hand over his face and sat back, his shoulders sagging. "I swear it, man. She wants there to be, but I'm not ready for that."

"So don't go there." Hunter didn't understand people who didn't take control of their lives. It was so easy to do. Make a plan and make it happen. Like he was doing with Jana. Everything had changed for him over the last few days, and now he understood how Pete and Sky could have fallen so hard so fast for Jenna and Sawyer. He'd not only already spent more time with Jana than he had with any other woman, but he couldn't get her out of his head.

He wondered if she'd slept okay last night, if she'd thought of him as much as he'd thought of her. If she was as nervous today about starting her own dance studio as she'd been last night. And if so, he wanted to be right there to help her realize she could achieve her dreams. All she had to do was get that stubborn mind of hers to listen. And last night? *Jesus, last night.* It had nearly killed him to leave her, when what he'd really wanted was to follow her inside, take her on every surface in every room, and make her realize that she wanted everything with him just as much as he wanted it with her.

"She texts all the time," Clark admitted. "She calls all the time. I'm not good at letting people down, and she listens, man. She really listens to every word I say."

Seeing his friend struggle made him realize he'd been selfish. Clark had come to him in his time of need. He hadn't gone to his family. He didn't try to figure it out on his own. He'd come to Hunter, and what did Hunter do? He got so wrapped up in Jana that he let his friend fend for himself when he was clearly too confused to do this alone.

He set a comforting hand on Clark's shoulder. "I'm sorry I haven't been there for you. With all the shit you have going on, I should have made myself more available."

"You did, Hunt. You even babysat for us. This isn't your issue."

"Yeah, it kinda is. If I were going through a rough time, you'd be there to listen so I didn't have to turn to a stranger.

You don't need this chick listening to your life story. You need your best friend and, dude, I'm going to be there from now on. I promise. Starting right now."

He picked up Clark's phone and navigated to the messages but didn't read them. He turned the screen toward Clark. "This her? Cherise?"

"Yeah."

"We're going to start by sending her a nice text telling her that you've decided to work on your marriage, that you appreciate her friendship, but you don't want your wife to get the wrong impression, so you need to break off contact." After typing all that in, he looked to Clark for approval.

Clark nodded. "Send it." He closed his eyes and let out a sigh. "Shit. Why the fuck did I need you to do that? What is wrong with me?"

"You feel like your life is spinning out of control. We've all been there, but it's not, Clark. We just need to get you back on track. Take today off. Go back to my place and sleep. We'll go out for dinner tonight and talk. Use me, man. I'm a great listener."

"What about your girl?" Clark rose to his feet, looking beyond worn out but mildly relieved.

He'd sent Jana a text when he'd arrived at work. *Had a great time on our date. Looking forward to the next one.* He'd heard the snarky tone of her voice when he'd read her response. *There may not be a next one if you don't put out.* "She's fighting being my girl, but no worries. I've got that, too."

They agreed to meet for dinner later. After Clark left, he

zipped off another text to Jana. *We're going to be more than fuck buddies. You might as well accept it.*

IT WAS ONLY one o'clock, and Jana had already met with Brock for her workout, taught three dance classes, and spoke to the local newspapers about ads that Marco wanted to run offering discounts for the next cycle of classes. Their classes ran in eight-week cycles, and he made a heavy marketing push a few weeks before each new registration period. Or rather, *Jana* handled the marketing push. Not for much longer, though. The thought comforted her enough to carry her through the busy afternoon ahead.

She'd been going back and forth about opening her own studio. Hunter and the girls made her feel like she could do it, but handling all of Marco's work plus teaching classes, she wondered how it would be any different if she owned the studio.

She'd already been through the pros and cons a million times, and she knew there were more pros than cons, but still she wavered.

Her phone vibrated, and she didn't have to look at it to know it would be from Hunter. She'd never answered his text about being more than fuck buddies. What was so wrong with being fuck buddies? Her stomach twisted. Why was he suddenly affecting her this way? The one thing she'd always been sure of was her sexuality. It was the one area she could control in her life, and she'd used it well, to clear her head, to handle her emotions. Now Hunter was trying to take that away from her and make her not only say she wanted him, but if she was reading him right, he wanted her to date only him, too.

She was perfectly happy being fuck buddies, and then he had to go and turn all nice and romantic. The Wicked Oyster? A walk? Mind-blowing kisses? She should be leaping off of cloud nine directly into his insanely muscled arms. Instead, she was beginning to panic. She wasn't dealing with Marco, who deserved a swift kick in the ass. She couldn't even commit to opening her own studio. Her mind flip-flopped like a fish out of water. How could she move forward with a relationship with Hunter? She couldn't commit to him until she could at least commit to herself.

Hours later, after teaching three more classes, dealing with a bitchy mother who always tried to hurry her daughter out of class early, and answering the studio emails, Jana finally checked her phone messages.

After seeing that the earlier text wasn't from Hunter, but from Bella, and a message from Leanna shortly thereafter, she clung to a thread of hope as she opened Bella's message.

Bad news. Theresa looked over the bylaws for Seaside, and apparently we're not allowed to rent out that space. It can only be used for community gatherings.

Jana's jaw dropped open. Tears burned in her eyes, and a lump of sadness clogged her throat. She hadn't realized that she'd been clinging to the hope of renting the space as desperately as she must have been.

She pressed her lips together, unwilling to fall apart over

something she hadn't even seriously considered doing a week ago. *It was a silly dream.*

She forced back the tears and responded to Bella's text. *That's okay. I knew it was a long shot.*

Wiping a tear that slipped free, she opened a group text to Harper and Sky. *I need to go out. Meet me at Undercover?*

She was contemplating texting Hunter, when her phone vibrated with a text from Sky. *Of course. What's up?*

As she sent her response to Sky—*Rec center is a no go*—she received one from Harper. *Just wrapped up my work. Meet you there!*

She forced a smile as more unwanted tears tumbled down her cheeks. She could always count on her sister and Sky. She tried to regain control of her emotions and reread Hunter's text from earlier: *We're going to be more than fuck buddies. You might as well accept it.*

She considered answering him honestly—*No, Hunter, we're not. I'm a mess, and right now I need a fuck buddy more than ever.* After last night, she figured if Hunter read that response, he'd want to know why, and why wasn't something she could understand, much less make him understand.

Instead, she texted an answer he couldn't argue with. *We make great fuck buddies. Why mess with perfection?* She bit back the pain that caused, which was made worse by the guilt threatening to strangle her over the blatant lie. But how could she offer him anything else?

She was working through administrative paperwork for the ads she'd scheduled when he responded.

Exactly. We're perfect together.

Yeah, they kind of were, but how long would Hunter really be happy with just one woman? She wasn't sure she even knew how to be someone's girlfriend anymore. She sent him a response that she hoped would end his pursuit for more. She wanted to be with him, but her life was complicated enough, and what they'd had before she'd been dumb enough to challenge him to be romantic wasn't complicated at all. They had hot sex. No questions, no strings. It was perfect.

Last night was fun, thank you. But I think I liked you better when you promised me sunsets and gave me orgasms.

She turned off her phone, crossed her arms over her desk, and rested her forehead on them. Jana hated liars, and she hated people who hurt others.

Right then, she hated herself most of all.

CHAPTER SIXTEEN

UNDERCOVER WAS PACKED. Hunter had forgotten that it was open mic night. At the moment, a redhead was butchering a Maroon Five song. Hunter and Clark had ordered a pizza and a pitcher of soda and they'd been talking for the past two hours, but every time Hunter brought up Nina, Clark skirted the issue. Hunter felt himself losing patience, and he knew it wasn't Clark's fault. It was the messages he'd received from Jana. She liked him better when he promised her sunsets and gave her orgasms? What the hell was that supposed to mean? She was the one who wanted sunsets. He wondered if he would ever understand women.

He topped off their drinks and looked at Clark. Clark wasn't a drunk, and the soda tonight was more to make a point than anything else, but he was getting the impression that there was more to his and Nina's separation than he was letting on.

"Just tell me this," Hunter said. "I'm trying to figure out how two people who loved each other so much that they couldn't imagine a future apart ended up where you two are now."

Clark shook his head and splayed his hands toward the ceiling, as if he had no idea. "I've been wondering the same thing for months. It's like…" His eyes searched the bar, but Hunter could tell he wasn't searching for someone. He was searching for answers.

"You really don't have any idea? You just woke up one morning and realized you felt trapped? You had to get out?"

Clark's brows drew together, and he stared into his drink for a minute before answering. "You know how you guys heat up the metal, and then you pound it on the anvil until it's the way you want it?"

"Sure."

"And when it cools, sometimes you have to reheat it and reconfigure it because you're not really happy with what you got out of it?"

Clark was speaking Hunter's language. This he could understand. "Yeah."

"Well, you know I adore Nina. My love for her hasn't changed, and to be honest, going through this—" Clark looked away, his eyes suspiciously damp. When he looked back, his voice was stronger. "Going through this has made me see her in a whole new light."

"But you hardly see her anymore. You've spent more time getting hammered than you have with Nina." That might not be true, but it was pretty damn close.

"Maybe so. But do you know how much I miss her? Do you know why I poured my guts out to a stranger?"

Hunter shook his head, hoping Clark wasn't going to admit he'd cheated on Nina, because that was something Hunter didn't think he could get past. Loyalty was everything when it came to family.

Clark leaned across the table and said with a serious tone, "Because I'm afraid that if I tell Nina how I really feel, it will make me seem weak and pathetic, and she might not take me back. But I have to get this shit off my back or I'm going to go fucking crazy."

Hunter looked at him for a long time before responding. As much as he didn't want to hear that his buddy had cheated, Clark was like family to him, and he couldn't turn him away. "What the hell did you do?"

"Why do you jump to that conclusion? I didn't *do* anything. I left for the exact reasons I told you I did. But come on, Hunter. How pathetic is that?"

"I don't get it. If you left because you felt like you were boxed in, like you weren't appreciated or noticed and you missed being intimate with your wife, why didn't you just tell her? Hire a babysitter? Fix it?" Hunter glanced up toward the bar. He could no longer see Colton serving drinks, or the stage for that matter. The crowd was standing room only, and his mind moved to Jana again. When they'd decided to come to Undercover, he'd hoped she might be working, but she was nowhere in sight.

"Because on the surface it was all those things." Clark leaned back. "But it wasn't until I was talking to that chick on the phone that I realized the rest, and the rest of it is what makes me really look like an asshole."

"You lost me. What's the *rest* of it?"

"I'm spilling my guts about how Nina doesn't notice me

anymore to this woman, telling her how nice it is to hear someone ask me how my day was and shit like that, and she moves straight from that to asking me if my wife still blows me. She says that's how I'd know if Nina loved me."

Hunter swallowed the bile rising in his throat. "Please tell me you didn't discuss the details of your sex life with her." His mind turned to Jana. Those were the types of details he'd share with Grayson or Clark about any other woman, but the thought of sharing those intimate details with them about Jana? That made his blood boil, and she wasn't even his wife.

"No, I didn't, but it made me realize that I have no business hanging around women who want to date. I know I'm not telling you anything you don't already know, but I just realized it. My life isn't about other women and partying. The idea that love is defined by a blow job made me sick. Seriously, I mean, I love a good blow job, but that's not love. My life is Nina and Billy, and it may have taken me a while to understand it, but sex doesn't equate to love." He finished his drink and said, "The whole time I was talking to that woman I was thinking, what would Nina think if she found this number on my phone and called to see whose it was? That's why I got drunk last night. I could barely stand to be around myself."

"So fix it, Clark. You know what you need to do."

"Yeah, I know what I need to do. But I'm not sure Nina will take me back when I admit the truth to her. And I *will* admit it to her, because otherwise we don't have a chance in hell of fixing what's wrong between us. I don't need a counselor to tell me that. But, Hunt...I've always been Nina's man, you know? The one she looks to when she needs something, or when she's down, or, shit, all the time, and suddenly I wasn't that guy anymore. She had Billy to care for, and she didn't need me as much. She'll see how selfish I was, thinking about myself and my needs when I should have sucked it up and dealt with it."

They talked for a while longer and agreed that Clark needed to take whatever steps were necessary to spend more time with Nina. He wasn't ready to move back in, because he feared they'd fight too much, but he was going to try harder and make more time for her, and that made Hunter feel a hell of a lot better.

They stood to leave, and a familiar voice sang out. Hunter's eyes shot in the direction of the stage. It was too crowded to confirm that the voice singing the Taylor Swift song was Jana, but his pulse was racing, and that was all the confirmation he needed.

"'Out of the Woods,'" Clark said. "I don't like Taylor Swift, but man, if that isn't the perfect song for tonight."

"I'll catch up with you at home," Hunter said to Clark, and pushed his way through the crowd so he could see the stage.

Jana, Sky, and Harper were center stage, singing into the microphone, and holy hell, Jana was wearing the skimpiest, tightest, reddest dress he'd ever seen and sky-high heels that made her gorgeous legs look a mile long. She wore a million necklaces and bracelets, and as she sang, she broke away from Sky and Harper, strutting across the stage like she was the star. Every guy in the place was practically drooling over her—

including Hunter.

JANA WAS THREE sheets to the wind by the time they arrived at Undercover. She'd received a text from Bella asking her to stop by. Jana had stayed for several glasses of wine as they all commiserated about losing the rec center space. Jenna and Amy decided that Jana should get ready to meet Sky while she was there, and they'd picked out her outfit, because according to Jenna, *Nights like this call for drastic measures.* They chose one of Leanna's dresses, which Bella had a field day with. *I always knew Leanna was a closet slut,* to which Leanna responded, *Only for Kurt, thank you very much.* By the time they were done, she was wearing a dress that was too tight, too short, and too red. Her outfit was completed with a pair of Bella's fuck-me heels. Jenna had gone from cottage to cottage collecting jewelry, and voila! Jana looked like a prostitute, and in her inebriated state, that made her feel sexy as hell. Several more glasses of wine later, Sky showed up to get her. Apparently the Seaside girls knew how to take care of their own. She hadn't even realized they'd called Sky.

Now, as she danced across the stage, she owned the look *and* the song. She, Sky, and Harper sang their hearts out. Jana sang the chorus, knowing she was nowhere near *out of the woods* in any respect. She was so deep in the fucking woods she couldn't see past the fucking trees, and that frustration fueled her voice.

She scanned the crowd, watching the hungry eyes of every

man in the place, which made her feel good and bad at once. She closed her eyes to sing the next verse, and when she opened them, the crowd before her parted like the Red Sea, to reveal broad shoulders and angry eyes. Eyes she'd know anywhere. Eyes she'd dreamed of every night for months.

Hunter broke through the crowd, his expression thunderous. Jana was in no mood to be judged or lectured. She was in the mood to forget the mess of emotions she'd gone through in the last twenty-four hours, and she knew of only one surefire way to do that. A good hard fucking.

Hunter was good at fucking. *Mighty good.*

She set a heated stare on him, ignoring the storm brewing in his eyes, and put all her energy into the song. When the music stopped she was breathing hard, and utterly powerless to tear her eyes away from the smokin' fire before her. She was vaguely aware of Sky and Harper pulling her off the stage and stumbling to keep up as they dragged her through the crowd to a booth in the back near the bar.

"Holy shit. That was incredible, Jana!" Sky was yelling to be heard over the crowd, but Jana could barely hear her over her pounding heart.

She glanced back toward the stage, desperately seeking Hunter. Had she conjured up his image because she wanted him so badly? Her eyes scanned the crowd, and her heart plummeted. Just as she was turning back, her eyes locked on Hunter, stalking toward her with a look so dark it could only be called predatory.

"I told you she was a great singer," Harper said. She sipped her drink and turned, following Jana's gaze. She turned back quickly, eyes wide, and reached for her sister's hand. "Jana…"

"Look! Hunter's here." Sky jumped up and went to hug him.

Hunter barely raised his arms, never taking his eyes off Jana. She was sobering up really fast. Sky didn't know she and Hunter had hooked up, other than the very first time. Oh God, that first time was coming back to her now. The tequila. Rolling around naked on the beach. Sex in the car. In his room. The confessions. *Oh God! The confessions.* He'd never been in love, never wanted to settle down. And hers…*I'd be the suckiest girlfriend on the planet.* She'd warned him of her weakness well before she'd forgotten his name and called him every other name she could think of.

He slid into the booth beside Harper, across from Sky and Jana. The rest of their first tryst replayed like a movie in her mind. He'd called her on not knowing his name, and she'd thrown it back in his face. *Oh, like you remember my name?* They'd been drinking all afternoon, and after their last round of tonsil hockey in the backseat of his car, they'd had to call a cab to get to his place. Even piss drunk he'd remembered her name. They'd argued—what else was new? And then he'd told her his name *again* and demanded she remember it. Did he ever not demand? Then there was more sex. *Lord.* The man fucked like the frigging Energizer Bunny, used his mouth like a lethal weapon, and made her come more times than she had in a month. That was when it had gone downhill. Midorgasm she'd called out the wrong name again. *Several times.*

She swallowed hard at the memory, hoping to push it far, far away, and tried to concentrate on what Sky and Harper were saying about dancing. Why was Hunter here at the table, anyway? Looking at her like he owned her and she'd wronged him?

Sobering up was short lived. She drew her shoulders back, feeling empowered by the alcohol. She refused to let that first night she'd spent with him make her feel weak, or the way he was looking at her now make her feel bad. She was having a great time, and she was going to continue.

"That was so fun!" Sky said. "Wasn't Jana amazing, Hunter?"

"Fucking incredible." The smile that spread his lips bordered on merciless, in a dark, sexual kind of way. Or maybe that was the alcohol twisting her interpretation.

Harper pushed Hunter out of the booth so she could get out. He stood behind her, eyes still locked on Jana as Harper leaned across the table for Jana's hand. "Dance with me," Harper said.

Even drunk, Jana could tell her sister was trying to rescue her from knocking heads with Hunter. Why did they always knock heads, when all she wanted to do was fall into his arms while he undressed her, whispering dirty promises in the dark?

"Yes, let's dance!" Sky slid out of the booth.

Jana followed her out, and as soon as Jana was free from the booth, Hunter grabbed her around the waist and growled, "Yes, let's dance."

He didn't give her time to respond as he nearly lifted her off her feet on the way to the dance floor. She looked over her shoulder just in time to catch the look of surprise in Harper's eyes before Hunter spun her in his arms and crushed her against him.

His scruff brushed against her cheek. *You didn't shave.* She didn't know why that thought pulsed through when nothing else was making any sense.

"Why are you here?" Her words came out slow and slightly slurred.

"I was here with Clark. Why are you here, Jana? Dressed like this?"

"What?" She pushed off his shoulder, swaying a little, and tried to give him a serious look, but it made her wobble even more, and she clutched at his shirt.

He glowered at her. "Looking so fucking hot that every guy in here is probably ready to come in his pants."

She felt her lips curve up and was too drunk to stop them. "Are you?"

"Jana." He crushed her to him again, and his masculine scent permeated her senses, sending ripples of desire straight to her core.

"This isn't you, Jana. You don't do this."

"Yes, I do. I met you on a night like tonight." *Oh shit...*

She felt his entire body go rigid against her. And she swore to erase that night from her memory so she never, ever brought it up again. He'd been so angry when she'd accidentally called him all those other men's names after he'd said sweeter things to her than any man had ever said before.

He put his mouth beside her ear and said, "You like me better when we're fuck buddies?" A chill hung on the edge of his words.

Her temper flared at her own words coming back at her, but as his hands moved up her waist, she got distracted from that anger, and when they brushed against the sides of her breasts, she rested her cheek against his shoulder. She wanted his touch, needed his touch. *Only Hunter's.* Hunter's touch made the noise and indecision fall away. His hands traveled slowly down over her hips, making it hard for her to hold on to anything but the desire to be consumed by him. When his hands clutched her ass, she gasped.

"Is that what you want, Jana? A good, hard fuck?" His hips gyrated against her belly, causing any remaining brain cells to shatter.

She opened her mouth, but no words came. Her body wanted what he offered, but her heart, her stupid, needy heart, wanted more—from him, only him—and that scared the shit out of her.

His hands moved down the back of her thighs and toyed with the edge of her dress. "You know I can give you that."

She closed her eyes, trying to decipher his tone, trying to read between the lines. But the lines blurred, and all she was left with were her desperate, warring emotions. Her greedy heart wanted Hunter, all of him: his caring touch, his possessive protection, and his sexual prowess. But panic roared through her meadow of love, trampling all over the beauty and safety of it and leaving behind darkness she couldn't comprehend.

ere a muted gold color. A pear-green dresser
dles in the shapes of flowers. He recognized
'd made them to fill a special order from the
That made his chest warm. Jana must like
e there was another one in the small bedroom.
ite plaid seat cushion conflicted with the pink
y upholstery that covered the back and arms of
nehow the gold frilly pillow made it fit right in
he mayhem in the bedroom. At the head of the
o sleeps in a double bed instead of a king? One
eping woman in his arms answered that—
green and blue curtains hung from a metal
that he also recognized, as it had come in as a
a the same store as the dresser handles.
brows together and wondered if she'd known
ho'd made them.
ave been fifteen pillows on the bed with crazy
color and size under the sun, piled on top of a
vhich was folded halfway down the bed, with a
nket beneath, also folded, and finished off with
nket lying across the foot of the bed. Even the
covers made him hot. It was summertime.
that many blankets?
v steps, quickly scanning the rest of the room.
lamp sat beside pottery pieces of various sizes.
were all in the same electric color. The entire
her with a painting hanging over the dresser
a child had painted mad streaks of the colors

CHAPTER SEVENTEEN

HUNTER CUT THE engine in front of Jana's house. After trying to practically climb onto his lap as they drove away from Undercover, Jana had passed out leaning against his shoulder. He shifted her gently so she wouldn't fall as he got out of the truck. He gathered her in his arms, struck by the angelic look on her peaceful face, contrasting sharply with the short dress and spiked heels. That was Jana, one big contradiction, even when she was asleep. He lifted her easily and kissed her forehead. She might be stubborn and antagonistic, but he'd seen her when her guard was down, and he knew this was a facade. She could push him as far and as hard as she wanted, but hell if he didn't want to make her his even more than before.

She snuggled against his chest as her arms wound around his neck.

"Keys," he mumbled. They'd left so quickly after he told Sky he was taking Jana home that they must have left her purse behind.

"Under the mat." She pressed her hand to his chest and blinked up at him with sleepy, sexy eyes.

Damn if he didn't get a little shiver. She'd gotten to him, all right. Hook, line, and sinker. He couldn't resist pressing a kiss

to her pink lips.

"We're going to ha

"No talk," she slur

He crouched, hol

trieved the key from

pocketed the key and

"We're going to t

the cadence of her b

passed out again.

Jana's house was

feminine, and too fuck

the other night, but

then, in the bedroom,

unable to see or think

look around. The hou

from the outside, but

room curtains were pa

pale blue couch clash

armchair definitely di

haphazardly on the cha

yellow, but as Hunter

bedroom door he'd sp

were pink. He smiled

as her life.

He stopped at the

make sense of the sigh

looking at something fr

catalog. How the hell

bedroom walls

boasted iron ha

them because h

Eclectic Shop.

armchairs, becau

The black and w

and purple paisl

the chair, but so

with the rest of

double bed—W

glance at the s

decorative brigh

twisted vine rod

special order fro

He drew his

he was the one v

There must

patterns, in ever

fuchsia blanket,

bright orange bl

an olive-green b

sight of all tho

Who slept unde

He took a f

A bright orange

Surprisingly, the

room came tog

that looked like

sprinkled throughout the room. He sat on the edge of the bed with Jana in his arms, thinking he'd just learned more about *his girl* than she ever could have told him.

Hunter carefully slipped off Jana's heels, hoping not to wake her. He set them on the floor and debated changing her out of the dress. Her breasts were vying for release from the binding material, plumping over the low neckline. Distracting himself from making the decision, he rose again with her in his arms and tossed the pillows to the floor, then pulled back the soft blankets and sheet. He couldn't imagine sleeping beneath that many blankets, and wondered why she needed them.

As he laid her on the bed, she sighed softly. Now he had another dilemma. He didn't want to leave her. Like, *really* didn't want to leave her. And it wasn't because he was worried she might throw up in her sleep and choke or anything as chivalrous as that. He just wanted to be near her. To hold her and wake up with her in his arms. He'd wanted that since the day he'd met her all those months ago. He sat beside her on the edge of the bed and brushed her hair from her forehead. Even the first time they'd hooked up, when she'd called him the wrong name and he'd wanted to throttle her, he'd been disappointed when she'd snuck out while he was asleep.

Weeks later, when Sky and Sawyer got together, he went to see Sawyer fight—and Jana walked in. He'd been drawn to her even more strongly than before. They fought, they challenged, they pushed each other to the limits, taking what they wanted and asking for nothing in return. Yet every time they'd come together since, she'd left him wanting more. He couldn't explain it, but he sure as hell couldn't deny that she had a string around his neck, and every time she walked away, she tugged a piece of him along with her.

He headed into her calm-within-the-storm bathroom, which was layered in pastel blue and yellow with a white tile floor and claw-foot tub, needing to figure out if he should stay or go. She *had* asked him to have sex. *That's kind of like an invitation.*

He was careful not to mess up her sink as he washed up. When he returned to the bedroom, Jana had pulled the sheets up over her shoulders. She looked so innocent, with her hair spread out beneath her. His body ached to hold her, and really, he shouldn't leave her alone, right? He took off his jeans and T-shirt, tossed them onto the chair, and slipped beneath the sheets. Lying on his back, contemplating his decision to stay when she hadn't asked him to, he locked his hands beneath his head.

As if she had a built in cock detector, Jana turned over. Her cheek landed on his chest, her hand palmed his half-alert cock through his briefs, and her leg draped over both of his. Where the hell were her clothes? Sweet Jesus, she was completely naked. A seductive *mmm* vibrated through her at the same time a greedy groan escaped his lips. This was *not* part of tonight's plan.

"Jana." He'd made a mistake. He was not doing this. Not when she was so drunk she couldn't even open her eyes. Her silence surprised him, and he dared a glance. She was sound asleep and making the not-quite-a-snore sound caused by too much alcohol, but she had a death grip on his now fully alert and ready erection.

Fuck.

He closed his eyes and tried to tame his mounting arousal, but all he saw was Jana up onstage, her eyes blazing, her body smokin', and that dirty little mouth of hers painted and willing. He must be in hell. This was going to be the longest night ever.

WHAT IS THAT yummy smell? Jana inhaled deeply as her senses came awake, recognizing the familiar scent of the only man she'd been with for months. Her body was splayed across Hunter's, only she was blissfully naked and he wasn't. She unfurled her hand from around his hard length. *Wow, even in your sleep you're ready.* She smiled to herself. *That's my Hunter. Always ready.* She tried to piece together what had happened last night, as panic tiptoed into her body again. She couldn't pick up her keys and disappear into the night. She certainly couldn't wake Hunter and ask him to leave. Well, she *could*, but that would only start a fight, and she rather liked this peaceful moment with him, when there was no tension between them.

Her eyes dropped to his erection.

Well, other than *that*.

She moved quietly off the bed, reminded of when she'd slipped away in the middle of the night in Provincetown the last time she and Hunter had been in an actual bed together. *When I promised I'd never sleep with you again.* The last time they were in her bedroom came rushing back. The night he'd bound her wrists. The tenderness he'd shown her afterward as he'd held her in his lap.

She felt a little dizzy knowing how much of herself she'd shown Hunter. She needed cold water. She needed space. A little room to think.

She tiptoed into the bathroom, brushed her teeth, and washed the makeup from her face. She debated her dilemma as she returned to the bedroom. Why wasn't Hunter naked? He always slept naked. At least after their hookups he'd never put on any clothes. Why was he here at all if they hadn't had sex? And she was sure they hadn't, even if her mind was fuzzy, because having sex with Hunter Lacroux was not something a girl forgot. *Ever.*

With her nerves doing a little uneasy dance, she slipped on his T-shirt and debated waking him again and asking him to leave. She quickly decided that it wasn't worth the fight. At least that was the story she tried to believe as she climbed back into bed with a smile on her lips and curled up with her back to him. The bed dipped as he rolled onto his side and his strong arm wrapped around her, tugging her back against his chest. Her body molded perfectly to his. She tried not to move as her heart went a little crazy and she debated this encroachment of her personal space.

"Close those pretty little eyes of yours and go to sleep."

Her eyes sprang open. "You're awake?"

"You glommed onto me all night. Of course I'm awake." He pressed a kiss to her cheek. "But I'd like to sleep, if you don't mind."

She smiled, loving that he wanted to stay, even as her rebellion left her lips.

"Then maybe you should go back home."

"No, pretty girl. This time I win. Sleep. Now."

"Hunt—"

He tucked her beneath him and gazed into her eyes. His arousal burned against her thigh. How he managed to take her brain apart with nothing more than one hot stare, she'd never understand.

"You never listen." He shifted his weight, pressing his rigid length between her legs.

"Now that we're awake…" She arched up and nipped at his chin. He searched her eyes with a hungry gaze. "I'm not still drunk, if that's what you're wondering."

He reached below the sheets and traced the curve of her waist. "I think I can tell when you're drunk." He clutched her hip. Hard. She sucked in air between her teeth. "I want to stay until morning. Right here. Holding you."

"Then let's fool around."

He scowled, but the rock of his hips told her he was fighting the desire, too.

She rolled her eyes. "Why do you have to make all the rules?"

"Because your rules suck." He lifted his hips, and she felt him pushing out of his briefs. "Fuck, Jana. I can't ever deny you." Seconds later the base of his hard length pressed against her wetness. "I should walk out the fucking door, because giving in to you is like feeding a kid candy. You'll keep coming back for more."

"And that's bad why…?" She rocked her hips against his.

He gritted his teeth and lifted his eyes away from hers for a moment as he groaned. She gyrated beneath him, pressing her hands to the back of his hips, knowing she'd get her way.

"Because you'll never agree to anything more than this if I keep giving in." She reached between them and fisted his cock. "Fuck," he grumbled. "You must enjoy torturing me."

"Almost as much as I enjoy pleasuring you." She pushed at his chest and he rolled to his side. Jana scooted lower on the bed, and without a moment's hesitation, she took him in her mouth.

He let out a hiss and a needy moan that spurred her into action. She loved the taste of him, the feel of him growing impossibly thicker as she stroked and licked, sucked and teased him. He fisted his hand in her hair, guiding her, controlling her speed. She shouldn't like it as much as she did, but she loved shattering his resolve.

"Fuck, baby. Come up here." He reached for her and she swatted at his hand.

Dragging her tongue along the tip of his arousal, she smiled up at him.

"Greedy, aren't you?"

"When it comes to you?" His eyes darkened. "Hell, yes."

She straddled his hips and pressed her hands to his wrists, her arousal heightened by the spark of restraint in his eyes. She knew he could easily break free of her hold, but she loved holding this particular man captive. Six-plus feet of sexual power and domination bending to her will. *Glorious.*

His gaze fell to her breasts. "Lean down here so I can taste you."

His command sent shivers of heat rippling over her. She lowered her left breast to his mouth. The first swipe of his tongue brought shocks of heat between her legs. She arched against his eager mouth, and he sucked the tip of her breast against the roof of his mouth. Her head fell forward with the delicious friction, and her hair curtained their faces, amplifying the sounds of their breathing and the sweet suckling of him devouring her. His mouth moved to her other breast; then his hands fisted in her hair and he crushed his mouth to hers. Fireworks sparked behind her closed eyes, and in the next second she was beneath him and the look in his eyes was pure sin.

"Condom." His eyes darted around her room.

"I don't keep any here." His face screwed up, and she explained. "I never bring men to my room."

"Fuck." His head fell heavily forward.

"Don't you have any?" She was on the pill, but she'd never chanced sex without a condom before.

"No, I don't have any. I was out to dinner with Clark, not you."

The way he said *not you* made her feel like she was the only woman he'd ever consider sleeping with, and she knew that wasn't true, but it still stopped her heart for a split second.

"I thought guys were always prepared," she snapped, as if

this were his fault, when she'd initiated the sex.

"I am, when I'm expecting to get laid." He kissed his way down her body, hovering over her sex as he pushed her legs open wide.

"Hunter. What are you doing?"

Without hesitation his mouth did what it did best, giving her the answer she sought as he dragged his tongue over her wet center. She was still enjoying the tingle of the slow drag when his mouth claimed her, his hands splayed across her thighs, holding them down. With determination and expertise, he brought her to the edge, and just when she was on the verge of coming apart, he withdrew that talented tongue and used his thumb to tease her sensitive clit, blowing lightly on the wetness between her legs. She ached against the tease, needing to feel him, wanting him to quell her desire.

"I'm taking care of my girl." His words came hard and fast, like he couldn't wait to take her over the edge.

She rocked her hips, his words playing in her ears like a threat—*or a promise*—as he pressed her thighs harder to the mattress. The rebellious words *I'm not your girl* were on the tip of her tongue, but when his mouth came down hard and his tongue drove deep as he masterfully shattered her last shred of control, lights exploded behind her eyelids. As her body rocked and pulsed against his mouth, the lie she'd nearly shared faded to bliss.

CHapter eiGHteen

HUNTER WAS SITTING on Jana's couch in the living room when she stumbled out of the bedroom at ten thirty the next morning wearing his shirt from the night before. She was rubbing her eyes, clearly oblivious to his presence as he watched her go up on tiptoes to reach a cup in the cabinet. Her shirt inched up, revealing her bare ass. Hunter smiled. He loved that ass. As she came down on flat feet and set her cup on the counter, he realized that there was a hell of a lot more than like going on inside his chest for the rest of her, too.

She reached for the coffeepot, which he'd brewed earlier, and a second later she whipped her head around. Her gaze found him and her eyes bloomed wide.

He smiled. "Morning, beautiful." He made no move to go to her, wanting to give her a moment to get used to seeing him there, in her living room, fully dressed and comfortable. Luckily, he kept an extra shirt or two in his truck in case he had to see a client with little warning.

"What…? You didn't leave?"

She brought her coffee to the couch, and he pulled her down on his lap. "What kind of a welcome is that for a guy who made you come several times last night?"

"You were a very good boy last night, but—"

He pressed his lips to hers and swept his tongue over the seam of her lips. She opened for him, returning his kiss with fervor, then suddenly pushed away.

"Don't freak out," he said quickly.

"You stayed over." Panic was evident in her wide eyes and in the tenor of her voice.

"I did. Thank you for giving me what I wanted. I woke up with you in my arms for once." He'd laid in bed with his body wrapped around her as she'd slept, and nothing had ever felt so right. Every so often she'd sigh, or make a soft sound, almost as if she were talking in her sleep, but he hadn't been able to make out what she was saying. He'd gotten up with the sun, showered, and taken care of a few things to prepare for the day.

"I'm sorry I didn't…you know…" She dropped her eyes. "Repay your efforts."

Since they'd had no condom, he'd made her come time and time again, using only his hands and mouth. She'd been so spent, between the alcohol and the orgasms, that she'd fallen asleep soon after, but he didn't mind. He'd even made it through the night without taking things into his own hands—until his shower this morning. Surrounded by the scents of her body wash and shampoo, with the images of her beneath him clawing at his mind, it hadn't taken long to relieve the pressure.

"You did repay my efforts." He smiled as he said, "You let me wake up with you in my arms."

She tried to move from his lap, but he held her in place. "You're not getting away that easily, not now that I have you without any distractions."

She rolled her eyes and yawned. "What time is it?" She glanced over her shoulder toward the clock on the kitchen wall. "Oh shit! I have to call Brock. He's going to be pissed."

He clutched her hips, keeping her in place. "I called him at six thirty and told him you wouldn't be there."

"Hunter! You had no right to do that. You should have woken me up."

"You're welcome." He laughed, and she stewed. "He has you signed up for an exhibition match against the Plymouth Fight Club, which I almost told him you wouldn't take part in, but I knew you'd get mad. I hate the idea of that pretty face of yours getting maimed."

The scowl on her face didn't soften. Hunter ignored it. "You'll probably need to train a little extra at some point before the match. But he was cool with you missing today."

"Yeah, I bet he wanted to kill you." She looked away.

Hunter gently moved her chin toward him, so he could see her eyes. "Don't worry, pretty girl. He thinks I drove you home last night because you'd had a little too much to drink and that I stayed to make sure you didn't puke and choke on it. I told him I slept on the couch."

She sighed. "Thank you for that."

"I've got a sister. I get it." And that brought him to the next thing he wanted to talk to her about. "I had Sky drop off your purse, and I got Marco's number from your phone and called him. I told him that you were sick and you wouldn't make it in today."

"Oh my God. Sky knows you stayed over? And my classes? I'm in so much trouble."

"First of all, yes, but Sky thinks I slept on the couch, too. We'll talk about that later." He let those words sink in despite the fact that her relieved sigh about Sky was immediately followed by a scowl. "And as far as your classes go, Marco's taking care of canceling them. The guy was pretty cool about it, actually. He wasn't the dick I expected." Marco had asked if Hunter was her brother, and he'd taken the liberty to say no, that he was *her man*. He wasn't about to tell her that.

"He wasn't pissed?" She shifted on his lap and her gaze softened.

"No. We had a nice talk."

She bonked her forehead on his shoulder. "Oh my God."

He lifted her chin again and smiled. "It was fine. He needed to understand that you couldn't be expected to work seven days a week or to take on the responsibilities of three people."

"I'm *so* fired." Jana closed her eyes.

"Actually, you're not. He said he had planned on coming back soon to help out. I have no idea if he was bullshitting or not, but at least now he knows someone is looking out for you."

She covered her face with her hands, and he pulled them down so she had to look at him. He wasn't going to let her pretend that the feelings between them weren't there, and he sure as hell wasn't going to allow her boss to continue taking advantage of her.

"Now, you're going to shower and dress, and then we're going to talk." He lifted her to her feet and patted her bare ass.

"Go on. We have a lot to do today."

"I have to go to work, Hunter. I can't spend today—"

He rose to his feet and swept her into his arms, ignoring the words streaming from her mouth as she flailed against him. *Hunter. Stop. I'm going to kill you. Asshole.*

Speaking calmly, as if she weren't punching and flailing in his arms, he said, "You're going to shower, and then we are going to talk. No work. No excuses." He set her on her feet in the bathroom, and when she said, "But—" he took her in a passionate kiss, leaving her breathless, and closed the bathroom door as he left the room.

JANA WASN'T SURE if it was nerves or anger making her body thrum, but she was glad that for once it wasn't desire. At least she had *that* aspect of her body under control. Who did he think he was, canceling her classes and calling her brother? She showered and dressed, stewing over his actions, and took her sweet time drying her hair, hoping Hunter would get sick of waiting and take off. Although, she had to admit that taking care of all of her commitments had been a thoughtful thing for him to do. It might even border on romantic. And didn't he have to work today?

She turned off the hair dryer and brushed her hair, thinking about last night and the way he'd said he was taking care of *his girl*. A thrill raced through her with the memory, despite the reality that she wasn't his girl. She wasn't anyone's girl, nor could she be, until she figured out her own life and what she really wanted. Besides, Hunter wanted to win. He always wanted to win. Surely this was all still part of a game to him.

Then why did he refuse to leave last night?

And why did he make all those arrangements today?

And want to talk?

She opened the bathroom door and listened to the silence. Hunter was gone. Her stomach knotted, and unexpected disappointment floated through her. Could she miss him already? No. This was *all* part of his stupid game. She swiped her cell phone from the table, pulled up DO NOT RESPOND! and typed in a fast text. *You left?*

She slumped onto the couch, confused and feeling betrayed, even though she had no right to feel that way. She'd told him she didn't have time to talk. Of course he left. Wouldn't she have left if the tables were turned? Hell, she probably would have left while he was sleeping. Still, anger and hurt simmered inside her. She typed another angry text at being ignored— *WTF?*

She got up and paced the living room, then glanced out the window, catching sight of Hunter pacing the backyard, talking on his phone.

Relief swept through her, followed quickly by regret for the angry texts she'd sent. She watched as he rubbed the back of his neck, squinting up at the sun. He ended the call and looked down at his phone. Before he could swipe and read the texts, she ran out the back door. His killer smile brought guilt to the forefront of her mind as she sank into his open arms.

"Shit," Hunter said with a laugh. "What did you do?"

"Nothing. I just…" *Was afraid you left.*

He pried her arms from around his waist and searched her eyes. "Spill it, pretty girl. We've already established that you're a sucky liar."

"I thought you left," she mumbled.

"What was that?" He leaned in closer.

"I thought you left! Okay? Jesus. And I might have sent you a few angry texts."

She walked away, and he quickly fell into step beside her, shoved his phone in his pocket, and draped an arm over her shoulder. She waited for him to laugh, or to give her shit, but he didn't say a word as he guided her to the swinging chair built for two hanging from one of the large trees at the edge of the back yard and pulled her down beside him.

She eyed him suspiciously as they sat in silence. He tucked her against his side, and she wasn't about to fight him on it. She wanted to be there, even though she was struggling to keep the dark, uncomfortable panic from taking over.

When he finally spoke, his tone was calm and confident, with no trace of his usual demands. "I want to tell Sky we're dating."

That was not at all what she'd anticipated. "That's why you want to talk?"

"No." He looked over at her. "Yes, partly, but not solely."

"But we're not even dating, Hunter. Why would you want to tell her anything?"

"Okay, then I want to officially date you, and then I want to tell her. I don't keep secrets from my family, Jana. Maybe I used to, but it's not the man I want to be with you. It's not the man I want to be anymore."

"I told you when we first met that I'm not the girlfriend type. And you said you never wanted to settle down. So where is this coming from?" The tentative tone of her voice didn't surprise her. It mirrored the conflicting emotions she'd been battling on a daily basis.

He turned so his entire body faced her, one arm across the back of the swing. He took her hand in his.

"Where?" He shrugged. "My heart, I guess. I'm not good at this stuff, and you know that, so you use it against me. I get it. You're scared to commit. Hell, Jana, I'm scared to commit."

She wasn't about to deny that. "Then why are you pushing for me to?"

"Because every time I look at you I want more of you. I want to understand why you do things, whether it's boxing or dancing, crying, or dressing like you did last night and singing your heart out onstage. I want to hold you in my arms at night after making love to you so many times you can't return the favor." A relieved smile spread his lips, like the words had been trapped inside too long. "Then I want to wake up in the morning and take you again. I want to bear the brunt of your stubbornness and your tenderness. I want to listen to your dreams and help them come true. I want it all with you, and I've never wanted that before."

Jana was sure her heart had stopped beating. That had to be it. She was dead.

He touched her cheek and her stomach flipped. *Nope. Not*

dead.

She took her hand from his and turned to face the yard, unable to think, much less speak.

"You're not going to ignore me, Jana. Not after everything I just said. Do you think that was easy for me?" The restraint in his voice was like a living thing between them.

She forced herself to respond. "No," she whispered.

He waited in silence for more. She waited in silence, too, because she was having trouble processing what he'd said, what he wanted. She wanted to be the girl who could say she wanted that, too, but panic spread through her chest like wildfire, trapping her words inside.

"So that's it? You've got nothing to say?" Hunter rose to his feet, and her stomach took a nosedive, reminding her of how she felt when she'd thought he'd left only moments earlier.

Panic brought her to her feet, too, and the truth poured out. "No. I have things to say. I'm not scared, Hunter. I'm petrified. I don't know how to be a girlfriend, and right now I can't even commit to getting my life in order. How can I possibly commit to you? And you…You're as much of a non-committer as I've always been. What makes you think we can work? I've never been a good girlfriend, not even when I was in high school and it was the thing to do."

Her voice softened as she admitted what he'd already known, but somehow saying it made her see it more clearly, and she didn't feel as proud of herself as she always had for being an independent woman.

His jaw tightened. "How many guys have you slept with in

the past six months?"

"What?" She shook her head, trying to think of dates and months, and even though she couldn't grasp the concept of time while her heart was racing and her palms were sweating, it didn't take long for the truth to become clear.

"How many, Jana?" He closed the distance between them. "Because yeah, I was the biggest fucking player there was, but in the last few months I haven't slept with anyone but you. Not once. Not one fucking kiss."

Her jaw dropped.

He shrugged, and the tension in his muscles drained away right before her eyes. "It's true. There's only been you, pretty girl."

She looked down at his hand as he reached for hers and brought it to his lips. "And I've never called a single woman a nickname, and with you, it just comes out." He stepped closer, their bodies touching from thigh to chest. "And I've sure as hell never asked anyone but you to tell me she wanted me. Do you know why?"

The blood was rushing through her ears so fast it took all of her focus to shake her head.

He cupped her cheeks, stroking her skin with his thumb as he gazed into her eyes with so much emotion there was no way it was anything short of real.

"Because I never cared. Until you."

CHAPTER NINETEEN

FEAR. THAT'S WHAT Hunter saw in Jana's eyes as he waited for her to respond. Every silent second felt like an eternity. He didn't dare rush her, for fear of her running away. He'd been a runner, too, but he was done with that, and he hoped to crack her walls enough that she'd consider being done, too.

"You're so sure of it all…" Jana said so quietly he almost didn't hear her. "It's like you have all the answers."

Love isn't about having all the answers. It's about not caring if you don't, because what happiness really comes down to is knowing that you don't need answers if your heart is full of the person you cherish most. As his mother's words came back to him, the ache of missing her settled into Hunter's bones. He thought about her often and missed the comfort of knowing she would always smile when she saw him, no matter what he'd done the night before. She'd open her arms and wrap him in unconditional love, and he'd probably soaked that up more than he'd deserved. Now it was his mother's words that confirmed what his heart had already known.

"I don't have all the answers. But I have the only one I need." Hunter wasn't good at deciphering Jana's silence. He knew she wasn't going to commit to him easily. Hell, she wouldn't even tell him she wanted him when they were naked and it was written in the blush on her skin.

A warning voice whispered through his mind, reminding him that he was laying his heart out for her to step on. Jana wasn't a dainty stepper. That smart mouth of hers knew how to trample. But he'd come this far. He wasn't about to be deterred.

"Maybe I'm reading us wrong," he finally said. "Maybe you don't want me the way I thought you did, but it doesn't change what I feel for you."

Jana tugged on a lock of hair. Her face clouded with uneasiness, and he feared he'd pushed too hard.

"I…" she stammered, and a second later she found her voice. "I haven't been with anyone else either, in several months."

He couldn't stop the smile tugging at his lips as relief nearly bowled him over.

She took a tentative step closer, and her vulnerability made his knees weak. With her bare feet, the top of her head didn't even reach his chin, making her seem even smaller and more fragile.

She gazed up at him with a mixture of hope and worry in her beautiful eyes. "What if we don't work?"

"What if we do?" he countered.

A soft laugh escaped her lips, and it was a magnificent sound.

"I'm being serious, Hunter. We're good at…hookups. What if we aren't good at something more?"

"Then we go back to hooking up." How else could he answer? He didn't believe they wouldn't be good together, but he didn't want the idea of their not being a *them* in her head.

"So, what exactly is it that you want from me?"

He arched a brow, biting back sexual innuendos. She laughed, and it shot straight to his heart.

"God. You're impossible," she said. "You know what I mean."

"I want to spend today together. I want to talk about your studio." If he wanted this to work—and man, did he ever—it was time for him to come clean and let her know what he already knew.

"When Sky dropped off your purse, she told me that you didn't get the space at Seaside. I want to talk about that, and other things." It was no wonder she'd dressed and acted like she had last night. She must have been heartbroken when she found out she had lost the space at Seaside, and if there was one thing he knew about Jana, it was that emotions scared her.

She nodded. "And this?" She waved her finger between them. "What do you want with regard to us?"

He didn't hesitate as he pulled her against him—hoping she wouldn't pull away and not spend the day with him. "I want there to be an *us*. A commitment. You see only me, and I'll see only you."

She rolled her eyes, but he knew it was a defense mechanism. "You want to win. To hear me say I want you."

Of course he wanted to hear that. What man wouldn't? What she didn't realize was that winning, to Hunter, meant having Jana all to himself.

"No. You don't have to tell me you want me. Just tell me you'll only be with me."

She laughed at that and quickly trapped her lower lip between her teeth. Her brows knitted. "Okay."

"Okay, what?"

"God, you're a pain. Okay, *fine*. I'll only be with you, but we're not boyfriend and girlfriend, and I can't promise—"

He pressed his lips to hers and lifted her off her feet and deepened the kiss. With kisses like this, how could she ever deny that they were so much more than a hookup?

"I can't," she said between kisses, "change, Hunter." He kissed her again, and she pushed his mouth away. "I'm selfish. My life is crazy. I'm not good at commitments, and I'm not sure you are either."

He huffed in annoyance, lifting her higher and guiding her legs around his waist. "You're also a stubborn pain in the ass, but I'm pretty sure I know what I'm getting into. Now shut the hell up and kiss me."

Hunter carried her inside and debated carrying her straight into the bedroom to show her just how much he wanted this to work, but he knew they'd never get any more talking done if he did. They had one day without distractions, and he intended to take full advantage of the time and show Jana just how right they were for each other.

JANA WATCHED HUNTER as he read through her lists and

the notes she'd taken about opening a studio. His confession had left her reeling and feeling a little overwhelmed, and they'd sat on the couch and talked for a long time about things that weren't as scary, like how she'd ended up in that tight dress and spiky heels. He'd laughed when she'd admitted that while onstage, she's been pretending she really was Taylor Swift. She'd told him about crying when she'd heard that she didn't get the space at Seaside and how she'd been taken by surprise by her tears. He'd told her that those tears should have been her first eye opener about how much the studio actually meant to her. And he'd held her when tears threatened again with her confession, and he'd whispered, *I wish I could have been there to help you feel better.* He offered comfort without judgment. He was the one person she thought she never wanted to see her weaknesses, and somehow, when he did, he made her feel stronger for it.

They'd picked up her car from Seaside and spent all afternoon talking. They'd talked about his mom and how much he missed her. He'd shared his heartache over his father's alcoholism, and she'd seen the relief of having his father whole again written all over his face. She realized how he must have felt, seeing her that drunk. Not just last night, but most of the times they'd hooked up, and she realized she'd been using alcohol as an escape, too, and it was time to stop.

Now, as she watched him reading over her notes, she was filled with emotion for the man who probably should have run from her, and instead, he'd not only opened himself up, but he was helping her slow down and do the same.

She'd expected him to skim her notes, at best, but he really seemed to care. He was concentrating, pointing to words, then looking away, as if he were thinking about what he'd read.

He closed the notebook and placed his hand over the top of it. "You've done your homework."

"Yeah, but it doesn't matter anymore. Maybe Marco will come back and things will be better." She reached for the notebook, but he wouldn't let it go.

"Since when are you a quitter?" he said harshly.

She was baffled by his swift attitude change. "I'm not a quitter." She yanked the notebook from his hands. God, would they always bump heads, even after such a nice few hours?

He scoffed. "You must not have wanted your own studio very badly, then."

"I just told you that I *cried* because I wanted it so badly, and you know I don't cry. I scream and yell, but I never cry," she challenged. "Having my own studio would mean that I could go back to doing theater. I could make my own hours, my own decisions. God, Hunter." She shifted her eyes away, annoyed at herself for snapping at him.

"Then why are you giving up? Just because you lost one space that was handed to you? Let's get out there and find you another space."

"Oh, like it's that easy?" She rolled her eyes.

"Nothing worth anything is easy. Jesus, look at you." His smile told her he was only half kidding, but he was right. Jana knew she was anything but easy. "Lucky for you, maybe it can be easier for you than for most people. You can use our empty building out on Route 6."

"I am not *using* your space." She got up and paced the living room.

"Why not?"

"Because we're involved. Mixing business and pleasure is never a good idea."

"Jana, it's in the perfect location, with plenty of parking, no retail neighbors to complain about loud music or whatever other concerns you might have, and it's mine, which means you can use it without worrying about a shitty landlord."

"No." She continued pacing. "It complicates things too much."

He rose to his feet and blocked her path, anger rolling off of him in waves.

"When will you step out of your own stubborn way? Open your eyes and take what's being offered. Everything you want is right here in front of you."

She flinched at the tone of his voice and wondered if he meant *him* or the space he was offering. "It's not a good idea."

"You made it very clear that we're not girlfriend and boyfriend, and I can deal with that, but, Jana…" He pulled her in close again—he was always pulling her in close lately, and not just for sex, but making her feel special and important. Like she was the only thing that mattered and he wanted to keep her safe. She wasn't used to that.

The tension in him eased as their bodies came together. "Baby, what I'm offering has nothing to do with sex, or us, or commitments. It has to do with you achieving your dreams."

She wanted to trust that he was telling her the truth, but she was still reeling from how much had changed between them—

and inside her—in the past few hours. She didn't fully trust it. They were both committing to something they'd fought forever. *But not really.* She honestly hadn't even tried to pick up a man in six months, and she'd only slept with Hunter. Whether she'd acknowledged it to herself or not before she was forced to, it was the truth.

"So, your offer has absolutely nothing to do with control?" she asked. "Or wanting to keep me under your thumb?"

He pushed away. "No. Jesus, is that what you think?" He fisted his hands and walked around the couch.

She wondered if he was going to walk right out the door, and the thought brought a rise of renewed panic. She was messing everything up between them, and she didn't want to mess them up; she just needed to slow them down. Or maybe it was her *life* she needed to slow down.

Thankfully, Hunter didn't head for the door. He went into the kitchen and leaned against the counter with his back to her. She had pushed him away so hard, so many times, and he never ran away. She took a step closer to where he stood and stopped when he turned around, his gorgeous dark eyes laden with defeat.

"Jana, I know I'm aggressive, and I get why you'd think I want to control things, but can't you see I'm trying here? I may be an asshole sometimes, but I'd never try to control you. You're like a wild horse. You can't be tamed or chained."

He searched her eyes as he had earlier, and this time she was sure he saw her heart opening up to him, because she couldn't stop it if she tried. No one had ever seen her so clearly before, understood what she'd felt like her whole life. There was so much she wanted to do—*boxing, dancing, theater…him.*

"That's one of your most alluring qualities." He smiled, shook his head. "Believe it or not, I like who you are, and I don't want to change you. I just want to be with you. To experience life with you and see you happy. When you talk about opening your own studio, your entire face lights up, and I'd hate to see you give that up so easily. Especially when easy isn't any part of who you are."

The sincerity in his voice was too genuine to deny. He really *was* interested in helping her, walking beside her, not carrying her. And at a time when he could have told her she was easy to get in bed, he didn't take that half-teasing stab. He'd somehow made her feel stronger again, and that overwhelmed her, softened her toward him even more.

"You are probably the only person who sees me for who I really am, and…" Her feelings for him warred with the fear of somehow hurting him—or herself. "I appreciate that more than you can know. And I love that you want to be with me, not control me. But can I think about it? See the space?" she asked as she came around the couch and joined him.

"Of course." He didn't look mad, just resigned, like he knew she'd need time.

"Shouldn't you talk to Grayson about it first?" She reached for his hand, and this time when he pulled her in close, she wrapped her arms around him and soaked in the comfort he offered. "I'm sorry. Everything is changing so fast. You're so sure of it all, and it's just going to take me some time."

"To trust me."

It wasn't a question, but she realized he only understood

part of what she was saying. It was also about trusting herself not to hurt him.

"To trust both of us. To trust the changes we're talking about. I'm sorry."

He drew back and lifted her chin, gazing into her eyes with a look that told her that everything *had* changed. Gone was the competition, the games, replaced with something real. Replaced with *more*.

She felt panic rising in her chest, and this time it was easier to push it back down.

"Don't ever apologize for being careful. We both have pasts, and they're not pretty. Hell, Jana, they're too much for most people to even try to understand. But you and me? I've said it before and I'll say it again. We're so similar. We're both stubborn, controlling, passionate. I want to cross this line with you. I want to build trust, but it goes both ways. We'll argue, and we might take seven steps back for every one we take forward, and that's okay."

You really do get me.

Maybe they could do this.

"Regardless of whether you tell me tomorrow that you made a mistake and we can't be together or not, the space I'm offering you stands. No strings attached. I'll talk to Gray, but he won't mind." He smiled and said, "You know where it is, right? Prime location. Right on Route 6 across the street from the Dunkin' Donuts, with plenty of parking. It's unfinished, and we can build it out however you'd like."

He held up their laced hands before lowering his lips to hers, sealing his hopes with a kiss and igniting hers.

CHAPTER TWENTY

THEY DIDN'T HAVE wild monkey sex that night, and they didn't go see the space off of Route 6. After Hunter made a trip home for the necessities—clothes and condoms—they made a quick dinner and watched a movie. Jana fell asleep with her head on Hunter's lap about halfway through *Million Dollar Baby*, for which Hunter was glad, because he knew she'd give him shit about his damp eyes. That movie got him every time, because he saw Jana in Hillary Swank's fierce determination. He'd carried Jana to bed, and for the second morning in a row, Hunter had woken up with Jana in his arms.

Then they'd had wild monkey sex.

In the days since, life had been hectic. Between Hunter's long hours working on the sculpture to make the deadline for the competition and the extra hours Jana was putting in at the studio, they rarely saw each other before nine at night. Thankfully, Jana hadn't fought him on staying over, and they'd woken up together every morning for the past week. He'd kicked her out of bed for her boxing practices, though he had a hard time letting her leave the house in her sexy little workout clothes, inciting her to roll her eyes and tell him that if he didn't stay over, she'd get out of the door quicker.

He loved every minute of their bickering and somehow knew it might never change. He sure as hell hoped it didn't.

Hunter had spoken to Grayson about letting Jana use the space, and as Hunter had assumed, Grayson was all for it. Meanwhile, Hunter and Jana discussed the what-ifs about her accepting the space ad nauseam. *What if we break up? What if we stay together but owning my own studio doesn't work out? What if I quit my job and no one wants to take my classes?* They'd become experts at talking about the space, and Jana's excitement about opening a dance studio had only increased. But Jana had successfully avoided or redirected every conversation about their relationship.

It was Sunday evening, and their schedules had finally eased enough to go see the space.

Hunter opened the passenger door of the truck and helped Jana out, handing her the keys. "Here you go, pretty girl. Check it out. See how it feels."

"This location *is* great," she said as she walked toward the front door. "And you're right. There's plenty of parking."

Like most of the buildings on the lower Cape, the cedar siding was weathered and gray, and the storefront looked more like a residential house than a commercial property.

"The gardens are overgrown, and the grass needs to be mowed, but those are easy fixes." Hunter pointed to the right side of the parking lot. "I was thinking that we could put a sign up there, that way the trees out front won't block it from traffic coming in either direction."

Jana turned and faced the street with a wide smile. "I can't believe you guys don't use this place. Or haven't already rented it out."

Hunter shrugged as they made their way to the front door. "We were going to open a showroom, but right after we bought it we were so busy with orders that we pushed the idea off for a while. And now we work on a custom-order basis, so we don't really have stock, and renting is a big time suck."

He placed his hand on her lower back as they walked up the front steps. "But I'd suck anything for you," he teased, with a flick of his tongue over her ear.

She giggled, and he watched her unlock the door. Lately he found himself studying her movements a little closer, capturing her energy to pour into the sculpture. He'd been so inspired this week that he'd completed the body. He'd begun fabricating thin, twisted strips of iron to create a skirt that looked like it was blowing in the wind, and over the next week or two he'd create a bodice out of hundreds of small pieces of metal and mirrors to simulate fabric for her top.

Every moment he and Jana spent together bonded them on a newer, deeper level, and he woke up each morning more inspired than the day before. The sculpture was changing as quickly as their relationship. When he looked at Jana, his muse, he saw a woman breaking free of her own confines and evolving right before his eyes, and because of that, the sculpture had taken on a life of its own.

Jana smiled as she pushed the door open. The property had been empty for so long, the hardwood floors were covered in a fine layer of dust, and Hunter realized his mistake. He'd been so excited to offer the space to her, knowing the location alone would practically assure her success, he'd forgotten about cleaning it.

"Sorry, babe. I probably should have had it cleaned before showing it to you."

"That's okay. I don't mind a little dirt." They went inside, and she turned in a slow circle, a sweet smile spreading her lips. "This is big enough to have a reception area up here with chairs for parents, and…" She walked across the floor, then turned to face him again.

He was right behind her and folded her in his arms. "A reception area, huh? I was thinking that this was the make-out lobby."

She went up on her toes and wound her arms around his neck. "Mm. I like that."

"Wait until you see the cunnilingus kitchen." He slanted his mouth over hers and clutched her ass.

"Hunter," she whispered. "Why didn't we start there?"

He nibbled her neck as they moved toward the doors in the back of the building. She was walking backward, stopping every few seconds as he sucked or nipped at her skin.

"Baby, I'll start anywhere you'd like." He lifted her into his arms and she wound her legs around his waist. How did she do this to him? Take him from a walk through a building to wanting to tear her clothes off in a matter of seconds? The rosy flush on her cheeks and lust in her eyes as her mouth met his in a hungry kiss always pulled him in.

He pushed open the door to the kitchen and lowered her onto the counter. "You're so fucking sexy. I swear, Jana, you totally own me." He crushed his mouth to hers as he hiked her skirt up around her waist and teased her through her silky panties.

"Oh God, yes," she hissed.

He tugged her panties to the side and slid two fingers in deep, burying his tongue in her mouth and moving his fingers and tongue with the same rhythm. She returned every stroke of his tongue with one of her own. When he used his thumb to tease her clit, her head tipped back, revealing the creamy expanse of her neck. Lord, he could come just watching her fall apart against him. He sank his teeth into her sensitive skin above the curve of her shoulder and her breathing became shallow. She clawed at his shoulders as he sank lower and brought his mouth to her hot, wet center.

"Hunt…Oh my Go…" Her words trailed off as he pressed her legs open wide and feasted on her.

Her thighs tensed, and he felt her climax build in the rock of her hips, her panting sighs. She cried out his name as she came apart, and just as she came down from the climax, he buried his fingers inside her again, quickly finding the spot that sent her right back to the peak, and took her in a wild, passionate kiss.

As the tension in her body eased and their lips parted, he said, "Want to see the naked stockroom?"

HUNTER. GOD, HUNTER. He was turning her inside out.

He'd taken care of her in so many ways over the last week. Sex had become the icing on the cake instead of the cake itself. She never thought she'd meet a guy who was as sexual as she was. Yes, guys were all sexual, but most had no imagination. Hunter had no inhibitions. He took and gave in equal measure, and she loved that about him. He wasn't put off when she was aggressive, and he was constantly surprising her in other ways, like texting just to say he was thinking about her. Sometimes they were sexy texts; other times they were so sweet they turned her mind to mush. When they'd argued last night, he'd taken out her boxing gloves and held up a pillow for her to work out her aggression. And probably the sweetest thing, which no one would ever believe if she told them, was that before bed, he'd begun rubbing her feet. *You're on these babies all day long. They need attention, too.* Even now he took care of her, fixing her skirt and putting her shirt back on, making sure she was properly covered.

She looked around the small break room as she tried to remember why they were there. The space would work well, but the idea of mixing business with pleasure still made her uneasy.

"You like?" He kissed her again. Remnants of her scent lingered on his mouth.

"What you just did? Do you even have to ask?" She knew he meant the space, but she could feel his arousal pressing against her belly, and she became too distracted to think about anything else.

"Mm. That's a great answer."

She hooked her finger in one of the belt loops on his jeans

and tugged him through the only other door she saw. "Show me the naked stockroom, please."

The door clicked shut behind them, surrounding them in total darkness.

"I feel like a teenager sneaking into a closet to make out." She was whispering, even though they were the only ones there. "It's my turn," she said as she tugged his shirt over his head.

"Come here." He pulled her close and kissed her. His skin was hot, and the muscles in his back bunched as he rocked his hips and deepened the kiss.

"I could kiss you all night," he said against her mouth.

"I have something else in mind." She unbuttoned his jeans and tugged them down his thighs.

She kissed her way down the treasure trail of dark hair to the tip of his erection. Licking the bead of wetness waiting for her, she closed her eyes and relished the greedy moan coming from deep within his lungs as he fisted his fingers in her hair. She licked him from base to tip, then teased his sensitive sac with one hand as she stroked his erection with the other. She loved the feel of him, thick and ready, in her hand, and when she took him in her mouth, the way he sucked in air between his teeth heightened her arousal.

"Oh yeah, that's it," he said as she moved along his eager length. "Christ, Jana, you've got me so hard I ache."

She smiled around his erection, quickening her efforts, pushing him back against the wall. He thrust his hips, and she knew he was close.

"Jana. Fuck. Jana." The restraint in his voice only spurred

her on. "Shit. Stop. I'm gonna come."

She loved that he warned her, but there was no way she was pulling away before she got a taste of him. His hips thrust once, twice, and the third hard thrust brought his salty, warm release. She struggled to swallow, but the desire to pleasure him, to give back to the man who was giving her so much, overrode her discomfort, and she accepted every last drop.

Afterward, while he stroked her hair, whispering about how incredible she was, she touched her forehead to his navel, savoring the feel of being so close to him.

"Baby. You spoil me." He lifted her to her feet, tucked her hair behind her ear, and kissed her tenderly. "Let's finish looking around, go home and clean up, and then let's go out to Race Point and watch the sunset."

As they drove back to her place, she wondered when it had become his home, too.

CHAPTER TWENTY-ONE

THE NEXT MORNING Brock took Jana through a grueling workout. They worked the heavy bag, the speed bag—her least favorite, because she wasn't very fast—and then he had her jumping rope and sparring for four rounds.

"You don't have as much steam as usual," Brock said as she took a drink from her water bottle. "Anything going on you want to talk about?"

She shook her head. "Not really. I just have so much going on right now." She'd been thinking about the exhibition match. As much as she loved to fight, she knew she wasn't up to par. She simply didn't carry the same level of aggression as she had a week ago, and she knew it was the change in her and Hunter's relationship. Maybe giving up the fight, easing up on her need to do absolutely everything, was the slowing down that she needed.

"Hunter told me about the exhibition match, but would you be upset if I don't fight in it? I'm just so crazed with trying to decide about the studio and everything right now. I feel like one more thing might push me over the edge."

He handed her a towel and she wiped her face.

"Not at all. Listen, fighting was your idea, and if it's causing you stress, or you're not enjoying it, don't continue because of me. Take some time off if you need it."

"Thanks, Brock. I'm okay. I just don't want the added pressure of an exhibition match. Thank you for understanding, though."

"I have to admit, I was surprised to hear from Hunter the other morning."

She'd wondered when Brock was going to get around to mentioning the call, and in the days since, she'd tried to figure out how to handle it when he finally got around to it.

"Sorry about missing that practice and not calling you myself. The night before had been a particularly rough night." She sat down on the bench and leaned her back against the wall.

"Yeah, Harper told me." His stare was steady, and she wondered just how much Harper had shared. "Sorry about the Seaside space. But I'm sure you'll find someplace else."

"Do you think it's a mistake?"

"Opening a dance studio? Hell, no. You're so talented, Jana, and you love teaching. Why work for a guy who doesn't appreciate it and takes advantage of you?"

She nodded, thinking about Hunter, who appreciated everything about her and pushed her to do the same. "Hunter offered me his place out on Route 6."

"Seriously?" Brock's eyes narrowed, as if he were questioning why Hunter would do that, and just as quickly the look faded and he smiled. "That's prime space. Can you afford the rent?"

"Gosh, we haven't even talked about the rent. I don't know

how I feel about renting from Hunter."

"Why?" He cocked his head in that older brother sort of way that said, *Do I need to hurt somebody?*

She shrugged, trying to act casual. "He's a friend. What if something goes wrong? It could kill our friendship."

"Listen, I might have warned you about dating Hunter because I think he plays around a lot, but he's a good man. Even if you burned the place down, he'd know it was an accident."

Hearing Brock talk about Hunter playing around and knowing that the only playing around he'd done in the last six months was with her made her want to defend him. She contemplated telling Brock that they were seeing each other, but she wasn't ready to take that step yet. She gazed up at him waiting patiently for her to respond, like he had all the time in the world, when she knew that he, like her, had a million things he had to take care of.

"Can I ask you something?" she finally asked.

"Anything, sis."

"Why do you think none of us have settled down with anyone? I mean, you're twenty-nine, superhot, nice as can be, and you don't have a steady girlfriend. Harper is, like, *made* to be married or something, and Colton's successful and truly the nicest guy around." She smiled at Brock. "No offense, but you're big and scary-looking when you're mad, and Colton doesn't have that same edge. Did Mom and Dad mess us all up somehow?"

Brock laughed. "Mom and Dad didn't mess us up. We had

great role models. They love each other; they just have old-fashioned values. Don't you think?"

"Yeah, that's the thing that worries me. I was kind of hoping you'd say that they did something that I don't remember, because if that were true, it wouldn't come down to me being too fucked up to commit to a relationship." She wasn't about to tell her brother that she had no idea why she was willing to give so much to a man who was obviously willing to give even more, but she was still having trouble fully committing. Hunter had called her his *girlfriend* that morning instead of his *girl,* and it had sent a wave of panic through her again.

Brock shrugged. "We all have our reasons. I'm busy with the club and I'm picky as hell. Harper's been working on her writing career, and Colton? Well, from what Colton says, it's different for gay guys. They're less into monogamy than chicks are."

"Maybe I'm really a gay man," Jana teased.

He pulled back to arm's length and searched her eyes. "Huh?"

"It scares me, committing to a relationship. I just know I'll mess it up."

Brock leaned his elbows on his knees and wrung his hands together. "The guys you dated when you were younger really did a job on you. And I think that mess with Spencer broke something in you, Jana. It's always worried me."

"That's just it, Brock. I don't think it was them, or specifically Spencer. This is all on me. I'm the one who screwed up my relationships."

"That's not true. All guys aren't all clingy like Spencer." His tone turned serious. "If you'd just give yourself a chance—"

"Thanks, but this isn't about Spencer. He's just the last guy I committed to. This is about me. You guys all have good reasons for not wanting to commit, and I don't have anything more solid than knowing I'm not good at relationships." She'd committed to *not* committing. It made no sense, and it worried her that she'd throw that away on a guy with a reputation that even her brother couldn't deny. But her heart told her otherwise.

"Jana, you're spinning all this in your head. You think we didn't get Mom and Dad's old-fashioned values, but I don't believe that. I think we're all good people. We care about others. We work hard. We're just on different timetables with our love lives. But that's okay. That doesn't mean we don't have solid values. It just means we're human."

She rose to her feet and took another drink from her water bottle. "I better take off. I'm teaching a class at ten, and I want to get in touch with Sky. Hunter's letting me do a test class at his place to see how I like it. I want to invite Sky and the girls for a Foxy Mamas class."

"Okay. But listen, if you want to talk more, text me. We can meet for a drink or something." He pulled her into a hug. "There's nothing you can't be good at Jana, including relationships. If you want to be good at relationships, you will be."

She gathered her gym bag and equipment and hurried out to her car, thinking about what Brock had said. Was that true? Did she not want this with Hunter? She stopped cold at the sight of Hunter leaning against her car. His booted feet were crossed at the ankles, and his thick arms were crossed over his broad chest. When he lifted his eyes to hers and pushed from the car, her steps faltered.

He'd left her house early to meet Grayson at a job site, and she hadn't been expecting to see him until that evening. "What are you doing here? How did your meeting go?"

"I missed you." He raked his eyes down her body, and she flamed from the inside out. "You look sexy as hell in that little boxing outfit."

It was no wonder that he made her head spin when he actually touched her; he could turn her on with nothing more than a graze of his eyes.

"Oh, and the meeting went well."

He bent down to kiss her, and as she went up on her toes to meet him halfway, she glanced over her shoulder to see if Brock was watching.

"Jesus, babe. How long are you going to keep this up?" Hunter snapped.

She tried to ignore the piercing guilt his question inspired and tossed her gear in the back of her car.

"You can't hide us forever, and I don't even understand why you are. It's starting to piss me off."

"I'm not trying to piss you off." He'd brought this up a lot lately, but no matter how many times he reassured her, she still worried. "Aren't you concerned at all about all our friendships? We hang out with all of our brothers and sisters. What if we break up? Then they'll feel weird around us anytime we're together."

He folded her in his arms and gave her that look that made her insides go all fluttery. He was pushing for her to give in. Hunter always pushed her past her comfort zones.

"Listen to me, pretty girl. The only thing coming between us is your fear of commitment."

She rolled her eyes, even though she knew he was right. She loved the way he pursued her, and his confidence in their relationship, but she still wasn't sure that letting everyone know they were together was the smartest thing to do. The thought of putting Sky in that weird position was enough to make her hold her ground.

"Okay, maybe it's your inability to trust that the guy I've become is here to stay, but that's all on you, babe, not me. I'm in this for the long haul. I know you're the woman for me, and I know I'm the *only* man for you." He pressed a kiss to her lips. "One day you'll realize that, too."

"Why do you always have to push so hard?"

"You think that's hard?" His smile turned wicked. "That's so soft it's practically liquid."

Her steely resolve instantly turned molten.

Hunter dug his hand into his pocket and handed her a key as he stepped in closer, bringing all that heat with him. "I know we talked about you getting the girls together for a class tonight, so I wanted to be sure you had a key. I'm going to babysit for Billy so Clark and Nina can go out."

"You are?" For some reason the thought of Hunter babysitting again melted her resolve even more. She looked down at the key and noticed it was on a key chain of a heart that said TAKEN. He was bossy even when he didn't say a word.

She arched a brow and he held his palm up toward the sky. "What? It's true."

She laughed.

"Want to come by after the class if I'm still babysitting?"

"Yeah, I'd like that."

He kissed her again. "Then it's a date. You, me, and the little guy. No dirty stuff, though."

"Okay. I'll try to behave myself." She climbed into the car and he closed the door, then leaned in to give her a kiss. "Thanks for bringing me the key and for letting me try out the space."

"Anything for you, pretty girl." He kissed her again. "You'd better take off, or I'm going to climb in that car and take off that sexy little outfit of yours and have my way with you."

"Promises, promises." She blew him a kiss and waved as she drove away, knowing he'd have kept that promise if she'd stayed. She was learning that Hunter's word was as good as gold.

CHAPTER TWENTY-TWO

ON THE WAY to meet the girls for the Foxy Mamas class, Jana turned up the radio. She needed a pick-me-up after getting into it with Marco. She'd asked him to hire another instructor, or an administrative assistant, and he'd finally revealed the real reason he'd stayed in Plymouth for so long. He'd gotten engaged to his head dance instructor from the new studio. Jana knew from the elation in his voice that he was never coming back, at least not for good.

Ella Henderson's "Ghost" came on the radio and she cranked it up. Listening to the words, she thought about how Hunter was her river. When she was in his arms, he washed everything away, her pain, her worries, her sins...Her chest burned as the chorus came on. She wanted to give up the ghosts of her past, the ghosts that pushed her to keep that last wall between Hunter and the rest of her life, but she wasn't sure exactly what those ghosts were, or how to finally let them go.

Leanna's colorful van was parked out front when Jana arrived for the class. Amy, Bella, Leanna, Jessica, Jenna, and Sky came around the side of the building as she stepped from the car. She wished Harper could have come, but she had a conference call with the production staff for her sitcom.

"This place is incredible," Jenna said.

"I had forgotten how perfect the location was." Sky hugged Jana. "My brother pulled out all the stops to help you."

"Yeah, it was really nice of him," Jana said as she fished out the key Hunter had given her, palming the TAKEN charm. She opened the door, and her jaw fell open as the girls pushed past her and went inside. The place was spotless. She had no idea how he could have gotten it cleaned so quickly.

"Look!" Jenna picked up the card from a vase of a dozen red roses on the far end of the counter. "Can I open it?"

Jana could hardly believe her eyes. Roses? How could she ever have doubted his ability to be romantic? She was so nervous about what Hunter might have written that she snagged the card from Jenna's hands. "I'll read it."

"Lizzie told me Hunter had ordered you flowers, but I had no idea that they were *roses*." Sky's voice reeked of curiosity.

Jana opened the card and noticed that it was Hunter's slant-ed handwriting, not Lizzie's curly script. Her heart beat a little faster as she read the note.

I hope your class is everything you dreamed it would be. H.

The simplicity of the note took her by surprise, and she wondered if that was difficult for him, or if he knew she'd have several sets of eyes peering over her shoulders, as she did now.

"That's so sweet," Amy said. "He's such a nice guy."

"Yeah." The confirmation came out as dreamily as she felt, and when she lifted her eyes, she met Sky's assessing gaze and tried to cover it up. She waved the card, as if it didn't mean anything special. "Okay, who's ready to become a foxy mama?"

"Hunter sent roses…" Jessica smiled.

"What do you think this means?" Leanna flashed a mischievous grin at Bella and the others.

Bella jumped right in. "Flowers usually mean sex."

"Oh my God, you guys." Jana laughed, even though she thought they might see right through her ruse. "It means he must be really eager to rent the place. Let's get started."

An hour later, they were sweaty, laughing, and leaning on one another as they drank from their water bottles.

"I feel sexier already," Jenna said as she ran her hands through her shiny dark hair. "Watch out, Petey, 'cause here I come."

"I definitely feel something." Leanna tugged her sweaty tank top off of her skin. "But I'm not sure it's sexy."

"Oh, please. Our men love to see us hot and sweaty." Bella hugged Jana. "This was so fun. And this space? With a few homey touches, it'll be perfect."

"Want to know what I think?" Jessica asked.

"Sure." Jana couldn't stop admiring the flowers, and the cleanliness of the room.

"I think you've got a sweet deal here that you shouldn't pass up." Jessica pointed to the flowers. "And how many landlords leave roses as incentive?"

Jana's mind reeled back to the other sexy things Hunter had used as incentive when he'd shown her the kitchen. She couldn't stop a dreamy sigh from escaping her lips.

Sweet deal doesn't even scratch the surface.

IT WAS BILLY'S bedtime when Jana arrived at Clark and Nina's, but the moment Billy saw her, he wanted nothing to do with bed—or Hunter, which was surprising, since Billy hadn't met Jana before. But as Hunter watched Jana sitting on the floor in Billy's playroom playing with wooden blocks with the cute little guy, Hunter had only two thoughts. Billy was a smart kid, and Jana had never looked more beautiful than she did right then. She picked up a square block and pretended to try to shove it into a round hole, earning the cutest belly laugh from Billy.

Jana swooped him into her lap and gave him Eskimo kisses. She hugged Billy cheek to cheek, and a look of peacefulness washed over her, drawing Hunter in even deeper.

Billy yawned, and Jana's lower lip plumped out in a cute pout.

"Aw, the little guy is tired." She rose with Billy in her arms, looking natural and happy and more at ease than he'd ever seen her. "We should put him to bed."

It took Hunter a moment to get his brain to work. "Uh, yeah. Okay."

They went into Billy's bedroom and he reached for Billy. "I'll change him."

She wrinkled her brow. "No way am I giving up this little guy for a second. We'll do it together. Do you have his jammies?"

He laughed. "Jammies?"

She changed his diaper while Hunter pulled pajamas out of the dresser.

"Yes, he's a baby. They're not called pajamas until he's at least…three."

"Three?"

She shrugged. "Seems right to me. Here." She handed him the dirty diaper and he tossed it in the Diaper Genie. "You didn't even cringe."

"Why would I?" He helped her put Billy's jammies on.

"Most guys wouldn't go near dirty diapers." She lifted Billy into her arms and sat in the rocking chair beside his crib.

"Most guys wouldn't do a lot of stuff." He crouched beside the rocker. "Want me to rock him?"

"No. If you don't mind, I'd really like to."

He shut off the light, leaving only the glow of the night-light, picked up the baby monitor, and left the room, pulling the door partially closed behind him. Jana began singing quietly. He stopped to listen and was surprised that she wasn't singing a lullaby, but Beyoncé's "If I Were a Boy," barely above a whisper. He leaned against the doorframe, listening as she poured her emotions into every word. She sang about having a group of guys to stick up for her and taking people for granted without being held responsible. When she sang about guys who didn't understand what it felt like to lose the one they wanted, he wondered why it sounded so personal coming from her lips. And when a tear tumbled down her cheek, it nearly tore his heart out.

Her voice faded to a thoughtful hum, and he tried to turn

away, but he was riveted in place. He pushed the door open, basking her face in light from the hall as she placed Billy in his crib. Their eyes met, and he swore time stood still.

He reached for her as she neared, and when she laid her hand in his, electricity sparked up his arm. He pressed a kiss to her temple, feeling as though he'd just heard her bare her soul to the darkness of the room, and he wanted to understand where all that hurt came from. He wanted to climb inside her and remove the anguish he'd heard, keep it from stealing any more of her, and protect her from ever feeling hurt again.

CHAPTER TWENTY-THREE

HUNTER TOSSED AND turned all night, worrying about what he'd heard in Jana's voice last night. Coupled with the swelling of his emotions over seeing her with Billy and the thoughts that image had brought to mind, his brain was a tangled mess. He had spent so much of his life avoiding relationships. They were complicated and took time and energy that he hadn't ever wanted to give. Jana was the epitome of *complicated*, but spending nights with her, seeing how much of herself she poured into everything she did, and seeing her last night with Billy, he didn't know how anyone could be around Jana Garner and not fall desperately in love with her.

He looked around her kitchen, seeing his keys beside hers, his designs rolled up on the edge of the table. He turned and saw two pairs of his shoes by the front door, his hoodie lying across the back of the couch. How, in the space of a few short months, had everything changed so much? Had *he* changed so much? Jana still wasn't willing to let everyone know they were dating, and he wondered why he was willing to put up with feeling locked out of that part of her life just to be with her.

Jana came out of the bedroom wearing his T-shirt from last night and looking completely adorable. He opened his arms and she walked right in, snuggling against him.

"Why are you up? It's only five." She yawned against his shoulder, pressed her warm lips to his skin.

"Couldn't sleep. I have a lot to get done for the competition. It's just under three weeks away." He kissed the top of her head. "Why don't you go back to sleep. I didn't mean to wake you."

She shook her head, causing her tousled hair to fall in front of her eyes.

"You've ruined me. I can't sleep when you're not with me."

He tucked her hair behind her ear and kissed her softly. "What was that? Are you admitting that you want me?"

She wiggled between his legs and wound her arms around his neck. "I never got to thank you for the flowers."

"You're avoiding the question." He pressed his lips to hers again, loving the sweet look in her eyes, even as she rolled them at his remark.

"You're avoiding the compliment."

He lifted her easily onto his lap. "I'm glad you liked the flowers. I was careful not to write anything that would *out* your secret lover." The truth stung. He'd had a hard time holding back his feelings when he'd written the card, but he and Jana had come so far, and he didn't want to make her uncomfortable around her friends. He had faith that she'd eventually come around and let him be her man the way he wanted to.

"Thank you for that. Although Sky looked at me like she knew something was up."

"I still don't understand why you feel like you need to keep our relationship from everyone. Sky would love knowing that we're a couple." He had no doubt that his sister would be ecstatic to know they were together.

"I just need a little more time. One thing at a time."

"I'm trying to give you time, but it's not easy, Jana. You're asking me to hold in all these emotions I've never felt for anyone else. It's pure torture." His tone made light of the ache he really felt. In an effort to distract himself before that ache could turn to frustration, he asked, "How did the space work out for the class?"

"It was pretty incredible, actually. How did you get it cleaned so fast?"

"With a little help from my friends." He hadn't been able to hire anyone to clean the space on such short notice, so he, Grayson, and Clark had done it. And the little white lie about where he was yesterday morning was worth hearing that the space was *pretty incredible*.

Her eyes widened, now fully awake. "*You* cleaned it? Hunter, you didn't have to do that. I could have cleaned it myself."

"Don't be silly. Let my girl work her pretty little fingers to the bone?" He kissed her fingertips. "The space is perfect for your studio, right?" He shifted his eyes upward. "I can see it now, a big sign that says 'Jana's Dance Studio.'"

Her smile reached her eyes and just as quickly fell flat. "Oh! I forgot to tell you. I spoke to Marco yesterday. He's engaged. *Engaged.*" The word was laden with disdain. "He's never coming back. He's marrying his head instructor. Head instructor. I'm only an *instructor*. How did she become a head instructor?"

They talked for a long while about Marco and what she had planned for the day, and it wasn't until much later, after they had thoroughly ravaged each other, showered and dressed for work, and finally kissed goodbye, that Hunter realized she'd never answered him about accepting the space.

CHAPTER TWENTY-FOUR

JANA'S LIFE CONTINUED to feel like it was on fast-forward, despite backing out of the exhibition match. Hunter was putting in extra hours on his sculpture, and Colton had asked Jana to fill in for the past three nights, which was great for her bank account, but it meant that she and Hunter were rarely together before midnight, and they usually ended up tangled in the sheets, with very little time to talk. She knew he was stressed about getting his sculpture done, and she made a point of trying to keep their conversations light when they did find time to talk.

Jana was meeting the girls for breakfast at Seaside, and Hunter was going into the shop early.

"Have fun telling the girls about us." He said it with a smirk. All week he'd been dropping not-so-subtle hints that he was tiring of waiting for her to publicly claim their relationship.

She smiled up at him. "It's not like I'm going to *announce* that we're seeing each other."

As he walked her out to her car, his tone became serious. "But you're going to let them know, right?"

She shrugged. "It's not like I'd lie about it. I just don't think I need to make a statement about it."

"Jana, you know that when we do go out with everyone—and eventually we will—I'm going to have an arm around you, or hold your hand, or kiss you, regardless of whether you let them know first or not."

"Why does it have to be such a big deal?"

"It's not like I want you to announce it, but come on. You could have told them when they saw the flowers, and you didn't. You could have told my sister any number of times, since she texts you a million times each week."

She was silent for so long, Hunter's gut clenched.

"What are you afraid of?"

"I'm not good at this, Hunter. I told you I suck as a girlfriend and I wasn't kidding." Hunter accepted her past, moving from one guy to the next with no strings attached, but he didn't know how badly she'd been hurt in the past or how badly she'd hurt Spencer.

"I don't understand what that means."

They'd never talked about specifics, and now she felt compelled to tell him—and the confession brought a thrum of panic. She knew the importance of this conversation, of his finally understanding where she was coming from, and she wanted to give him that. Desperately. She drew her shoulders back, swallowing the fear that accompanied the dull ache in her gut, and forced herself to explain.

"What if...? I don't know. What if I flirt and don't realize I'm doing it?"

He gritted his teeth. "Seriously? I'd better be the only man you flirt with."

"That's what I mean. Do you know why I never date, Hunter?" She couldn't slow down, and the truth roared out. "Because men suck. They make promises they can't keep, and they manipulate you until you open your heart up and lay it out on the table. Because all they care about is winning—and then they leave, they hurt, they fucking take that trust and shred it to pieces." His eyes filled with empathy as he reached for her, but she shifted out of his grip, unable to stop the rest from being set free.

"And it's not just that. A string of guys hurt me, yes, and that was bad, but honestly...I get so caught up in having fun that I must not see clearly. Every guy I've ever dated has accused me of flirting with other men, and maybe they were right. I don't know anymore. Every boy I ever dated thought I wanted to cheat even if I never did. I must give off really slutty vibes or something." Her eyes filled with tears. She turned away to keep him from seeing. Her chest ached like an open wound. He'd walk away now for sure. How could he not? She couldn't bear to look at him, to see the disdain that she imagined she'd see in his eyes. The disappointment and judgment that she surely deserved.

"Because you probably were," he said so softly, the pit of her stomach felt like she'd swallowed lead. He put his arms around her from behind and held her. She braced herself for a breakup.

Please make it quick, because while I could take losing anyone else, I can't take losing you.

"Hell, Jana. I was doing that back then, too. I was doing that until I found you." He turned her in his arms and pressed his lips to hers. Salty tears slipped between their lips. "That was then, pretty girl. This is now. I have total faith in you."

Her lower lip trembled. "You still don't understand."

HUNTER'S INSTINCTS WERE to force her to see the difference between who she was then—who they both were before finding each other—and who she was now. But the look on Jana's face told him there was much more than she was letting on.

"Then tell me, Jana. I don't want to play games. If you don't want me, you better step up now and tell me."

Her chin fell to her chest. "It's not that."

He forced his insecurities aside and held her. "Then tell me what it is. I can't help if you don't tell me what's going on."

"I don't want to hurt you."

"Hurt me?" He was totally confused. She might be afraid to commit, but he couldn't imagine her purposely hurting him.

"When I tell you the rest, you're going to think I'm a slut and probably a bitch."

"Every single one of your tears destroys me, baby." He wiped them away and kissed her damp cheeks. "Unless you've slept with some other guy since we agreed to be exclusive, I've got no right to judge anything you've done."

She shook her head. "I didn't. I wouldn't. I could never do that to you."

A relieved sigh escaped his lips. "Then tell me what's going on. I don't understand."

"A few years ago I dated this guy Spencer. He was a really nice guy. The kind of guy who is serially monogamous, brings you flowers every week, dresses nicely, asks you how your day was. You know, the—"

"The kind of guy every girl dreams of. Yeah, I get it." He had no idea where she was going with this, but he knew he was the antithesis of the man she described, and that made him even more tense.

"I guess." She wiped her eyes and said, "Every girl except me."

"Baby," he whispered, wishing he could ease the pain he heard in her voice.

"Every time I tried to break up with him, he begged me not to. You know me, Hunter. I'm not a pushover. I told him I didn't want to settle down and get married. I told him I didn't love him. But he kept showing up everywhere I went. He pushed and pushed, no matter what I said or did. And finally I did what I felt was my only option, and it ended really badly."

"What did you do?" A bad breakup was something he could deal with, and the fact that she was so torn up over whatever had happened only emphasized how vulnerable she felt. Sometimes that was hard to remember, because she acted so strong and in control all the time.

Fresh tears tumbled down her cheeks. She covered her mouth with her hand and looked away. The pain in her eyes was enough to make him want to find Spencer and strangle him.

"Whatever it is, Jana, you can tell me."

"It's embarrassing." She looked down at her hands as she explained. "I was only twenty, and all I wanted was to live my life. All he wanted was to settle down and have a family. After trying to break it off for a few weeks…" She looked at him and said, "Weeks, not days." Then she looked down at her hands again. "I couldn't see any other way out, so I made a play for his best friend, who I knew was into me. I made sure Spencer would see us together."

"Okay, so you messed around with his friend. You felt trapped. What does that have to do with us?"

Her eyes shot to his. "Hunter, look at how I handled it. He hated me after that, called me all sorts of names, and then…"

Hunter fisted his hands. "And then?"

"To get back at me, he posted about it on Facebook. I've never been so humiliated in all my life, because of course he didn't say I'd tried to break up with him for weeks. He just said he caught me and his friend making out and that I was a slut and he was now a 'free agent.' My family saw it, of course, because he tagged me in the post, which is why I refuse to be on any kind of social media anymore. My closest friends knew the real story, but I had to explain it all to my brothers and sister, even my parents, and that was so hard."

The song she sang to Billy came back to him loud and clear. Jana's inability to commit was born of hurt, and that cut him to his core. She'd boxed herself off from relationships in the same way he had. *Like a guy.* But while Hunter had simply not ever met a woman worth the effort until Jana, Jana had cordoned off her heart so she wouldn't ever be hurt again. And she'd struck back the only way she knew how, to do what had been done to her in the past. To dish out the hurt she'd suffered. Who could blame her for that?

"I hope Brock beat the shit out of the asshole." *Because if he didn't, I'm going to.*

"Spencer's really not an asshole. He was hurt." She must have recognized his mounting anger, because when he opened his mouth to refute what she'd said, she cut him off. "I've felt horribly guilty ever since. I should have handled it better, differently, and I swore I'd never be in that position again."

He roped in his anger at the sight of more tears filling her eyes, and he gathered her in closer. "That's why you're afraid to fully commit?"

"I don't want to get hurt and I can't take a chance of hurting you," she whispered. "I don't want to hide us. I'm just not ready to let everyone know. My life is such a mess right now. I need a little more time to be sure we're going to make it."

In that moment, Hunter realized the magnitude of her insecurities and how a string of bad relationships and one desperate act had led her to become the tough-as-nails-on-the-outside, sensitive-as-an-open-wound-on-the-inside woman she was. The woman he was falling deeply in love with.

Hunter was used to taking what he wanted, and in the past he probably would have forced her to tell everyone about them. But with Jana—*only with Jana*—what he wanted didn't matter. All that mattered was making Jana feel safe and earning her trust, so that she could finally let go of all those insecurities that were eating her up inside and allow herself to live the life she deserved.

"I'm sorry you went through that."

She tipped her face up.

"I'm not Spencer, and I sure as hell am not the guy women dream of marrying. But there's one thing I'm damn sure of, and that's my feelings for you." He tried to lighten the mood by saying, "Even if that means I have to work extra hard to keep your attention on me when we're out, I'm one hundred percent, totally and completely, all in."

He cupped her beautiful face in his hands and looked deeply into her eyes. "I have total faith in us, and because of that I'm not going to push you to claim our relationship in front of our family and friends right now. I wish I could say I'd wait forever, but you know me. I feel too much for you to hide it that long, because even if you say you don't want to hide it, that's what we're doing. But I know you need to trust what's happening between us, and I understand that. After all you've been through, you need to develop your own faith in us, and maybe more importantly, in yourself."

He let those words sink in. "Hopefully one day you'll realize that I don't ever want to hold you back from doing all the things you dream of. I want to help you set yourself free."

CHAPTER TWENTY-FIVE

JANA DROVE TO Seaside thinking about her conversation with Hunter and trying to wrap her head around her feelings. She'd never opened herself up to judgment like that before with anyone but her family when all that stuff first went down with Spencer. And even then, she'd done it only because she'd had no choice. But Hunter deserved the truth, and she felt better for having told him.

How had she gotten lucky enough to connect with probably the only man on earth who wouldn't judge her for her past? He could have called her out on the inappropriateness of her behavior with Spencer. Instead, he'd not only understood, but he'd helped relieve some of her guilt. By the time she arrived at Seaside, she realized that she was letting her past control her life, and she'd taken baby steps toward change. Telling her friends about her and Hunter was just another baby step. Even if it felt like she was stepping over a giant ravine.

She greeted the girls and their babies and sat beside Amy, listening to them rave about their husbands, who were out on Pete's boat this morning for a little *guy time*. It made her want to tell them how awesome Hunter was. But every time she opened her mouth, she struggled to tear down the walls she'd lived behind for so long, and no words came.

"What did you decide about the space for your studio?" Sky asked as they passed around a plate of muffins Leanna had made.

"I haven't made a decision yet. There's a lot to consider."

Sky rolled her eyes. "Like how quickly you can quit your job? Come on, Jana. If I can open my own tattoo parlor, you can open your own dance studio. You're more organized than me, less afraid of, well, anything at all, and from the way I was sore in places I didn't know could be sore after that Foxy Mamas dance class, I know you're a kick-ass instructor."

If only Sky knew how big her fears were and that they all centered on falling for her brother. "Yes, but what if I can't get any students? I wouldn't feel right stealing Marco's students."

"Seriously?" Amy shook her head. Her blond hair was pinned up in a ponytail, and Hannah, sitting in her high chair between Amy and Bella, kept trying to grab it. "You don't owe that man anything. Besides, he'll probably close the studio if you leave. Then they'll come to you on their own."

"Maybe." She twisted a lock of hair around her finger. "And you don't think that renting from Hunter is a huge mistake?"

"Why would it be?" Sky asked. "It's the same as renting the building here, isn't it?"

I'm not sleeping with you guys. "Yeah, I guess."

"Then it's settled," Bella said as she wiped Summer's chubby cheeks. "Call Hunter and tell him you'll take the space."

"Why is it that every time I come over here you guys change my life?"

"Speaking of lives changing." Sky looked like she was ready to burst. "Sawyer and I set a date for our wedding!"

"Oh my goodness!" Amy jumped up and hugged her.

"That's great!" Jana said, happy for the change of subject and truly thrilled for her friends.

"Yay, another wedding." Jessica said as Leanna circled the table and hugged Sky.

Bella lifted Summer into her arms and stood with one hand on Sky's shoulder. "We have to celebrate."

"We are," Sky said. "Sawyer's arranged to play his guitar at the Bombshelter next Friday night, and you guys are all coming."

"Definitely," Jenna said. "We wouldn't miss it."

"And tonight we'll have a barbecue in the quad, followed by a little chunky-dunking action." Bella raised her brows in quick succession.

"Bella." Amy's tone was stern. "You know Theresa's here all week, and you promised no more doing things that would bother her. Skinny-dipping definitely bothers her."

"No, I didn't. I promised not to do any more pranks, and I'm not breaking that promise." Bella kissed Summer's nose. "Chunky-dunking is like a rite of passage, and Jana hasn't ever joined us. It's time to christen her, and what better time than now, when we're celebrating her new studio and Sky and Sawyer's wedding date?"

Jana's phone vibrated, and when DO NOT RESPOND! flashed on her screen, she made a mental note to change it to Hunter's name. She opened and read the text.

I got tickets to the theater in Wellfleet for tonight since you only teach until six.

She couldn't imagine Hunter willingly going to a theater. That he would do that for her made her body hum with excitement. She texted a reply. *Really? Did someone hold a gun to your head?*

His reply came seconds later. *No. To my heart.* A sigh escaped her lips before she could stop it. *Be ready by 7:30. Wear that blue dress I love so much.*

"I think I need a rain check for the chunky-dunking." Jana pressed her lips into a tight line to keep from saying more as she typed a response and sent it off. *I see my bossy boy is back.*

"Why, and who's your *bossy boy*?" Bella's voice startled Jana.

She turned her phone over against her leg, panic clawing at her again.

"Oh, *bossy boy*, I love that," Amy said. "Tony can be bossy sometimes, and it's such a turn-on."

"Pete is always bossy," Jenna said. "I think it runs in their family."

Jana's pulse quickened as Sky's knowing gaze pierced through her veil of secrecy.

"Bossiness does run in our family." Sky crossed her arms and sat back in her chair, eyes pinned on Jana, a smile playing on her lips. "It's hard to avoid, and from what Sawyer tells me, it's even harder to resist."

You're telling me? The words *it was Hunter* were on the tip of her tongue, but she'd lived within the confines of her self-imposed prison for so long that without thought she was rising to her feet and saying, "I've got to go."

Bella put a firm hand on her shoulder and pushed her back

down. "Oh, no you don't. Spill it, girlfriend."

Her mind told her to bolt from the deck, save herself from the peer pressure that was about to be unleashed upon her, but the weight of their inquisitive gazes, coupled with the mischievous look in Sky's eyes, had her pinned in place.

As panic bloomed inside her, dark and petrifying, she thought of Hunter and the look in his eyes as he'd listened to her share her past with him, and she knew she wasn't being fair. He was working so hard to help her, *to set me free*, she wanted, needed, to do the same for him. But when she opened her mouth, her words betrayed her.

"There's nothing to spill." She'd never felt so low in her life. Lying to her friends was worse than sneaking out of a room that charged by the hour.

Jenna shook her head and looked down at Bea, sleeping soundly in her arms. "That lie was loud enough to wake my precious girl, wasn't it, Bea?" As if on cue, Bea sighed in her sleep.

"Wait." Jana pressed her palms to the table as all the girls leaned in closer.

"I'm sorry. I should have told you guys earlier. Hunter and I have been seeing each other."

"Well, duh," Jenna said.

Duh?

"Like we didn't already figure that out?" Amy added. "What do you think we are, amateurs?"

"Shh. Let her talk." Sky's smile widened. "And…?"

She felt tears sting her eyes with her confession, and their support only made her that much more emotional. And made her want to share more, to tell them everything.

"And, I don't know. You guys know me. I suck at dating. I just...I'm afraid something will happen and I'll hurt him, or he'll hurt me, and then you guys won't know how to act around us, and everything will be a mess, and I'll lose the best friends I've had in a long time." She met their eyes, wondering if her face had turned blue from the exhaustive sentence.

Amy covered Jana's hand with her own. "You're one of us now. Friends don't abandon ship over a man."

"I knew it the night he drove you home from Undercover, when you were so drunk you could barely walk." Jenna looked around the table. "Didn't I tell you guys that when Sky said he was still there the next morning? I mean, really, what guy stays overnight with a girl he's not sleeping with?"

Bella, Sky, and Amy said "Blue" in unison. Blue was Sky's closest male friend, and they used to sleep over at each other's houses all the time, without ever once leaving the *friend zone*.

"And the roses. That's what sealed it for me," Jessica said.

"The roses threw me for a loop, because come on. Hunter? Flowers? I never thought I'd see the day," Sky admitted.

"So, Sky, you're okay with me and Hunter seeing each other?" Jana twisted a lock of her hair, hoping Sky's smile wasn't feigned.

"Are you kidding? I'm totally okay with it, but, honestly, you are right about you two. Neither one of you has a great track record with dating. Are *you* okay with it?"

"To be honest, it was really hard for me to let him in, and sometimes it's still difficult. But he's so..." She searched her brain for the right words to describe Hunter, and there were too many that fit, so she shared them all. "He's romantic and caring. Thoughtful and patient." She held back on saying that he was a lion in bed and a kitten when she least expected it, and instead said, "He's got to be the most generous and understanding person I know, and yeah, he's a stubborn mule of a man, but…he's just the right amount of soft and hard."

"There's nothing soft about that man," Jenna mumbled.

Amy giggled.

Jana laughed. "You know what I mean. Before Hunter, I was never used to, you know, dealing with real emotions beyond an hour or two of great sex."

"Wow, you get an hour or two?" Leanna nibbled on her lower lip. "Ever since Sloan was born, we're lucky if we get fifteen minutes."

"Tell me about it." Jessica nodded in agreement. "We've snuck into the bedroom for a quickie more than once while Dustin was in his bouncy seat."

"God, you guys are great birth control," Sky teased. "More importantly, Jana, just tell me one thing. How long have you guys been seeing each other?"

She dropped her eyes, and for a split second she debated not telling them the truth, but she'd come this far, and she had to admit that getting it off her chest felt too good to keep it in any longer.

"Remember the grand opening of your tattoo parlor?" She told them about how she and Hunter had hooked up after the grand opening and how they'd bumped into each other every few weeks afterward, always happenstance, and at the end of the night, they'd almost always hooked up.

"But it wasn't until that night at the Governor Bradford when we were listening to Sawyer play and Hunter was giving me crap about boxing." She looked around the table at the curious and supportive eyes of the women who had become her closest friends, and she knew she was doing the right thing. "Remember that night?"

"Boy, do I ever," Jenna said. "I thought you were going to rip each other's heads off." She shifted her eyes up for a moment, her brows knitted, and then a smile crept across her lips. "Now I totally see it. Wow, that's a totally different kind of hot."

"I honestly thought you were going to rip each other's clothes off right there in the bar," Bella said. "But Sky pointed out that you guys would probably tear each other's heads off first."

"Well, we, um…find other uses for all that energy." Relief washed through her. How could Hunter have known that telling her friends was exactly what she needed?

Because you're setting me free.

CHAPTER TWENTY-SIX

THE WELLFLEET THEATER was buzzing by the end of the last act, and Jana was positively glowing. It wasn't just her gorgeous smile that sparked glints of delight in her baby blues, either. It was the way she squared her shoulders and craned her neck to make sure she didn't miss a single thing happening on the stage. She mouthed the words to the songs, and even some of the lines, as if she'd acted in the play before, which she probably had, since up until this summer she'd been in musicals with nearly all the theaters on the Cape.

When the musical ended, Jana pushed to her feet, her cheeks flushed with excitement as she applauded.

"Let's go backstage." She dragged Hunter across the crowded floor toward the doors that he assumed led to the private actor area. She stopped to greet a large man who stood eye to eye with Hunter and blocked the doorway.

The big man's harsh features softened when Jana opened her arms and said, "Micah! I've missed you. This is Hunter. I want to go back and say hi to everyone."

Micah embraced her. "Good to see you, Jayjay." He held a hand out to Hunter. "How's it going, Hunter?"

"Great. Nice to meet you."

Micah held the door open for them. "Go on back. Everyone will be thrilled to see you."

Hunter leaned in close to Jana and whispered, "Jayjay?"

She laughed. "Stage name. Everyone here calls me something different. Jayjay, Jana girl, Garner. Whatever comes to them, I guess."

They entered a large room cordoned off by heavy dark curtains. The room hummed with excitement as the actors' voices rose and fell, each talking over the next.

"Jana girl!" A redheaded woman ran across the room, calling the attention of the others, and within seconds Jana was engulfed by welcoming hugs and shouts about missing her.

Hunter stood off to the side, soaking it all in, his chest tight with conflicting emotions. He was overjoyed to see Jana among so many friends who were not only excited to see her, but asking her when they could expect her back among them. That joy was underscored by sadness over how much she'd missed out on because of her work situation. Now, more than ever, he was determined to help her see the light and open her own studio, so she could go back to taking part in this other, obviously very meaningful part of her life.

After the whirlwind calmed, Jana introduced Hunter to her friends, and a while later, when they left the theater, Jana sighed dreamily as they walked toward the car.

"Thank you for that." She gazed up at him and he couldn't think of a time, except when he'd seen her dancing in the studio, when she'd looked so content. A gentle breeze blew her hair off her shoulders, the sweet scent of her perfume mingled with the scents of the sea, and Hunter slid his hand to the nape of her neck.

"It was my pleasure. I want you to be happy, Jana. I want you to wake up every morning excited to jump into the day instead of feeling like you're trapped by your life. Between boxing and teaching and handling the studio, I thought you could use a reminder of something you loved." He stopped walking a few feet from the car and reached for her hands.

"I know you have a hard time with commitment, and you worry about taking the space I offered in case things don't work out between us, but as I've said a million times, I'm in this for the long haul, and I wish you'd take the space and let your dreams come true. All I want is for you to be happy."

"I believe you." She smiled and went up on her toes to kiss him. "I want to take the space, but only if you allow me to pay a fair rent and you treat me like you'd treat any other renter."

He lifted her off her feet and spun her around as he kissed her with all the emotions he'd been holding in. When he set her feet back on the ground, they were both laughing.

"You're taking it? You're really going to follow your dreams? I'm so..." He reached for the right words—*proud, happy, thankful*—and finally decided that he couldn't say what he wanted to in a single word.

"Seeing you soar is almost everything I've ever hoped for." He slanted his mouth over hers, and she pushed him away.

"Wait, wait, wait." She was still smiling so wide it made him laugh again. "Almost?"

"I'm still waiting for you to have enough faith in us that I don't have to hide my feelings in front of our friends and family," he teased. "Now hurry up and get those lips back here."

"Oh, please," she said with a dismissive wave of her hand. "I told the girls about us this morning."

She laughed as he lifted her into his arms again.

"Thank Christ and Moses and the stars above. It's about damn time, pretty girl."

CHAPTER TWENTY-SEVEN

THE NEXT MORNING Jana was on fire during boxing practice. She felt lighter on her feet, invigorated with enthusiasm. Every punch felt stronger, more effective, and her mind was less cluttered. And she realized as she wrapped up the last thirty seconds of a sparring match that she no longer felt trapped.

"That was awesome," Brock said as she and her sparring partner knocked gloves and left the ring. "You were strong in there today. Quicker, less aggressive but more focused."

She removed her gloves and mouthpiece and gulped down water.

"My life is finally falling into place. It feels good." She looked up at her big brother and realized she hadn't told him about Hunter yet. She waited for panic to set in, and when all that came was a nervous flutter in her stomach, she knew she'd made the right decision—about the space for the studio and about Hunter.

"I accepted Hunter's offer for the space on Route 6."

"Jana, that's great." Brock wrapped her in his strong arms.

"Yeah, now all I have to do is give Marco my notice. I'm not looking forward to that, but I'm doing it today so I don't chicken out."

"You never chicken out of anything." Brock picked up her gear and she followed him up to the front of the gym.

"That's not exactly true."

"*Pfft*. Right. Jana, you wanted to do musicals, so you learned how to sing and dance—when you were six. You wanted to prove you could fight, and you nailed it. And now you want your own studio, and you're going for it." He touched the tip of her nose as he'd done a million times when she was a little girl and said, "You're unstoppable."

She gathered her courage, and before she could overthink his potential responses, she said, "I'm seeing Hunter."

"No shit." Brock said with a serious tone.

"You knew?" *Did everyone know?*

"The guy called me at six thirty in the morning that day you were drunk off your ass, remember? I can put two and two together. I wouldn't have batted an eye if Sky had called me, but Hunter? Shit." He laughed. "I was sort of tipped off when Sawyer asked if Hunter got you home safely, too. I'm not an idiot."

"Apparently I'm the only idiot around, because I was trying to save our friendships and not clue anyone in, but everyone apparently already knew." She grabbed her bag from the counter. "So? Aren't you going to tell me all the reasons I shouldn't date him?"

Brock smiled and began leafing through papers on the desk. "Nope."

"Why not?"

"Because a certain someone told me to stay out of her personal life. For what it's worth, I like Hunter. And from what I can tell, he's really into you."

"What makes you say that?"

He leaned across the counter so they were nose to nose. "Hunter left about ten minutes before you arrived this morning and asked me if I would mind if he dated you."

Jana's jaw dropped open. "He came to see you when I was trying to keep it quiet? That little—"

"Before you go all bat-shit crazy on him, he said you'd already told everyone else. Besides, if you told him not to speak to me specifically, then you've got to give the guy credit. He's got bigger balls than most."

"I never told him not to talk to you specifically, and I told him last night that I already told the girls."

"Listen, if it helps, I already knew that you two were together, like I said. The guy risked the wrath of the *Beast* coming down on him, which is bad enough. But it sounds like he also risked an argument with you for asking. Want to hear what he said that won me over?"

"Oh God. Do I even want to know?" Jana closed her eyes for a beat. When she opened them Brock was chuckling. "Just for the record, he's going to be sorry for going behind my back." She was only half kidding.

"Hey, the guy did a stand-up thing. And it sounds like he waited until you told everyone else." Brock narrowed his eyes. "Which, by the way, tells me where I stand with you, little sister."

"No, it doesn't. I just hadn't seen you since I told the girls. Besides, they pretty much guessed. It's not like I announced it."

"Fair enough." Brock smiled, and she knew his feelings weren't really hurt. "He said he'd wanted to talk to me sooner but that you weren't ready, and he apologized for keeping it from me. He could have hidden your relationship forever, but now that I know that it was you trying to keep it a secret, I guess I can see how that would be hard for a guy like Hunter."

"What does that mean? *A guy like Hunter?*" Feeling protective of Hunter, her fingers curled tightly around her bag.

"Just that he said hiding your relationship wasn't in the game plan for him. That he used to be a guy who would do that, but that with you, he wanted to be a better man. *A stand-up guy* was how he put it. And while he might not have told me the whole truth—that you two were already dating—what he did say, baby sister, said it all."

Half an hour later Jana walked into Hunter's shop, determined to talk to him about telling Brock before she had a chance to. Regardless of the wonderful things he'd said, she was still slightly annoyed.

"Hey, Jana." Clark turned from where he was working on the computer. "Thanks for helping Hunter out the other night. Nina and I really appreciated the time together."

"It was fun. Billy is really cute, and I hope you and Nina are doing okay." She glanced at the photo on the desk of Clark, Nina, and Billy, and it warmed her to see them smiling.

"We're working on it. At least we're talking now. That's a start." He rose from his seat and pushed open the door to the shop. "Go on back. Just stay away from the forge."

Jana peeked around him at the interior of the shop. She'd always been fascinated by their work and had been thrilled when Hunter told her that he'd designed the dresser handles and curtain rod she had in her bedroom. But she'd never actually seen Hunter in action. She'd never been inside his workshop, and it was nothing like she'd expected. The walls were made of old barn wood and the floors were concrete. She thought it would feel cold, because she'd always associated *metal* with *cold* in her mind, but there was nothing cold about the space. Besides the large pieces of equipment that looked complicated and sturdy, there were several long tables, both wooden and metal. Heavy anvils were set upon enormous tree trunks, giving the workshop an old-fashioned feel.

She spotted Grayson first, standing at the forge, holding something over the red-hot coals, and then she saw Hunter leaning over a table near the back of the room. His back was to her, his shirt stretched tight over his muscles. She suddenly felt like she was interrupting him for something that wasn't nearly as important as concentrating on his work.

Grayson turned to set the glowing red metal clamped in the end of what looked like heavy iron tongs on an anvil. He lifted his safety goggles and raised his chin. "Hey, Jana. Come on back."

Hunter turned, and the surprise in his eyes quickly faded as a smile spread across his lips, instantly warming her all over. Her annoyance at his talking to Brock faded with each step as he closed the distance between them.

"Hey there." He leaned in for a kiss. "I wasn't expecting to see you. Everything okay?"

"Yeah, I, um. I just came from boxing practice."

"Ah," he said, as if he knew why she'd come. "Let's go into my office and talk." He turned to his brother and said, "We'll be right back."

He led her around the equipment, and when they passed the table he'd been leaning over, she glanced over and stopped to get a better look.

Hunter followed her gaze. "It's just something I was working on for you."

"For me?" she asked softly, her eyes focusing on the script lettering, which read, *Jana's Dance Studio*. Her eyes shot to his. *Ohmygod.*

"There's only you, pretty girl." He placed his hand on the small of her back and guided her toward the table.

Her heartbeat quickened as she took in the distressed metal mounted on planks of rustic wood. Delicate metal flowers were sprinkled over the upper right corner of the sign, and beautiful lettering that curled at the edges spelled out her hopes and dreams. Hunter had created an image of a dancer with her hand over her head and her legs crossed as she stood on her toes and arched back gracefully. The time he must have put into the sign and the thoughtfulness of the design brought her emotions rushing forth. Her eyes dampened, and when she lifted her gaze to his, she felt herself tumbling into the well of affection she saw there.

"Do you like it?" His eyes filled with hope.

"Hunter," she said breathlessly. "Like doesn't even come close to how much I adore it. You must be so busy, and you still went to all this trouble."

He stepped closer, tucking the lock of hair she was nervously twirling behind her ear. "Baby, you have revitalized my creativity." He lowered his voice and said, "In more ways than one," with a seductive tone. "There's nothing I'd rather do than make a sign for my girl."

My girl. The words swirled inside her.

"Thank you. I…No one has ever done anything like this for me before, and you've already given so much of yourself. You're letting me rent the space, and—"

"Baby, don't you get it?" He searched her eyes. He did that a lot lately, searching for answers that she thought only he could see. "There's nothing I wouldn't do for you." He lowered his lips to hers.

"Grayson?" she said against his mouth, wondering how she could have ever doubted that they were right for each other.

Hunter smiled. "He left when you looked at me like you wanted to tear my clothes off."

His mouth moved over hers, swallowing her laugh in a smoldering kiss that left her head spinning and her body humming.

"What did you come to tell me?" he asked, gazing at her sweetly.

His words were still swirling in her mind—*Baby, don't you get it? There's nothing I wouldn't do for you*—making any further thought, beyond her need for another kiss, impossible.

"Nothing important," she whispered as she went up on her toes, and he met her in another soul-binding kiss.

CHAPTER TWENTY-EIGHT

THE COOKOUT WITH their friends and siblings was exactly what Jana needed. Hunter was glad he'd pushed her to go, when he knew all she'd really wanted to do was climb into bed and forget about the hellish time she'd had giving her notice to Marco. He watched her laughing with the girls as she bounced baby Hannah on her hip.

"She looks pretty natural with a baby." Pete draped an arm over his younger brother's shoulder and lowered his voice before saying, "You know, babies are contagious."

Hunter laughed. "Funny. When my oldest brother gave me the sex talk, he made it perfectly clear how to avoid that situation. Maybe you should have taken your own advice."

Pete looked down at Bea sleeping soundly in the playpen. "She's the best thing that's ever happened in my life, besides Jenna, of course."

"I never thought I'd say this about any woman, but that's how I feel about Jana. My girl has changed my life in too many ways to count." Bea sighed softly in her sleep and Hunter's heart squeezed, knowing, without a shadow of a doubt, that if Jana were to get pregnant, he'd be proud to step up to the plate, marry her, and raise their children together. His eyes sought

Jana again, and when he saw her whispering something to Amy, he imagined coming home to her every night, waking with her every morning, and he realized…they were already there.

"That's how you know she's the one. Before Jenna, I never really gave women the time of day, like you." Pete leaned in closer and said, "Grayson's the same way. Matt and Sky are the only normal ones in our family when it comes to dating."

"The hell with that," Hunter said. "I think it's totally normal to wait for the right woman."

Blue and Grayson crossed in front of Jana as they neared.

Grayson's eyes jumped between Hunter and Pete. "Why does it look like you guys are talking about me?"

"We were. I was thinking that since the sculpture and the model of the gazebo are almost done, I could swindle you, Blue, and Pete to help me get the space out on Route 6 ready for Jana's studio." He knew that seeing progress, having her vision come to fruition, would help ease the pain of still having to finish out her four-week commitment to Marco.

"I can swing it," Grayson said.

"For Jana? Absolutely," Blue said. "I can move my schedule around and clear a few days, but you need a permit."

"Already done. I got it when I first mentioned it to her."

"Pretty sure of himself, isn't he?" Grayson said to Blue.

Hunter lifted his chin in a silent *miss you* as Jana smiled from across the quad. "Always." He nudged Pete. "You free to help?"

"Why not. This could be fun." Pete eyed Caden, who was bouncing Summer on his shoulder a few feet away. He raised his voice and said, "As long as Caden will be there wearing his sexy tool belt and boots."

"Anything for you, sweetheart," Caden called to Pete.

Ten minutes later they'd recruited Jamie, Kurt, Sawyer, and Tony and had a plan to meet the next morning to begin the renovations.

"IT'S TIME," JENNA whispered in Jana's ear. It was nearly midnight and the babies were asleep in their playpens on Bella's deck.

"But Theresa is here, and she was nice enough to consider letting me use that space. I don't want to upset her." Jana had seen Theresa down by the pool earlier, locking the gate.

"She went to bed hours ago," Bella said. "We're not going to wake her, and besides, I'm done pranking. Chunky-dunking is not a prank."

"Maybe not, but it's definitely against the community rules," Jessica pointed out.

"Yeah, but I guess it's not really a prank. Besides, it's tradition. Come on," Amy said, carrying a bunch of towels. "The guys will watch the babies, and I've got..." She pulled a tube of cookie dough out from beneath the stack of towels. "Cookie dough!"

"Okay, but I'll feel really bad if she catches us after how nice she was to me." Jana followed them down to the pool.

It was so dark that they couldn't see but a few feet in front of them. They clung to one another, whispering about the babies and how they *needed* this break. They huddled together as Jessica unlocked the gate, because she was deemed to have the softest touch. And she did, because she made almost no noise whatsoever as she held it open for the girls to pass through. They pulled the gate closed behind them.

Jenna began taking her clothes off right there by the gate, while the others hurried down to the other side of the pool, where the steps were, and stripped in silence.

"Here I come," Jenna whispered loudly as she ran naked from one end of the pool to the other, making the rest of them laugh.

They descended the steps in a huddle of giggles and hushes.

"This is frigging cold!" Bella whispered.

"Shh. Just get in. You'll get warm soon." Amy gave Bella a little shove, sending her sprawling into the water, chest deep, earning more laughter and another round of shushes.

They formed a circle in the middle of the pool, treading water while Leanna and Jessica gathered the Styrofoam noodles and handed one to each of the girls.

"I feel so privileged to be included in your chunky-dunking, but I have to tell you. I can't believe you do this all the time and the guys behave. Honestly, I can't believe Hunter didn't follow me down here." Jana had never been chunky-dunking with them before, but Sky had told her all about their midnight jaunts into the pool.

"Speaking of Hunter," Jenna said. "Ames, grab the cookie dough. I want to ply her with sweets so she spills her guts."

"I'm on it!" Amy swam to the edge of the pool to retrieve the cookie dough.

"He's my brother," Sky reminded them. "Please be discreet with the things I definitely don't want to know."

"Like I'd share the yummiest parts of him with anyone?" Jana thought about the way he looked at her, like he wanted to consume her and care for her at once, and the things he said that made her heart turn inside out.

Amy handed her the cookie dough. "Yummier than this?"

"Sorry, girls, but…definitely!" Jana took a hunk of cookie dough and passed the rest to Leanna. "But don't worry, Sky. There's plenty of PG stuff I can share, like how in the heck we've come so far so fast. It seems like just yesterday we were fighting over everything, and we only fell into bed when we were arguing—"

Sky held her hand up and said in a harsh whisper, "No bed talk. Brother, brother, brother."

"I *wasn't* going there," Jana whispered. "What I mean is, your brother surprises me every single day. I never knew I could care about anyone as deeply, or as fast, as I'm falling for Hunter."

"That's a good thing," Bella said quietly. "Love has a way of finding us even when we don't want to be found."

"You can say that again," Leanna said. "With Kurt I feel like I've discovered who I really am for the first time."

"That's it exactly," Jana said, forgetting to whisper.

"Shh!" Jenna and Bella said in unison. "You'll wake Theresa."

Jana cringed. "Sorry," she whispered. "But that's exactly it. He calls me on my shit, but he does it in the most wonderful ways."

"Aww." Amy reached for the cookie dough. "That's so sweet."

Theresa's porch light went on, and all the girls gasped.

"Get to the far end of the pool," Bella whispered.

They huddled together in the corner of the pool.

"Get your boobs off of me," Bella whispered to Jenna.

"Oh, like I can control them?" Jenna giggled.

"Shh!" Amy put her hand over Jenna's mouth.

"Let's get out so she doesn't catch us." Leanna headed for the stairs with all the girls on her heels. They were quiet as they wrapped towels around their bodies and walked along the fence line with their clothes bundled in their arms, hiding in the shadows.

Bella pressed her finger to her lips, then opened the gate as quietly as she could. They slipped out and walked along the far side of the grass up toward the cottages.

"Were we that loud?" Amy whispered.

Huddled under the cover of the trees, they stared, wide-eyed, at the beacon of light coming from Theresa's porch. Before anyone could answer Amy, the light went off and there was a collective sigh of relief.

"Oh my God," Bella snapped. "Do you think she did that just to piss us off? Like she knew we were chunky-dunking?"

"Well, you did call a truce," Jenna reminded her. "And chunky-dunking is against the rules."

"Whatever." Bella stomped across the grass.

Hunter stepped off the deck, and even in the dark Jana could feel the heat of his wanton stare.

"Here comes your hunky heartthrob," Sky whispered. She strutted past Hunter and sang, "I know all your secrets."

"I swear she doesn't!" Jana said with a laugh, as the other girls headed for the quad.

Hunter's lips curved up in a smile that nearly made her towel catch flames.

"Pretty girl, do you know what kind of torture that was?" he whispered to her. "Knowing you were down there, naked and wet, and I had to pretend I wasn't hard for you every single second you were gone?" His erection pressed against her belly.

Heat roared through her as he clutched her ass beneath the towel and backed her into the darkness beside the cottage, out of eyesight of the others. He nudged her legs apart and slipped a hand between them. She gasped at the intense invasion as he teased her, hitting the perfect spot to drive her over the edge quickly.

"Home. Now," he growled. "Or I swear I'll take you right here."

"Holy shit!" Bella's voice carried from around the front of the cottage.

"Shh!" Amy said. "You'll wake the babies."

Pete and Caden's laughter sparked a chaotic din of exclamations.

Hunter withdrew his hand from between her legs, leaving her bereft and trembling with need.

"We're not done," he promised. He kissed her quickly before taking her hand and walking around front to see what all the commotion was.

Standing in the light from the cottage window Bella stared up at Theresa's house, her face red with anger. Amy, Jenna, Leanna, Jessica, and Sky were bent over in fits of laughter, as were their men.

"You look like Smurfs!" Grayson said.

Jana looked down at her arms and legs, which were tinged a bright shade of blue, like the other girls'.

"Holy crap. We're blue." Her eyes shot to Hunter.

He spun her around so her back faced the others, opened her towel, and his eyes blazed as he drank in her blue skin. "Holy fuck, that's hot. Zoe Saldana has nothing on you. Come on Na'vi girl, let's play Avatar." He closed her towel and dragged her toward the truck, calling out a goodbye over his shoulder to the others. "I'm taking her home to wash the dye off."

Hunter backed her up against the passenger's side door, crashed his mouth to hers, and kissed her until her legs went weak.

"God you're gorgeous." He opened the truck and lifted her in, then came down over her, pressing all those hard muscles against her, and his eager arousal in the most perfect spot. The friction fried Jana's brain cells. Somewhere in the darkness of lust she realized they were still parked at Seaside.

"Drive," she panted against his mouth as his hands moved over her flesh, threatening to make her give up any remaining care about being caught.

He made a guttural sound that tightened the lust coiling low in her belly and reluctantly went around to the drivers' side. Jana was lost in a fog of desire, her body buzzing with need. She reached for his zipper as he drove out of the community and felt his body tense as she bent to take his hard length in her mouth.

"Jana," he said through gritted teeth.

She felt the truck make a sharp turn. There was no light coming in the windows, and Jana didn't bother asking where they were headed. She knew Hunter was too possessive to chance anyone seeing them. She focused on pleasuring him, moaning as she swallowed him deep. The truck rattled to a stop and he cut the engine. Hunter fisted his hands in her hair, tugging her up and crashing his mouth to hers. Their tongues fought for dominance, plundering roughly.

"Can't...get enough of you." He bit her lower lip, and she gasped at the sting and taste of blood. He sucked that lip into his mouth and tore her towel off.

"Fuckin'a, Jana. How did I get lucky enough to be the man you picked?"

Her body ignited with his words. "Like you'd have it any other way?"

Their mouths came together in another frenetic kiss as she tugged at his shirt. They parted just long enough for him to rip it off and push his pants down to his knees. He lifted her easily, and she straddled his lap and sank onto his hard length.

"Hunter—" She closed her eyes with the blissful, overwhelming sensation of his bare shaft filling her so completely.

He clutched her hips, and she wondered if his hands would turn blue, too. "Don't move." He gritted his teeth. "This feels too good. I'll lose it. Fuck. I'm sorry, Jana. I'm too into you. I forgot the condom."

The restraint on his face and the feel of his hot, hard length stretching her made her ache with the need to move. Her heart was racing as she quickly contemplated the ultimate show of trust.

"Have you been tested?" It felt wrong to ask him, but she had to. She needed to know.

"Every year at my physical." His eyes narrowed. "Last time was four months ago." He sat up with a wicked grin, driving deeper into her. She let out a needful moan. "*Four months ago*, pretty girl. I haven't slept with anyone but you for six months, and I never had sex without a condom. Ever. Not once."

She read the silent question in his eyes and whispered, "Me either."

His arms circled her in a tight embrace that pulled him deeper into her, but before he moved any more, he cupped her cheeks and said, "I want this. I want you. But it's up to you, pretty girl. I'll wait forever to make love to you without a condom if that's what you want. We can drive to your place and get protection."

Her body was on fire, and her sex swelled with every word he spoke. As she gazed into Hunter's eyes, the adoration and deep emotions she saw made her feel like this was her first time. Like she was eighteen all over again. But she wasn't that girl any longer. She wasn't even the woman she'd been a month ago.

The ache consuming her wasn't about sex and consumption; it was about respect and fulfillment, wanting to be closer in every way possible, wanting to experience *all* of Hunter, the physical, emotional, and everything in between. It was her heart that spoke the loudest, and her trusting words fell easily from her lips. "Take me, Hunter. All of me."

CHAPTER TWENTY-NINE

HUNTER COULD HARDLY believe he'd finished the sculpture in time for the competition. He'd been so wrapped up in Jana that his creativity had flowed like a river, and he was able to spend the last two weeks getting Jana's studio ready. It took a few days for him and the guys to build two rooms for classes and extend the registration desk. He'd since painted and was getting the final touches ready. He'd found furniture online from a designer in Harborside, just a short drive from the Cape. He'd ordered wooden chairs with elaborate carvings of trees and giant leaves as backings, and then he'd designed two end tables using wood and iron to complete the lobby area.

He'd finished making the sign, and Jana had loved it so much she'd ordered business cards with the same design. He'd stopped by earlier to check out the landscaping. He'd hired a crew to make the entrance as beautiful as Jana. They'd come close, but nothing could top his girl.

He glanced at her now, as she stepped from the truck, her pretty painted toes on display in a pair of cute leather sandals. She wore tan shorts with a blousy top, which went well with Hunter's tan pants and short-sleeved white button-down shirt. Her hair fell loose, like a mane down her back, just the way he loved it. She was beyond gorgeous, and she no longer looked like she wanted to throttle him and fuck him all at once, like she used to. As he came around the car, she looped her arm into his, looking like she wanted to fuck him and climb beneath his skin.

Little did she know that she already had.

"Ready?" They were going to the Bombshelter, a local pub where their friends were celebrating that Sky and Sawyer had chosen their wedding date.

"Yup." She smiled up at him and wound her arms around his neck.

He loved when she claimed him. He pressed his lips to hers and couldn't resist backing her up against the truck to deepen the kiss. She had this incredible sensuality that resonated in everything she did and said, and he knew he'd never get enough of her.

"I forgot to tell you," he said between kisses. "I made a key to your place so I could run over and change before the competition tomorrow, since your place is closer."

She pushed back and wrinkled her brow. "You made a key?"

"Yeah. I figured—"

"Hunter, don't you think you should have asked me about that first?"

Surprised by her response, he took a step back to clear the desire from his mind and focus on the conversation. "Jana, we've been practically living together for weeks."

"Living together? We're not living together."

The panic in her eyes sent his mind back in time, and he tempered his annoyance at her attitude, reminding himself that this was classic Jana. One step forward, two steps back, until she slammed into a wall, beat it for a while, and finally leapt—because she was too rebellious and stubborn to take two steps forward and one step back like others did.

He softened his tone. "Baby, we stay together almost every night of the week. You cleared out a drawer for me. I have my stuff in your closet, your bathroom."

Her brows knitted together and her hand went to a lock of her hair, twisting it furiously. "You…We…When did that happen?"

"Over time, I guess." He pulled his keys from his pocket, removed the key he'd made from the key ring, and placed it in her palm. He closed her fingers over it and brought her hand to his lips, pressing a kiss to her knuckles.

"Take the key, baby. I'm sorry I overstepped my boundaries." He knew she just needed time, and maybe he had assumed too much, but hell if her denial of their situation didn't sting.

"Hey, guys!" Sky hollered as she and Sawyer crossed the parking lot to greet them. "I'm *so* excited."

Sawyer pulled Hunter into a manly embrace. "Ready to get your ass kicked in pool, dude?"

My ass was just kicked in love. Why not pool?

THE BOMBSHELTER WAS a dimly lit dive located beside the Bookstore Restaurant in Wellfleet, and it was one of Jana's favorite places. She loved everything about the pub, from the crowded dance floor to the clanking of the billiard balls and cheers for the sports teams on the televisions above the bar. The place smelled of testosterone, perfume, and anonymity. Tonight, as she sat with her friends, she wished she could feel anonymous, but she felt…panicked.

Hunter staying over all the time wasn't the same thing as actually living together, was it? Living together meant sharing bills, planning dinners, getting a dog or a cat, and *having his own key*. Living together was the opening act to a much bigger and more permanent commitment. Shouldn't he have talked to her about that instead of making the determination on his own and assuming it was okay for him to make a key? What if she wasn't ready for the opening act, or even the main event?

What if I am?

Holy shit. She needed another drink, stat.

She searched for the waitress, but the perky little brunette was busy eyeing *her* man. *Bitch.* Hunter, however, was solely focused on the pool table. Leaning over to take his shot, his long, strong arms held the pool cue as he lined up his shot. Her fingers curled with the desire to stand behind him, grab his hips, and press her body to his. *Tonight you're all mine.*

Aren't you?

Oh God. Panic trickled back in. Now that she was thinking about it, he'd hurried off with the guys awfully quickly when they'd entered the bar. That was unusual for him. He didn't seem angry on the outside, but he was definitely put out.

Well, damn it. So was she. Why was he making assumptions instead of talking with her about what she wanted?

Maybe I do want the main event…

Lord. She was driving herself crazy. If this was what relationships did to a person, no wonder she was never any good at them.

No, she wasn't going down that road. She and Hunter were good together.

Great. They were *great* together.

Then why was she panicking?

That's it. She couldn't deal with this right now. She was *done* with this circular thought process. She scanned the floor for the other waitress. It wasn't until Amy's voice cracked through her confusion that she realized she was completely ignoring her friends.

"How is Marco treating you?" Amy asked. "You're almost done right? Just another few weeks and then you're on your own?"

Jana pushed the thoughts of their argument aside and tried to focus on Amy and her friends. They were supposed to be celebrating. She was not going to allow herself to get tied in knots over a stupid key.

Over her life.

Oh God, she'd just begun to love her life.

Where's that damn waitress?

"Marco's not happy that he has to come back to town, so he's hardly talking to me." *Like Hunter, tonight.* "It's probably better that way." Her heart ached.

"Probably so," Sky said. "I saw the website Jamie made. It's incredible."

"I tried out the online registration process," Jenna added. She wiggled her shoulders and eyebrows and said, "I signed up for the Foxy Mamas class. Petey's so excited."

"Pete's excited anytime you're excited," Amy said with a laugh. "Speaking of which, how about that blue dye? Bella is dying to get Theresa back with another prank, so I guess the games are on again."

"We didn't have too much trouble getting it off," Jana said distractedly.

"It made Pete's teeth blue," Jenna said with an eyebrow waggle. "And not from kissing."

"Ohmygod." Amy laughed. "I'm calling TMI on that one. Let's talk about something else." She turned to Jana, stifling a giggle. "On a more important note, Jana, I was in Stop & Shop the other day and saw the flyers you hung up. There were three women talking about joining, and I told them how wonderful you are."

"Thank you, Amy." Jana reached across the table and squeezed her hand, catching sight of the sexy waitress who was still eyeing Hunter. She tried to ignore the claws of jealousy tearing at her gut, but how could she when it felt like a wild animal digging its way out from beneath her skin?

She shifted her eyes to the dance floor, where Jamie and Jessica were dancing cheek to cheek to a way-too-fast beat. Bella and Leanna were dancing near the pool tables, calling her attention back to that big, sexy key maker.

Ugh. She pushed from the table. "Excuse me, ladies. I'm grabbing a drink." She strutted over to the bar. Fuck the skanky, flirty, gorgeous waitress who was eyeing her man. She could get her own damn drink.

After downing two fireballs, she ordered a round of shots for the table and, feeling warm and light from the alcohol, joined Bella and Leanna on the dance floor.

"I ordered a round of shots to celebrate!" Jana yelled over the music.

"Awesome. Caden's the designated driver, so Mama gets to drink tonight." Bella bumped hips with Jana.

Jana closed her eyes and raised her arms above her head, allowing the music to seep past her irritation over what that tiny key signified, past thoughts of the flirty waitress, past the heartache she was trying to ignore. When the edginess subsided and she felt suspended by the beat, she opened her eyes and let her body take over. Her hips swayed, and her shoulders flowed from side to side as she moved around Bella. When she came full circle, her shoulders drew right, pairing her up with Leanna in a slow, sultry dance. She was mildly aware of Leanna's movements stopping and a crowd forming around them. She closed her eyes again, unwilling to let anything break her from the comfortable zone she'd fallen into.

The music calmed her, the alcohol eased her worries, and when she opened her eyes, she danced without thought. Her body knew how to move, what to feel. And in that moment, she decided she was done drinking. Just like that. Done. She didn't need alcohol to deal with her problems, and Hunter didn't need to worry about her falling into the bottle like his father had. She was opening a business. She could make clearheaded decisions, and right now she needed to dance.

Leanna and Bella pointed to the table.

"We'll meet you back there," Bella said.

Jana nodded. "After this song."

She felt free and untethered, but when she noticed a tall, muscular guy encroaching into her personal space, the contented smile fell from her lips.

He reached for her and she sidestepped his touch. "I'm here with someone," she said. She could handle herself with most guys, but the feeling inside her wasn't one of fear or intimidation. It was a twisting in her gut, telling her that things had changed. She'd changed. The unsettled feeling from earlier returned.

The burly guy reached for her again, and she stepped away with a sharp, "Not interested. Sorry. I'm involved with someone."

The guy began gyrating his hips in front of her, so close she could smell the alcohol on his breath. She was used to this. Before Hunter she would have probably enjoyed the dirty dancing, but now she had no interest in anyone other than Hunter.

She stepped backward, tripping over another dancer. As she found her footing, the big guy was lifted by the back of his shirt off his feet. Hunter came into view, his face burning with rage, the veins in his neck bulging as he seethed.

"Don't touch my girl, asshole."

The guy held his arms up. "I didn't know, man."

"She said she wasn't interested loud and clear," Hunter growled.

"Hunter!" Jana yelled. "Put him down."

Hunter's angry eyes moved between the guy and Jana, his brow wrinkled in confusion.

"Hunter. Seriously."

"Learn some fucking manners," he said before dropping the guy to the floor.

Jana stormed through the crowd and out the front door.

CHAPTER THIRTY

HUNTER FLEW OUT the door and caught up to Jana. "Where the hell are you going?"

"Nowhere." She paced, hands clenched tight.

"Jana, what's going on? Why are you pissed?"

"Because," she spat. "Why do you have to act like a Neanderthal? I can handle myself."

"Seriously?" He closed the distance between them. "Did you want that asshole to touch you? Because if you did, then fuck me, Jana. I thought you were mine." And then it hit him like a brick in the face, and he stopped cold. His entire body turned to ice as his words hung in the air between them.

First the key, now this? What the hell is going on?

"Hunter..." She reached for him, but he took a step away.

"Jana...?"

"I don't need you to go all caveman crazy. I'm allowed to dance. I'm allowed to move my body to the music, and yes, guys are going to look. They might even approach me, but Jesus Christ, Hunter, don't you trust me to handle myself?"

"Do you want me, Jana?" As soon as he said it, her lips curved up in that fucking sweet smile that turned him inside out, and he realized he'd asked for the three words she was never going to give him.

She crossed her arms and rolled her eyes.

He laughed, despite the anger that was coursing through him. "You're a pain in the ass."

"So are you," she pointed out. "I'm not a delicate flower, Hunter. I can tell a guy to fuck off if I need to."

She was so fucking sexy when she was ornery, and he loved her so much, he couldn't hold on to his anger any longer. "No shit. You've done it to me." He stepped in closer, wrapping his arms around her waist.

"I never told you to fuck off. I told you to learn how to be romantic." She flashed a sassy smirk.

"Fuck..." He slanted his mouth over hers, taking her in a deliciously warm kiss. "You're mine, Jana, and I'll be damned if any woman of mine is going to dance like that and turn on other guys."

She pushed away from him. "God. You're infuriating sometimes. It's not the 1950s."

"You're right, it's not. But hell if you don't make me want to beat the shit out of any guy who looks at you."

She stood with her hands on her hips, looking impossibly stern and sexy at once. "You always tell me to trust you. Well, what about you, Hunter? Don't you have to trust me, too?" Before he could respond, she said, "I'm going back in to party with everyone. It's a celebration, remember? Sky and Sawyer deserve a happy night. They don't need us fighting about keys and assholes."

As she disappeared through the pub door, Hunter groaned,

hoping to hell that was the second step back and that the next one would be a step forward. He knew Jana too well to hope for the leap.

Two hours later, after a tense celebration, they pulled up in front of Jana's house. Hunter cut the engine and they sat in silence.

"I'm sorry we argued," he said into the dark.

"Me too."

His phone rang, and he pulled it out and groaned. "It's Clark. I've got to take it." He stepped from the truck as he answered.

"Hunter, Nina and I had a big fight. Can I crash at your place?" Clark sounded horrible, defeated. His voice was scratchy and rough, as if he'd been yelling.

He ran his hand through his hair. Going home was the last thing he wanted to do. He and Jana didn't argue, not like this. Their arguments weren't arguments at all. They were mating dances. But tonight felt different—and it had all started with the stupid key. But he couldn't blow off his buddy because of their shitty night. "Of course. I'm at Jana's. Give me twenty minutes to get there."

After ending the call he helped Jana out of the truck and told her he had to go let Clark in.

"That's okay. We're both tired. A little space will do us good." Her eyes were filled with sadness, and it made him want to stay right there and figure their shit out, but it was after midnight and he knew from experience a little space would probably do them more good than staying up all night, especially with the competition tomorrow.

"I'm sorry, Jana. He sounded awful, and God knows what's going on, but I'd imagine we'll be up for a while talking about whatever he's going through."

She shrugged. "It's fine. He needs you."

Part of him wished she'd ask *what about me?* and say she needed him, too. Or beg him to come over after he was done talking with Clark. But that wasn't Jana.

Jana was the woman who freaked out about a key.

"My competition is tomorrow afternoon. You're still planning to come?"

She hooked her finger in his belt loop, and that simple, familiar touch eased his worries.

"Of course." She went up on her toes and pressed her lips to his.

His phone vibrated again, cutting their kiss short. After one more chaste kiss, they gazed into each other's eyes. A world of questions passed between them, falling into the crevice that had formed between them.

JANA STOOD IN the foyer of her house listening to the sound of Hunter's truck fade into the night. The silence of the room closed in on her. How long had it been since she'd been home alone at night?

She walked down the hall to her bedroom, feeling exhausted. Depleted. Ready to drop. She'd gone through so many emotions lately that maybe a night alone would be a good thing. She'd never needed company before. Why should she now? And besides, she could use the rest. They both could.

She took off her jewelry and stripped off her clothes. She needed a shower, but she was too tired to make it happen. Instead, she brushed her teeth and washed her face. Hunter's scent lingered on the towel. She glanced around the bathroom at his toiletries mingling with hers. *We're practically living together.*

Jana turned off the light and padded into the bedroom, taking a T-shirt from Hunter's drawer and pulling it over her head. Then she slipped beneath the covers and closed her eyes.

She'd never been one for opening acts, but she'd take the opening act instead of standing on an empty stage.

CHAPTER THIRTY-ONE

HUNTER SPENT HALF the night listening to Clark and Nina's newest battle, which he still wasn't sure he understood. It sounded to him like they were going around and around about the same issues without any resolution. Nina felt like she was a single parent, and Clark felt like he was undervalued. Hunter had witnessed many happy marriages: his parents, Pete and Jenna, and all their friends at Seaside. They made Clark and Nina's troubles seem out of the ordinary. But he wasn't dumb enough to believe that every couple wasn't fighting their own private battles.

He left his house early to head down to his father's hardware store. Some guys turned to alcohol when things got tough, as his father had after they'd lost his mother. Hunter usually turned to his work, but after spending so many hours working on the sculpture for which Jana was his muse, he knew the shop would only further confuse him. The next best thing to working with his hands was being around power tools—and his father. A double dose of calming influences.

Hunter had grown up in the small town of Brewster, where thankfully, not much ever changed. He parked beside the hardware store and headed around front. His phone rang as he reached for the door, and he smiled when he saw Jana's beautiful face on the screen. But his mind zipped back to last night, to their argument over the key and her sexy dancing, tempering his emotions.

Running a hand over his closely shorn hair, he paced the sidewalk as he answered. "Hey."

"Hi."

Silence stretched uncomfortably between them.

"I just got a call from Brock. The girl who was fighting in the exhibition match today got food poisoning, and he needs me to fill in for my weight class, so…"

Hunter's gut clenched.

"I know your competition is today, and I hate to miss it, but he's really in a bind, and I kinda thought—"

He hadn't made a big deal about the competition because they'd been dealing with Jana's studio, but it *was* important to him. He debated asking her not to go to the fight, but that didn't feel right, either. Especially after he'd given her a hard time about the way she'd danced last night. Everything he was saying lately came out wrong. Everything he did pushed her further away. Hunter never claimed to know how to handle women or relationships, but with Jana, together they'd somehow figured it out. He had faith that this, too, would somehow work out.

"Sure, good luck."

"I guess we'll catch up later?" she asked tentatively. "I'll try to make it after the fight. I just never know how late they'll run."

"Yeah, whatever." His biting tone surprised him, but he couldn't have covered the sting of her missing his competition if his life depended on it.

He ended the call before his voice could shoot any more darts, then headed inside. How many times had he and his siblings walked into their father's shop on their mother's heels? Running up and down the aisles as his parents talked or kissed or whatever adults did when their kids were busy terrorizing a store.

He thought about his childhood. He'd had a good one, and as he'd grown into a man, no one had ever questioned his playing around with women. Hell, no one had ever held him accountable, either. Men were lucky like that. He thought of Jana and all that she'd been through, and an empathetic ache weighed heavily inside him.

She'd poured her heart out to him, and he'd made it even worse by judging one of the very things that drew him to her. Her dancing. His heart ached at how stupid he'd been. She'd become vital to him. Essential.

As he opened the door to his father's shop, he realized that he'd always thought there were four essential elements to life: earth, wind, fire, and water. But he'd been so very wrong. There were five, at least for him, and he had a feeling *Jana* was the only element he needed.

His father looked up from behind the counter. A wide smile graced his handsome face as he came around the counter with open arms.

"Hunt. How're you doing, son?"

Hunter welcomed his father's warm embrace. Neil Lacroux had hair the color of sand after a harsh rain. When he'd been drinking, his belly had gone soft and his face had aged, but now that he'd been sober for a few years, he'd lost the weight. Losing his wife had stolen a piece of his spirit and left behind a shadow of emptiness that Hunter assumed would always be there. But he was glad his father had climbed out of the bottle and gotten back to the business of living his life.

"I'm okay, Pop. I thought I'd come down and walk the aisles for a bit." He smiled, knowing his father would laugh at the reminder of what he'd said to his son so often in his youth when Hunter had had a bad day. *Come on down to the shop with me. Walk the aisles. We'll talk tools and you'll feel better.*

"Gotchya." His father's large hand landed on Hunter's shoulder and squeezed gently. "What's on your mind?" He picked up a can of paint from the counter and placed it on the shelves beside the others. "Is it the competition? I've got Mira, the young gal I hired last month, coming in later so I can be there."

"Thanks, Pop." Thinking of Jana and the sculpture he'd created in her image, he said, "It's not that. I'm pretty sure we've got that nailed."

"That's what Grayson said, too. He said you'd finally found your muse."

"Yeah, you could say that." Was there such thing as a life muse? Because that's what he felt like Jana had become. She inspired so much more than his creativity.

They walked up and down the aisles. His father pointed out a few new tools and a new brand of electric screwdriver he carried. Normally the distraction would be enough to ease Hunter's mind no matter what he was dealing with, but today he couldn't shake the churning in his gut.

His father looked at him with an assessing gaze and tilted his head toward his office. "Come see what I found last week."

Hunter followed him into the small office just beyond the counter. Neil waved to a chair, and Hunter sat down, watching his father push aside stacks of papers. The wall in front of his desk was littered with pictures of Hunter and their family.

"I was digging around in your mother's sewing room, looking for something I'd misplaced." He opened his file drawer and withdrew a green hanging file folder. "And I found these." He set the folder on his desk and opened it, revealing Hunter's original drawings of his very first sculpture.

"She kept them?" The image of his parents standing across from Wellfleet Harbor came rushing back, the smell of the bay, the glimmer of love in his mother's eyes. God, he missed her. He reached for the drawings, poring over the notes he'd written in the margins. *Remember her fingers. His arm.*

"She kept everything," his father said. "Those drawings were the catalyst for what you've become, Hunter. I saw it as kind of a sign, seeing as how your work is going to be judged in the very spot where you saw us standing."

Hunter nodded, smiling to himself with the memory of that afternoon. "You know, Pop, there was a time when my work was everything. I lived for it. I craved the feel of the cold metal in my hands. Knowing that whatever I had inside me would come out in what I created." He gazed into his father's deep-set eyes. Eyes he'd looked into his whole life and seen endless support.

"And now?" his father asked.

"Now I still feel the same love of my work. I could never stand in front of a class and teach, like Matt, or tattoo people's skin, like Sky. And the way you and Pete refinish boats is incredible, but it's also too regimented for me. I need the freedom my work offers. I need to be able to visualize what I want and turn those visions into reality." He inhaled and blew it out slowly. "But for the first time in my life, I found something else that fulfills me in ways I never imagined possible, some*one* else. She challenges me, Pop, and makes me want to be a better person. More caring. Stronger, but in a different sort of way."

"Sounds like me when I met your mother."

He smiled, thinking of his mother. "The funny thing is, with her it's not about fulfilling my hopes and dreams. It's about fulfilling hers."

Hunter pushed to his feet, filled with purpose and determination. "Pop, I have an idea."

"You usually do," his father mumbled as he got to his feet. "You know, you don't always have to act on your impulses, Hunter. You could contemplate, let things settle for a little while, and then make a decision with a level head."

He smiled and draped an arm over his father's shoulder. "Wasn't it you who told me that levelheaded decisions have no place where women are concerned?"

His father laughed. "Probably so."

"Well, then, you should say 'I told you so.' Because it's

definitely true where my woman is concerned."

WHY DID EXHIBITION matches always run late? The match was supposed to begin at two o'clock, and by four o'clock they were just finishing the third weight class. Jana was up next, and she was a nervous wreck. She was running on no sleep, too much coffee, too little training, and a heart that felt like it had been filled up like a helium balloon that soared to cloud nine, only to find it had a pinhole leak and was making a slow descent back down to earth.

"Ready, sis?" Brock helped her put on her gloves while he spoke. "Whatever's got you more jittery than a coke addict, kick it to the curb, because, baby, you've got this. You're fierce, determined, and you've got a harder punch than any woman in your weight class. Focus, Jana."

How could she focus when she felt like her world was careening out of control again? She should be at the competition with Hunter, not fighting in a match she didn't really care about.

She held up her boxing gloves. "Can you just check my texts for me quickly? Hunter had his competition today for a sculpture he was making, and I was supposed to go. I just want to know if he won."

"That's what you're stewing over? Jana, we could have forfeited this match." Brock grabbed her cell phone and checked her text messages. "You've got, like, a zillion messages from Sky and one from Hunter. Which do you want first?"

"Sky." *Because Hunter's might not be as nice.*

Brock began reading Sky's message. "'OMG. Hunter is a finalist. SQUEE! He is one of three finalists, fingers crossed.'" He arched a brow. "Squee?"

Jana smiled, too happy to respond to his question. "He's a finalist. That's amazing."

"There's more. Do I really have to read them all? You go up in seven minutes—"

"Read them!" Her happiness was layered in guilt. Hunter had placed as a finalist, but she'd missed it. He never asked her for a thing, and here she was, fighting instead of going to the event he'd been working toward for weeks. She really did suck as a girlfriend. She made a decision right then and there that from now on she would focus on Hunter. No matter what else was going on in her life, she was going to make sure she was there for him. And if he needed her to modify her sexy dancing in order to feel more comfortable, then she'd do that, too. It was a small concession, wasn't it? He'd done so much for her.

Brock sighed and continued reading Sky's texts. "'He looks so nervous. And OMG if you could see the guy he's up against. He's such a nerd LOL.'" He lifted his eyes. "Jana. I'm not doing this."

"Fine, just skip to the last message from her and read that." She waited, hoping Hunter had won the competition.

"'They're not doing the final judging until later. Maybe you can still make it.'"

"Good," Jana said. "Everyone's late today. Maybe I can

make it."

The announcer called for Jana and her competitor.

"You're up, sis." Brock set her phone in her bag and took her by the shoulders. "I want you to use that feel-good energy to win this fight, you got it?"

Jana nodded. "Just tell me what Hunter's text says."

"Damn it, Jana. That's not focusing." He grabbed the phone with a huff, swiped the screen, and read, "'We need to talk.'"

CHAPTER THIRTY-TWO

THE CROWD CHEERED as the winner pranced around the ring with her hands in the air. Jana took her wounded ego and battered body back to the locker room, shrugging off Brock's consoling words and trying to ignore the blood dripping down her cheek. She'd been so sidetracked about Hunter's cursory text, and the guilt of missing his competition, that she'd completely lost focus.

She reached into her purse for her phone, and the key Hunter had made fell to the floor, landing with a hollow *ping*. She swiped at the sweat dripping from her brow, then scrubbed her hand over her face, wincing as her hand touched the welt below her right eye where she'd taken a nasty blow.

Wiping the blood from her hand on her shorts, she leaned down and picked up the simple reminder of their argument. Staring at it lying in her palm, she lowered herself to the bench. Hunter had taken the effort to make the key, when she'd been too busy to even notice that they were living together. His clothes *were* in her dresser, in her closet. He was there nearly every night. It wasn't a matter of *if* she was ready for the opening act. They *were* the opening act, and had been for quite some time. They were the *best* opening act! She'd made such a big deal out of the key, and he hadn't thrown it in her face, or given her an ultimatum. He'd wrapped it gently in her hand and kissed her knuckles.

He loved her. It was evident in everything he did, everything he said—and everything he didn't say.

And I missed the first part of his competition for a stupid fight and dirty danced like he didn't matter. What the fuck is wrong with me?

She rose to her feet and stuffed her gear into her bag, gathered her purse in her arms, and breathing so hard she felt on the brink of tears, she burst through the locker room doors.

How could she have been so stupid?

"Jana!" Brock caught up to her. "Let me clean up your cut."

"Can't. I've got to go." How could she have said those things to him? *We're not living together.* Of course they were. Jesus, he must think she was crazy.

"But we're having a—"

Jana spun around and pressed one hand to her brother's chest. "I hate to let you down, Brock, but I have a key to deliver."

His confused gaze made her laugh. She kissed his cheek and ran out the front door.

Her phone vibrated as she tossed her things in the backseat.

She started the car, feeling like she'd won something much bigger than a stupid boxing match. Hunter was right. Everything she wanted was right there in front of her, and she was done being too stubborn to see it.

She drove too fast, making the long drive in record time.

Jana drove down to Wellfleet Harbor, searching for a parking place. Crowds of people spilled from the grass, where the competition was being held, into the street. There were lights shining on a makeshift stage, and after driving up to the parking lot at the pier and finding that lot full, too, she gave up and double-parked.

With Hunter's key in her hand, she ran down the road, past the Pearl Restaurant, past the gallery and the Bookstore Restaurant, where she was swallowed into the crowd. Her heart was beating so hard, and people were looking at her funny, but she didn't care. All she cared about was seeing Hunter. She hadn't even seen his sculpture. God, she really did suck, but she was done being sucky. She was there, with the key to her house, and she was ready to give him everything he wanted. Everything she wanted.

She pushed through the crowd, going up on her toes to look over people's shoulders and squeezing between couples and children. Until finally. *Finally.* She could see the stage.

Hunter looked so handsome, in his dark slacks and white shirt, standing beside Grayson. There were six other men and women standing with them. Parker Collins looked as gorgeous as she did on the big screen, and for a millisecond, jealousy clawed at Jana. She shook it off, too focused on why she was there to let anything else rattle her. Parker stood with a man Jana didn't recognize at the center of the stage, holding microphones.

Please let him win. Please let him win.

Her hands were shaking, and her heart was so full of hope. He'd given her everything. He deserved this more than any other person on earth.

Parker stepped forward and spoke into the microphone. "Thank you all for bearing with us while we took the extra time this afternoon to make our final decisions. Let's give a hand to each of our talented participants."

The crowd clapped, and Jana's stomach sank. Had she missed the award?

When the crowd quieted, Parker turned to face Hunter and the others.

"The reason we took a little longer to make our decision was that we were not only blown away by each of the artists, but we've also decided to extend a bigger prize to the winner."

Please, please say Hunter Lacroux.

"We have two winners of the competition, two very talented brothers, who have lived on the Cape their whole lives. Please give a hand to Hunter and Grayson Lacroux, of Grunter's Ironworks."

Tears sprang from Jana's eyes as she applauded. *You won. Thank you, God. Thank you so much.*

Parker shook Hunter's and Grayson's hands. "Your work is incredible, and we're proud to offer you not only the two-year contract to work with the Collins Children's Foundation, but we'd like to have you work on-site."

Hunter and Grayson exchanged a glance, and Jana listened intently.

"You'll be joining our team of artists not only to work in the LA office," Parker said excitedly, "but traveling around the country for the next two years, working at our satellite offices, all expenses paid."

The pit of Jana's stomach knotted. She stumbled backward, tripping over a woman's leg.

"Sorry," she mumbled as she pushed her way back through the crowd toward her car. She felt her heart breaking with every unsteady step. *LA. Two years of all-expenses-paid traveling.* She couldn't give Hunter the key now. Not when he had a once-in-a-lifetime opportunity in the palm of his hands.

CHAPTER THIRTY-THREE

JANA DROVE AROUND town in a blur of tears and heartache, topped with a hefty helping of self-loathing. Half an hour after she'd left the competition she'd gotten another cursory text from Hunter. *We need to talk.* She'd sobbed so hard her chest ached. She'd driven to the beach where they'd watched the sunrise. How could she have been so blind to what was right in front of her? To the love that was growing inside her heart from the very moment she and Hunter had reconnected months ago, when she'd stopped even flirting with other guys? None of that mattered anymore, because she'd already been too selfish.

She drove up to Provincetown just to see the Governor Bradford, the bar where she and Hunter had hooked up a few times. But seeing it only stabbed the knife deeper into her chest. She got on the highway and drove all the way down to Yarmouth, where she pulled into an empty parking lot and sobbed some more. There was no way she was going to tell Hunter how she felt now and make him choose between her and his career. He deserved everything good that came to him.

He deserved a woman who didn't panic at the thought of a key.

He deserved a woman who didn't miss the first half of his

competition.

Why did those thoughts hurt so much? She wanted to be that woman so badly she could taste it. She wanted to kick her insecurities in their wretched little asses. She wanted a do-over.

When she felt depleted of every ounce of energy, she finally gave up and drove toward home. She couldn't escape her devastation. There was no escaping a broken heart. She'd been avoiding going home, because one night at home without Hunter had been enough to make her hate her sweet cottage just a little, and the thought of another night without him— forever without him—was too much to bear.

Hunter's truck came into focus as she drove down her street, and the lump in her throat expanded. She wasn't ready for the conversation that would end their relationship. Wasn't losing her fight enough of a beating for one day? Couldn't she pretend for one more day that he hadn't won something amazing and that she and Hunter had a chance at making things right? That he'd accept her apology, and the key, and they could go back to the incredible, loving path they'd been on? She'd liked that path. A lot.

She pulled up beside his empty truck. Her house was pitch-dark, and there was no sign of Hunter anywhere. Her phone vibrated on the passenger seat. Hunter's name appeared above his number, bringing fresh tears with it. She'd finally changed his contact information. How could such a small, silly thing like seeing Hunter's name on her phone hurt so badly?

She swiped the screen and read the text. *Can we talk?*

Her pulse quickened as she looked up, scanning her yard. A

figure of a man standing in her side yard came into focus. She would know him anywhere. The confident stance, his broad, powerful shoulders, and she was sure if she could see his face, the muscles in his jaw would be jumping with tension. She dried her eyes, pulled her shoulders back, and stepped out of the car. She refused to fall apart in front of him. She didn't want him to feel guilty for taking the incredible opportunity he'd been given. She wasn't going to be the woman who stood in his way.

The twenty feet between them seemed to pass in slow motion. As her eyes adjusted to the darkness, she saw that he was wearing a suit and tie. Her heart skipped a beat. She'd never seen him dressed up like this. A piercing pain shot through her stomach with the realization that he wasn't wearing the suit for her, but for the competition. He must have left the tie and coat in the car or something.

She couldn't help but notice that he was clean-shaven and he smelled like cologne. Jealousy prickled her limbs, knowing that *that* wasn't meant for her, either.

"Hi." Her voice sounded as frayed as she felt.

He took a step closer, his eyes raking over her face, then lower, taking all of her in more quickly than usual. Just another reminder of the distance between them. He curled a finger under her chin and studied her face.

"You're bleeding."

She swallowed hard. Could he see the blood draining from her heart, too? She lifted one shoulder in a halfhearted shrug. "I lost."

"I'm so sorry I wasn't there to cheer you on." His tone was serious, and another half shrug made his jaw do that jumping thing she worried about.

"Can we talk?" he asked.

She nodded, and when he waved a hand toward the backyard, she realized that he didn't even want to step into her house. That twisted the stake that was shattering her heart.

The backyard was dark, and she stumbled over something on the grass.

"What…?"

"Stay here. Let me get the lights." He walked to the back porch and plugged something into the outlet, illuminating the entire yard with tiny white lights strewn through the trees, over the bushes, and around the patio door, transforming her backyard into a magical wonderland.

"What…?" She couldn't process what she was seeing. Bouquets of roses formed a heart in the grass, and she was standing in the center of it. A sculpture came into full view at the point where the two sides of the heart connected.

Hunter followed her gaze. "You haven't seen that yet, have you?"

She shook her head. He hadn't told her what he was making for the competition, but she'd never in her wildest dreams thought he'd sculpt a dancer. Mesmerized by the elegant piece of art, she finally found her voice.

"This is what you made for the competition? May I touch it?"

"Of course." He placed his hand on her lower back, urging

her closer, but she didn't want to move away from him. She stayed where she was, lost in his touch, lost in the beauty before her, lost in confusion.

"It's so graceful. The arch of her neck, the movement of her legs and shoulders." She absently reached up and touched her neck. "It's powerful, and beautiful, and looks like she's actually in motion, the way the skirt appears to be moving. I've never seen anything so…so…feminine and natural."

"You were the perfect muse."

She glanced up at Hunter, tears filling her eyes again, and mouthed, *Me?*

He shoved his hands into his pockets and shrugged shyly. "Who else?"

Her knees weakened at the love in his voice and the idea that he saw her in the magnificent sculpture he'd created. Drawn to this piece of him, this vision he'd had, she stepped forward and ran her fingers over the circles and oblong pieces of shiny metal and mirrors that covered the woman's breasts. Her hand came back to her own body, and she touched the curve of her hip.

"Me?" she repeated, unable to see herself in the glorious woman before her. "But she looks so *free*." Was this his way of telling her he was leaving? Setting her free? Showing her this incredible piece of art first, so she wouldn't stand in his way?

"I call her *Emerging Elegance*." He looked at the sculpture, as if he were studying it. His eyes were narrowed, focused, as he spoke. "I watched you dance that night at the studio, and you looked freer than I'd ever seen you before. Like you disappeared into the music, as if it transported you somewhere only you could see."

Her breathing became shallow as she listened to him describe exactly what she felt every time she danced. He saw what no one else had ever taken the time to notice.

"Last night you were stunning on the dance floor. I'm surprised there weren't more guys pawing at you."

She lifted tear-filled eyes to apologize and he pressed his finger to her lips.

"Shh. Let me finish. Please."

He walked around the sculpture, and touched a corded piece of metal that wound around the upper thigh, across the lower belly, then frayed up by the shoulder.

"At first, with us. With me," he said. "You were bound by your own tethers. Rigid. Closed off. But slowly you've broken free of the memories, the heartaches, that imprisoned you."

My ghosts.

He touched the shiny metal pieces that formed a tank top, the strap on the left shoulder whole, while the strap on the right was shredded apart, jagged and torn, leaving that shoulder bare. "You've opened up to me, and you've trusted yourself enough to try to trust me."

Life is so much better with you in it.

Jana was no longer looking at the sculpture; she was watching him. In awe of his ability to see into her heart, into her soul, and understand exactly what she'd been feeling over the last few weeks. But why now? Why would he choose this moment to show her how well he knew her? She tried to swallow the emotions clogging her throat, but when he turned his warm gaze on her, their visual connection deepened the significance of his words, and she realized he'd been trying to tell her all along.

"I purposely didn't create a face, because your face…God, Jana, your face…"

The way he said it, breathless and painful, like something about her face destroyed and completed him at once, had her reaching up and touching her cheek.

He lifted his eyes to hers again, and everything else faded away. The air pulsed. His energy drew her closer. For a moment she didn't think he was going to say another word, and she wasn't sure she'd be able to hear it if he did. And then he touched her fingers, and sparks radiated up her arm, shocking her brain back to life.

"Jana." The lapels of his suit coat rose with each inhalation as he stepped closer. "Your eyes tell the world you're strong, that you don't need anyone's approval or help, while they unveil all your truths to me. I see your desire to be loved, cherished, adored, and I see your fear of the same." He smiled, paused briefly, like he was remembering her in those moments. "The set of your lovely, rounded chin"—he curled his finger under her chin again—"tells others of your iron will, but it shows me what lies beneath, your heart, afraid of being hurt."

He brushed his thumb over her lower lip. "And this sassy, smart mouth tells everyone else that there's nothing in the world you can't handle, but a single press of your lips, a whisper of my name in a certain cadence, reveals your deepest fears and insecurities. I couldn't create your face, Jana, because I couldn't share all of that specialness with the world. Selfishly, I wanted to keep something just for me."

He leaned in close, and she clutched at his jacket, needing his strength to counter her wobbly knees and expanding heart, which felt like it might burst through her chest.

It took all of her focus to push his name from her lips. "Hunter?" She tightened her hold on his jacket, her eyes moving over the lighted trees, the flowers, the sculpture, and finally, the face of the man she loved more than life itself. "What is all this?"

He got down on one knee and reached behind the sculpture, presenting her with a large wooden box. "This is romance. My girl likes romance."

Her limbs trembled. "But—"

"Please, pretty girl. Please don't fight me on everything tonight."

Pretty girl brought a rush of tears, and she closed her eyes against them.

"Open your eyes, baby. Everything you want is right in front of you." He opened the box, revealing some type of doorknob with a lot of buttons beneath it.

"I don't understand. You're offering me a doorknob?"

His smile made her laugh, despite her tears, as he rose to his feet.

"Yes, a doorknob for a coded entrance. No key necessary. I want to come home to you every night and eat you for breakfast every morning."

She felt her cheeks heat up as he aligned their bodies from head to toe, causing the rest of her to heat up, too.

"You can dance as dirty as you want, as long as the only body yours physically touches is mine." The restraint in his voice told her how difficult that was for him to say. "I'll be your bodyguard when you're in the zone and your lover when we're home. I can't promise I won't be a Neanderthal sometimes, but I can promise you that even if you need to take ten steps backward for every step forward, I will be here waiting when you're ready."

"But you won the competition." *Oh God, this is too hard.* She forced herself to continue, though her voice was barely above a whisper. "And you're going to LA, and traveling. I won't hold you back from that."

His eyes warmed. "How did you know I won?"

"I..." Fresh tears spilled down her cheeks. "I was there. I didn't want to miss it...and...and I heard—" She couldn't manage another word. It hurt too bad.

"Jana, I won the competition *because* of you." His smile widened. "But going to LA and traveling was never part of the plan. I would never leave you."

"But—"

He brushed his lips over hers and whispered, "Do you ever stop arguing? Grayson can travel. You're the only thing I want to win, and I'll spend the rest of my life trying to show you just how much I want you. Lord knows you'll test me in every way known to man. I'm not leaving you, Jana. Not now, not six months from now, not ever. No matter how many obstacles you put in our way."

"But I don't want the doorknob," she confessed through

more tears. "I want you to have the key."

"God, I love you." He sealed his lips over hers and she pushed at his chest.

"*What,* pretty girl? What could you *possibly* have to say now?" The fierceness in his voice rivaled the desire in his eyes, making what she was about to say even more important.

"Just..." She paused to gain control of her emotions. She didn't want to leave anything out. "Thank you for loving me for who I am. Thank you for loving me through my insecurities and helping me put my ghosts to rest. I want you, Hunter. Only you. I love you." His loving smile pulled more tears as she said, "I don't want just the opening act. I want the main event, the encore, and a standing ovation."

She saw a question fill his eyes and said, "Don't ask. Just kiss me already."

CHAPTER THIRTY-FOUR

JANA STOOD ON the front stoop of her studio with a silk tie covering her eyes—the tie Hunter had used to bind her wrists the night before. She'd been surprised when he'd confessed that he'd changed into his suit, showered, shaved, and put on cologne to see her last night, *after* the celebratory dinner he had attended. And after they'd talked, they'd made love well into the morning. Clark was right; there was a world of difference between making love to a woman you adored and having sex.

Hunter stood behind Jana now, guiding her by the shoulders. When Jana had said she loved him, he felt like the luckiest guy on earth. He knew their relationship would probably always have its ups and downs. They were both stubborn, after all. He didn't claim to have all the answers, but he had the only answer that mattered. He loved Jana, and he vowed to spend the rest of her life making her happy.

"Just promise me that if you don't like what I've done, you'll tell me."

She laughed. "Has that *ever* been a problem for me? Just because you have me blindfolded doesn't mean my mouth doesn't work."

"Christ, you do have a smart mouth."

"You love my smart mouth."

He moved in front of her and pulled her body against him. Her nipples instantly hardened against his chest. He couldn't resist brushing his scruffy cheek to the sensitive skin just beneath her ear.

"Hunter…" Her needy voice sent a rush of heat straight to his groin.

He sank his teeth into her neck and wrapped his arm around her waist, catching her as her knees wobbled. "You look so tempting, blindfolded and wearing that slinky little miniskirt and tight frilly top. I can't believe you're mine. Tell me again." He'd been teasing her all morning about finally admitting she wanted him.

She sighed dramatically. He could practically see her rolling her eyes. "Hunter Lacroux, I want you."

He ran a hand along her waist, over her rib cage, and brushed the sides of her breasts. "Tell me like you mean it," he teased.

"Why would I do that?"

He tore the blindfold off, and her eyes blazed with desire.

"Because you mean it." He tugged her tighter against him.

"Maybe so, but this is *so* much more fun." She raised her brows with a sexy giggle. "Now kiss me or fuck me, but stop this teasing nonsense."

"Christ, you're a pain in the ass. I'll do everything to you, but first…" He pushed open the door of the studio, and Jana gasped as they stepped inside.

"Hunter! This is gorgeous!" She launched herself into his

arms and wrapped her legs around his waist. "How about we check out the cunnilingus kitchen?" A pretty blush rose on her cheeks.

He carried her through the hallway that led to the kitchen. "There's a fee for entrance now."

"Let me guess. Does it start with a six and end with a nine?"

"From your lips to my ears."

She slanted her mouth over his as he pushed through the kitchen doors. They were met with cheers of "surprise" and "congratulations" from all their friends and family. Harper, Brock, and Colton were front and center, beside Clark, who was holding little Billy in one arm, his other draped around Nina. Blue and Lizzie were standing arm in arm beside Bella and the girls and all their babies and husbands. Everyone was smiling and laughing and moving in for hugs.

Jana looked at him with wonder and love in her eyes, and that alone nearly brought him to his knees. Jana was finally *his*. Really, truly his, one hundred percent his. "How did you arrange all this?"

"Don't you get it yet, pretty girl? There's nothing I wouldn't do for you."

CHAPTER ONE

PARKER COLLINS SHOVED a handful of M&M's in her mouth, eyes glued to *Saw III*. A burst of light illuminated the pitch-black media room, followed by a scream of terror. Christmas, her four-year-old English mastiff, sacked out beside her on the couch, pushed his big head beneath her legs as darkness shrouded them again. Another shrill scream brought her big chicken of a dog deeper into her leg tunnel.

"Whoever said dogs were a *man's* best friend was an idiot. *My* best friend." *Especially now that Bert's gone.* A few tears slipped down her cheek.

Christmas whimpered, pulled his head from beneath her legs, and licked her from chin to eyes, getting every last one of her tears and coming back for more. He'd been lapping up her tears for two weeks, ever since she'd lost her friend, mentor, and the only family she'd ever known. Bert Stein had suffered a massive heart attack while Parker was in Italy filming her latest movie, and she'd been moving on autopilot ever since: picking up Christmas from his housekeeper in Los Angeles because Bert had been watching him while she was away, attending Bert's funeral, *trying to remember how to breathe*, and finally, coming to her house in Wellfleet to mourn—and, she hoped, to mend a fence Bert was never able to with his estranged brother.

Holing up in the bay-front home she'd built for the Collins Children's Foundation, where no one would look for her, was the only way she could grieve without negative ramifications. God forbid an A-list actress went out looking like an average woman whose heart had been ripped from her chest. Rag magazines would pay big bucks for pictures of her puffy, tired eyes and I-don't-give-a-shit tangled hair. She could just imagine the headlines: *Parker Collins's New Drug Addiction*, or *Unplanned Pregnancy for Parker*, or anything else that would sell magazines. Nobody cared that she'd never even smoked a cigarette, that she needed to have sex in order to get pregnant, or that she'd gone so long without, she wondered if her best parts even worked anymore.

She pressed her hands to Christmas's droopy cheeks, kissed her bewildered boy's snout, and reached for the bottle of tequila she'd been nursing. She'd never had tequila before tonight, but it was the perfect addition to her chocolate–horror movie grief remedy. After pouring herself another shot, she tossed it back in one gulp, savoring the warmth as it slid down her throat and drowned her sadness.

She set the glass beside her on the couch and shoved her hand into the jumbo bag of peanut M&M's that had consoled her throughout the evening—because a big lazy dog was great for licking tears, but nothing quenched sadness like candy-coated chocolate. And tequila. *Definitely tequila.* Her fingers scraped the bottom of the bag. *Damn it.* She tossed the empty bag to the floor. Christmas hung his head over the side of the couch and whimpered.

"Don't judge me. It can't be that bad." She leaned forward to assess the damage, knocking an empty pizza box to the floor, and reached for the coffee table to stop the room from spinning. "Whoa."

Another scream brought her eyes to the movie, then toward the movement in her peripheral vision, where a shadowy figure blocked the entrance to the media room. It took her alcohol-drenched mind a minute to realize the tall, broad man filling the doorway wasn't supposed to be in her house. Panic spread through her veins, catapulting her to her feet. Christmas darted to the stranger with a friendly *woof.*

"Oh God." She reached for the wall to steady the spinning room, fighting to push through her drunken haze. She'd seen enough movies to know she was going to die in the media room of this lonely house, wearing chocolate-stained sweatpants—or more accurately, ice-cream-, tequila-, pizza-sauce-, *and* chocolate-stained sweatpants—while her dog made a new friend of her killer.

"Stay back. He's a killer. One command and you're dead!" Not likely with her loving dog.

The man sank to one knee, his face hidden by her big, traitorous dog.

"Yeah, I can see that," he said casually, as only a coldhearted psycho killer could.

Searching for a weapon, she grabbed the tequila bottle, only too late realizing it was spilling down her wrist. She flipped it upright, wishing this was a movie and someone would yell, *Cut!*

A piercing scream drew their attention to the heart-pounding terror on the projection screen. Suddenly the room was showered in light. Parker's eyes slammed shut against the sensory invasion, then flew open to get a look at the man who would probably find fame as the *Parker Collins Killer.*

Her breath caught in her throat, and her hand flew to her frantically beating heart, as she took in the Greek god rising to his feet before her. His smoldering dark eyes nearly brought her to her knees. *Grayson Lacroux.*

"Grayson?" *Do I sound scared, drunk, or like I want to jump your bones?* Probably all three, which wasn't good. Grayson had won a two-year contract in a design competition last summer, and for the past ten months he'd been designing artwork for the Collins Children's Foundation. As the founder of CCF, Parker headed up the project, and they'd exchanged hundreds of emails—emails that felt intimate and meaningful and had pulled her through too many long, lonely nights to count.

"What are you doing here?" She cringed at how breathless she sounded. Even in her drunken state she knew it had nothing to do with her initial fears and everything to do with the towering male across the room.

His lips curved up as he surveyed the room. She'd come straight down to the media room in full-on holing-up mode after arriving from LA. Her open suitcase lay in the middle of the floor, lace and silk seeping over the sides. The clothes she'd worn on the flight were strewn across the hardwood floor. One pink high heel peeked out from beneath an empty bag of Twizzlers; the other was nowhere in sight. An orgy of fun-size candy bar wrappers and M&M's littered the floor.

"I might ask you the same thing." His voice was low and rich and made the room feel fifty degrees hotter.

Maybe that's the tequila.

"I came to take measurements for the railing and heard a noise. I didn't know you were here."

Measurements? She couldn't think with his dark, assessing gaze trained on her as he crossed the room. Each step was a declaration of power and control—the same air of confidence he relayed in his emails. Parker was used to beautiful people, but holy mother of hot and sexy men, Grayson brought manliness and sex appeal to a whole new level. An *enticingly tempting* level. She was five nine, and he had several delicious inches on her. His bulbous biceps and massive breadth made her feel more delicate than she was. His tousled, thick dark hair and unwavering air of command made her knees wobble. She took a deep, unsteady breath and backed against the wall to stabilize those wobbly knees, but he stepped closer, assaulting her senses with his musky, and somehow summery, scent.

Nope. Definitely not the tequila. The man was a walking heat wave.

He eyed the tequila bottle in her hand, and his eyes filled with amusement. "Having a little party?" He plucked a sticky piece of candy from her hair and held it between his large finger and thumb with a cocky grin.

A crazy-hot cocky grin that sent dirty thoughts about his mouth rushing to the front of her mind. "Not exactly," she mumbled.

"You've been avoiding my emails."

She'd been avoiding email, voicemail, and *life* since Bert's funeral. Grayson was on her callback list, along with her agent, a few foundation staff members, and about a dozen so-called friends.

"I…Um…" *Can't really think clearly.* She lifted the tequila bottle. "Care to join me?"

His gaze dragged down her tank top, bringing her nipples to attention and reminding her she'd taken off her bra. As if on cue, Christmas *woofed*, Parker's pink lace bra dangling from his mouth. Grayson's eyes brimmed with heat, making her want to put him on a totally different kind of *to-do* list.

He'd been the subject of her late-night fantasies for so many months she felt like she already knew him well enough for him to own that list.

This was bad.

Very, very bad.

Parker didn't have that kind of *to-do* list. She *did* relationships. Or rather, *didn't* do them, based on her dating history.

Ugh! Her head was too fuzzy to try to untangle the web of lust she'd weaved with every email, every intimate glance into his private world of family, friends, and his love of his craft. Grayson worked with heavy metals, as evident from his insanely perfect physique, which no gym in the world could produce, and his designs were excruciatingly unique and beautiful. Parker had probably driven him crazy making changes, but if she had, he'd never let on. She loved reading his descriptions about why he designed certain pieces and how he felt when he was creating them. Sometimes he wrote about missing his family, or about bonfires and outings he'd gone on when he flew home to work with his brother on specific designs for CCF. She'd been careful not to ask personal questions, so she wouldn't feel inclined to share her personal life, but she had secretly clung to each of his tales, treasuring the emotions he'd so eloquently shared. She'd made excessive design changes just to keep those intimate glances of him coming.

And now he was here, all six-something feet of him, close enough to see and touch and taste—and between her grief and his godliness, she was clearly losing her mind.

She pushed past him, grabbed the lingerie from Christmas, and tossed it into her suitcase. "Lie down."

Christmas walked in a circle and plopped onto a pile of clothes with a huff.

Parker grabbed a shot glass from the bar, determined to remain in her inebriated state so she could deal with all the testosterone flinging around the room, and sank down to the couch. "Coming, big guy?"

HELL YEAH, I'D totally be into coming. Grayson scrubbed his hand down his face to try to clear that thought from his brain and sat down beside Parker, silently reminding himself that she was technically his boss *and* a client. That was only one reason he should stop thinking about how incredibly sexy she was. They'd been emailing for almost a year, and he'd sensed affection brewing between them, even if neither one had directly addressed it. Three weeks ago she'd sent him an email pulling him from the foundation project to design a railing for this mini-mansion and had followed it up with a note about being *excited to finally get together in person*—and he hadn't heard from her since.

Another reason he needed to keep his sexual urges at bay—because he really needed to find as many reasons as possible right this very second—was the inebriated state and slightly red, puffy eyes of the scrumptious blonde currently reaching across his lap. Her hair tumbled sexily over her bare shoulders as she fished for something between the leather sofa cushions. There was no ignoring the feel of her pert nipples against his thigh, making him hard and hungry for what he shouldn't have. *At least not tonight, with all that alcohol muddying your thoughts.*

She crawled off his lap and held up another shot glass. "Voilà! Fill 'er up!"

Needing the alcohol to calm the inferno inside him, he gladly filled their glasses and handed her one. She wrapped her delicate fingers around his, giving him ideas about what else he'd like to see those slender digits wrapped around. Her blue eyes filled with determination, which he also found incredibly sexy.

"Don't tell anyone you saw me like this."

Seriously? Who did she think he'd tell? "I'll cross putting an article in the paper tomorrow off my list."

She pushed her face to within an inch of his. His eyes fell to her luscious lips as more erotic thoughts raced through his mind. He was skating on very thin ice.

"*Parker* can't do things like cry, or curse, or eat an entire jumbo bag of M&M's and watch horror movies until her eyes nearly bleed without being judged. Only Polly can do that."

"Polly?" He reached for her glass, figuring she'd had enough and needed more babysitting than his sexual urges did at the moment.

She pulled her glass out of his reach with a devilish glint in her eyes and *clinked* it to his. "To Bert. I miss him *so* much I ache." She downed the drink in one swallow.

Bert? Jealousy clawed at him. He shifted his gaze away from her, taking in the room again. *Tequila, chocolate, pizza? Two weeks of radio silence. Aw, hell. Hallmarks of a rough breakup.* That thought bugged the shit out of him, so he moved on to another. Maybe this was her typical go-to stress release after filming and Bert was her...*director?* No way she'd *ache* for her director. Unless...*Christ*, something else, *anything* else. No matter how hard he tried, he couldn't get past his first assessment. Had their emails only *felt* personal? It was difficult to assess a lot of things over email, so it wasn't out of the realm of possibility that he'd misinterpreted the depth of their friendship, regardless of the heat simmering between them now.

As she refilled their glasses, he realized she'd never mentioned her dog. He'd talked about his family and friends, and if he'd had a dog, he sure as shit would have mentioned it. Who would leave out their dog? Feeling like a complete numskull, he realized she'd never mentioned her family, either. Had he been sucked in by her musings over how pretty the countryside was and how she wished *he* was there to see it? And her off-the-cuff remarks about how acting would be easier if the other actors were as confident as *he* was?

Another look around the room told him he was an idiot.

This is a post breakup breakdown. So much for babysitting. He could deal with a lot of things, but picking up the pieces from some other guy's mistakes was not one of them. He downed the shot, thankful she'd refilled their glasses.

"Bert?" he mumbled to himself, thinking about how he'd like to wring the asshole's neck—right after he wrung his own for being such a fool. Parker was America's sweetheart. Right up there with Julia Roberts. While he'd been slowly falling for the sweet, gorgeous woman a million miles away, she'd probably been out with dozens of Hollywood heartthrobs. He didn't like knowing he'd misinterpreted their friendship, but he only had himself to blame for that. But he didn't appreciate being blown off or having his time wasted. He couldn't move forward with the railing designs he'd sent her over the past two weeks without her approval—and she'd obviously been too wrapped up in whoever the fuck Bert was to answer a single email.

It was time for him to leave.

She turned her big, tear-filled baby blues on him, making

him sorry he'd come by to get the final measurements for the railing. "Bert was the best man on the planet. He was—" Tequila spilled over the top of the glass. "Oh, gosh! Darn it! I…"

"I've got it." Grayson pushed to his feet, needing to put distance between them anyway, because regardless of his not wanting to still be attracted to her, every fiber of his being had been consumed with her for months. He found a towel behind the bar.

Christmas lumbered over, sniffed the spillage, and went back to lying on the pile of clothes, leaving Grayson to mop up the mess—and scrub out his urge to be an asshole and walk out the door, leaving her alone to deal with her breakup woes. Hearing about some guy—other than him—that she thought was *the best man on the planet* was nowhere on tonight's agenda.

"Maybe you've had enough." He tossed the wet towel on the bar, grabbed another and wet it down.

"Oh no." She shook her head, waving a finger at him. "No amount of tequila is enough right now. I've never had tequila before, and you know what? I like it. It's delicious. Numbing. Truly helpful right now."

He wiped down the coffee table with the clean, wet towel and tried to keep the distaste from coming out in his voice. "I'm sure there are plenty of other guys to take his place."

Her mouth gaped.

He turned away and tossed the towel on the bar, having no patience for women who pretended they didn't know they were pretty. "You're Parker Collins. Tons of guys want y—" He turned around and nearly bowled her over. His arm circled her waist to keep her from falling. "Whoa. You okay?" Apparently she wasn't only a skilled actress, but she also had wicked ninja skills.

Tears slid down her cheek, conflicting with the anger in her eyes.

"Bert Stein wasn't a *guy*. You shouldn't assume. You're…infuriatingly *male*." She twisted from his grip, downed another shot, and sank down to the couch again. More tears fell, turning the anger in her eyes to sadness and filling him with guilt.

Grayson's compassion overpowered his hatred of drama. He had a younger sister, and if she was this sad and a guy was with her but didn't try to help, he'd pummel the asshole. He sat beside Parker and gave himself over to five minutes of hell. "All right, I'll bite. Who was he?" *And by the way, why didn't you tell me you were here? I wouldn't have barged in.*

She reached for the tequila, and he reached for her hand. Their eyes connected. Hers were so full of conflicting emotions—heat and sorrow—it stirred all the affection he was trying to push aside. He kept ahold of her hand and guided her back from the edge of the couch, taking her emotions more seriously, unwilling to let her fall any further into the blankness alcohol had to offer. He knew about that crutch all too well, having dealt with his father's alcoholism a few years ago.

"Tell me about Bert," he said in a softer tone. At Bert's name, Christmas's head popped up. The dog surveyed the room, then lowered his chin to his paws again and closed his eyes. At least Bert knew she had a dog.

"He was my…*everything*," she said just above a whisper.

"And now he's gone."

His heart ached at the sadness in her voice, pushing the jealousy in him to the pit of his stomach. When she lifted her eyes, another tear slid down her cheek, forcing that ache a little deeper.

"Gone, as in he went somewhere?" Grayson asked, hoping she hadn't lost her lover forever. "Or gone as in, *gone?*"

"*Gone.* He was like a father to me, and two weeks ago he passed away." She swallowed hard, more tears spilling from her beautiful eyes.

His breath hitched in his throat. *A father?* They'd emailed for nearly a year. How could he not know about someone so important to her? Now he was not only an idiot, but an asshole for assuming she was overreacting to a rough breakup.

She turned away, causing a torrent of emotions in him. The desire to pull her in to his arms until her sadness subsided obliterated every other thought. He gathered her close, soothingly stroking her back, remembering the gut-wrenching devastation he'd experienced after he'd unexpectedly lost his mother to an aneurysm. He closed his eyes with the memory, pushing his own painful past aside, and pressed a kiss to the top of Parker's head.

"I'm so sorry," he whispered. He held her until her breathing evened out and her tears stopped. He wiped her tears with the pads of his thumbs, wishing he could do something more and knowing time and compassion were the only things that would help.

"You came here to grieve?"

She nodded. "Flew in this morning."

"What about your family? Don't you want to be with them?" When he'd lost his mother, he'd needed family as much as he'd needed air to breathe. "Friends?" he asked hopefully.

"There's only me." Her eyes shifted to the dog. "And Christmas."

You're going through this alone? I should have fucking known you had no family. As painful as that thought was, he realized she'd had no reason to include family in their email conversations. Maybe he hadn't misinterpreted everything after all. Despite his waffling on the meaning of their interactions, his protective urges surged forth, driving his need to ease her heartache. He slid his hands to either side of her neck, brushing his thumbs over her jaw as he lifted her face so she had no choice but to meet his gaze. She was vulnerable and hurting, so different from the strong, sunny actress the world knew her to be. But grief didn't care about social status, and neither did he. All he saw was the woman he'd spent almost a year thinking about night and day looking at him with sad, soulful eyes. Despite the warning bells going off in his head about their professional relationship and his potential misinterpretation of their emails, he wanted to hold her all night, to kiss her until her pain subsided, and to protect her from ever being hurt again.

He fought the urge to kiss her and said what remained true regardless of whether he'd misinterpreted their relationship or not. "And me, Parker. Now you've got me, too."

To continue reading, buy **SEASIDE LOVERS**

DUKE RYDER BALANCED his cell phone against his shoulder, listening to his buddy and investment partner Pierce Braden talk about their newest potential investment property as he followed the rickety wooden dock onto the white sandy beach.

"The dock just might be the most stable thing on Elpitha Island," Pierce said. "Try to soak in a little sand and sun while you're there. That's the best part of the island."

Duke's eyes were immediately drawn to the sprawling oak trees he'd read about, standing sentinel over the forested acreage beyond. Long, thick branches spread like languid arms draped in moss, reaching for...*what?* One glance told him that there wasn't much to reach for, save for a building that looked more like a forgotten Mediterranean villa than the welcome center of the small Southern island. The stone and wood building had a deep porch that spanned the entire length of the left side with stone pillars. A wooden trellis laced with the most captivating flowering vines shaded the area. Although the structure itself was in need of repair, it was surrounded by perfectly manicured, ornate gardens, which contrasted sharply with overgrown and unkempt bushes littering the far edges of the property.

"The proximity to the mainland isn't bad," Duke said to Pierce. He set his suitcase on the sand and looked back at the Atlantic. "It only took an hour fifteen to get here." Elpitha was the smallest of the vacation islands off of South Carolina, and more than half of the land had been owned by the Liakos family for centuries. It was just over eight square miles, and not many investors wanted such a small tract of land, or to deal with families that were as entrenched as the Liakos family was thought to be. Some families might sell out, but they would fight tooth and nail against change, which could cause discourse on an island this small. Duke and Pierce weren't deterred. The restrictive size of the property would only increase the value, making it an exclusive vacation spot for the elite.

"With Hilton Head and the other islands so overrun," Pierce said, "Elpitha is ripe for development. Although we'll have to work around that name. Who wants to go to an island called Elpitha? It sounds more like a disease than an island."

Duke squinted up at the blazing sun and loosened his tie. "I don't know. I kind of like it." He noticed a plantation-style home tucked behind the trees in the distance. "They weren't kidding about the strange mix of Mediterranean and Southern feel of the place. This should be interesting." Duke knew some of the island's history, and though he still didn't understand why Greeks would immigrate to the South and try to re-create their country's feel, it didn't much matter. If he and Pierce decided to purchase the land, they would bulldoze every structure and give the island a complete Southern overhaul, making it the most desirable resort area in the South.

"Chuck called earlier and said Liakos's granddaughter Gabriella is an attorney," Pierce explained. "He thinks they might bring her in on things. Apparently their family keeps things tight. So if you meet her, play nice."

The hollow clank of a screen door hitting its frame drew Duke's attention. A woman stood on the porch of the old building, shading her eyes from the sun as she looked out at the water. Her long dark hair hung halfway down her back. Duke was too far away to see her features, but there was no missing her curvaceous ass and full breasts, not to mention legs that seemed to go on forever beneath her short summery dress. Duke watched with interest as he listened to Pierce relay the most recent information from the attorneys and engineers.

The woman glanced at her watch, then settled her hand on her hip. A voice rang out from inside the building, and the pretty woman hurried back inside.

"I just found proof of life," he said to Pierce as he stepped onto the sandy path. "I'll call you once I've done some recon."

His black leather shoes quickly lost their shine from the

dusty road as he approached the building. Voices filtered out the open windows as he mounted the steps. He glanced through the screen door, spotting the brunette he'd just seen. She was facing away from him, speaking heatedly in Greek, hands flailing as her exasperated voice pitched higher.

A thick-waisted man with salt-and-pepper hair sat at a table near the counter, amusement shining in his dark eyes as the brunette ranted to an older woman, and then the man said something Duke couldn't hear.

"*Ugh!* Baba!" The younger woman threw her hands up in the air and flew out the screen door, nearly smacking Duke in the face.

He stumbled backward, giving the angry woman a wide breadth as she paced the front porch. She mumbled something in Greek and then crossed her arms, raised her shoulders, and dropped them quickly with a loud *harrumph*. Duke couldn't help but drink in the flush on her smooth, sun-kissed cheeks. Her nose was small and straight, and her almond-shaped, dark—and currently angry—eyes were shadowed by lashes so long they brushed her cheeks.

Having grown up with a younger sister, Duke bided his time in announcing his presence, not wanting to take the brunt of her reaction to whatever the man had said to upset her.

She inhaled a deep breath, her breasts rising and pressing against the sheer fabric, then falling as she exhaled loudly. Her shoulders lowered, and the tightness around her mouth softened. She turned a full-lipped, mind-numbing smile to Duke, as if she hadn't just come out in a firestorm.

"My father believes that no matter what he says, I hear something else." She tilted her head to the side in a thoughtful pose, and in the space of a second her eyes filled with rebellion, making her even sexier. "Hearing and agreeing are two different things."

Duke wondered what her father had just said that got her panties in a bunch. *Christ.* Now he was thinking about her panties.

"I'm Gabriella Liakos. Welcome to Elpitha Island."

The granddaughter? Playing nice would not be a problem with this feisty beauty. Duke shook her hand, holding it a beat longer than he probably should, still mesmerized by the whirlwind of energy radiating from her. "Duke Ryder. It's nice to meet you. I didn't mean to intrude."

"No one intrudes on Elpitha," she said sweetly.

Duke shifted his eyes to the screen door, and she laughed softly. It was the rare type of laugh that floated like the wind and wasn't easily forgotten.

"We're Greek," she said with a shrug, as if that explained it all.

He arched a brow.

"When you combine a Greek father and a Southern mother, who learned *all* the best Greek ways, that's what you get. Food, yelling, guilt, more food. Sweet love. Crazy love. More food. That's who we are." She dragged her gorgeous eyes down his suit to his shoes and put one hand on her hip as she had earlier, tapping her lips with the other.

Duke wouldn't mind getting his mouth on those succulent

lips for some *crazy love.*

"You're the investor, checking out our island so you can line your pockets, right?"

He couldn't tell if the look in her eyes was teasing or serious, but her sharp tongue piqued his interest even more. Duke respected confidence, and even though it wasn't the greeting he'd hoped for, he liked knowing that Gabriella wasn't a pushover.

"Something like that," he answered casually.

As a real estate investor, Duke knew his clients were vulnerable and, more often than not, taking a deal they didn't really care for because, by the time he swooped in to save the day, they had gotten a strong dose of what failure tasted like. A hard pill to swallow. Which was why Duke didn't flinch as Gabriella measured everything about him, from his appearance to his answers. While other investors were cold as sharks, Duke had never quite mastered making ice flow through his veins. But he always got the job done.

Her eyes flicked toward the water, where another boat was nearing the dock. Her smiled turned genuine at the sight of a handful of children waving from the boat. She waved both arms over her head and yelled something in Greek, then settled her hands on her hips as she watched the children file from the boat.

"It was nice to meet you, Gabriella," Duke said, hoping he'd see her later. The island had a population of just over two hundred and fifty people, so he imagined it would be hard not to see the same people throughout his stay. "I'll just step inside and see about my room and a tour.”

“Lucky you,” she said, turning a steady gaze back to him, “I’m your tour host.” She didn’t wait for him to reply as she opened the screen door and hollered something in Greek to the people inside. Over her shoulder, she said to Duke, “Give me a sec to get your keys and the cart, and I’ll show you around and drop you at your place.”

It took a moment for him to remember that they drove golf carts or used bicycles on the island and that cars were prohibited.

She hurried inside and headed directly to her *Baba*, which Duke now knew meant he was her father, and said something that made the man laugh. She leaned in to kiss and hug her father, and her dress crept up, exposing the backs of her thighs and hugging her ass. He tried to ignore the stroke of awareness racing through him. She walked around the counter and grabbed a set of keys from a hook, then draped an arm around the shoulders of the woman with whom she was speaking earlier.

“Mama,” Gabriella said to the woman. Her mother’s hair was a shade lighter than hers. “Talk some sense into him, will you, please?” She whispered something, then kissed her, too.

The woman wiped her hands on an apron and smiled at Duke, catching him observing them. “Welcome to our island, Mr. Ryder. I’m Peggy Ann, and this is my husband, Niko.”

Her warm Southern drawl took Duke by surprise after hearing her speak fluent Greek, and he realized it shouldn’t have. They were in the South, after all.

He stepped inside. "It's a pleasure to be here, and to meet you both."

Gabriella's father nodded. "Nice to meet you, Mr. Ryder."

"I'll meet you out front," Gabriella said as she grabbed a large basket from the counter, then disappeared through a door in the back of the room.

As he stepped onto the porch, Duke had a feeling Pierce was wrong about the sand and sun being the best part of the island. Those things had nothing on the intriguing woman who'd just slipped out the back door.

To continue reading, buy **CLAIMED BY LOVE**

BLAIN'S MOUTH BLAZED a path up her inner thigh. His hot breath teased over her wet flesh. Kenya fisted her hands in the sheets, dug her heels into the mattress, and rocked her hips, aching for his talented tongue in the place she needed him most. Blaine lifted smoldering dark eyes, a hint of wickedness shining through, as his tongue slicked over his lips. He was a master at seduction, but Kenya didn't give a shit about seduction. She wanted to be fucked hard. Now. She needed his—

A large hand landed on Janie Jansen's desk beside her braille device. She nearly jumped out of her skin and nervously yanked out her earbuds. *Holy shit.* She was supposed to be finishing a technical editing assignment, not listening to the latest hot romance audiobook.

"Nice article in the newsletter this week, Jansen. *The Oxford Comma Revolution.* Catchy." Her boss, Clay Bishop, was slightly less arid than a desert, but Janie didn't mind. He'd hired her to work at Tech Ed Co, or TEC, on a trial basis, and four years later, her respect for him had only grown. He was a fair and equitable boss, and was currently considering her for a promotion.

It was difficult to spice up a weekly column geared toward grammar and editing, but Janie tried. It was just one more step toward the promotion of technical writer she'd been vying for, a nice step up from editor.

"You're here late. Trouble with the ARKENS handbook?"

"I'm just catching up on a few things. The handbook is almost done." Well, technically not *almost* done, but she'd meet the deadline. She had yet to miss one. She loved editing, but she hadn't set out to be an editor after college. She'd wanted to be a journalist, but that door had closed and she'd tabled her dream and settled for editing. Usually the intensity of her job didn't get to her, but after weeks of grueling revisions on this particular medical equipment handbook, she'd needed a short mental break. But Clay would never think to take a break. He was all business all the time, even hours after their workday officially ended.

"Perfect. Don't forget, Monday afternoon we have the peer review of your writing sample. If that goes well, your promotion will be in the hands of the management team. I'm not worried—you're always on top of your game."

"Yeah, she is." Boyd Hudson's amused voice brought a smile to Janie's lips.

Boyd consulted at TEC only a few days a month, and though Janie didn't know him well, he was quippy and flirtatious, bringing a spark of amusement into her otherwise quiet days.

"Hudson," Clay said dryly. "Okay, well, it's late, so…"

"See you Monday, Clay." Janie listened to his retreating footsteps and let out a relieved sigh.

"He almost caught you again, didn't he?"

She heard the smirk in Boyd's voice. "He didn't *catch* me last time. I was on my lunch break last week. And besides, I was just studying the nuances of the romance genre."

"If by *study* you mean *getting swept away in the sexy fantasy life of some fictional, ridiculously unattainable hero*, then yeah, I'd buy that."

"Why do you trash the genre when you know it's my favorite escape?" She began gathering her things to leave for the day.

"Because it's fun. You're too smart to be a cliché, Janie. You know that, right? Girl who's blind whiles away hours of her youth reading romances because her parents are too controlling. Grows up wanting a fictional life that can never exist. Break free from it." His voice rose with excitement. "Let it go. Romance isn't real. It's crap writing about fake people."

She never should have revealed that tidbit about her parents in the break room last month. They'd been talking about their childhoods, and while others had fun stories of hanging out at the mall, or going on spur-of-the-moment outings with groups of friends, Janie had very few spur-of-the-moment anything to share. Her parents worried about every step she made, questioning her safety and whether this or that location would be difficult for her to navigate without them to hold her hand. They'd been a noose around her neck, and it had often been easier to escape into fictional worlds than to battle for the chance to go out.

"And your sci-fi adventures are more real than romance? Ha!" She hefted her bag over her shoulder. "I bet you've never even read a romance."

"Don't need to. It's crap."

"It's not crap. I bet I could write a romance that you'd not only read, but love." Janie turned off her computer and braille device.

"Not unless it's got a heroine who likes sci-fi, is smarter than me, *and* is into kinky sex."

"God, you're a pig. Fine, sci-fi and kinky sex. It shouldn't be hard to make her smarter than you." She lifted her brows with the tease. "But if I write it, you not only have to read every single page of it, but you also have to go to the Romance Writer's Festival with me in October and stay all day. Plus," she added, getting excited about the bet, "you have to buy me every romance book I want for a month."

He placed Janie's cane in her hand. "A little greedy, aren't you?"

"Hey, if I'm writing a whole novel, it's got to be worth it."

"Fine, but I'm not buying you romance books for a month."

"Whatever. Torturing you with the festival for an entire day will be worth it. It's Friday night. What are you doing here so late?" It was after nine o'clock, and a group of people from work had gone down to NightCaps, a local bar where they often hung out.

"Had a busy day before coming here," Boyd answered.

"Are you going to NightCaps, or are you going to *while away the hours* with your nose in outer space?" Janie loved the constant vibration of laughter, hushed whispers, and the hum of sexual tension at NightCaps, but her best friend, Kiki Vernon, was out of town, and she didn't like to go to bars without her. She'd planned on spending a quiet weekend at home, but she assumed Boyd would want to go.

"I've got a date, so I'm pretty sure my nose won't be any-where near space, but I'll walk with you. I'm headed that way anyway. But first, shake on our bet."

"Game on, dude," she said as she shook his hand. "And you're *so* gonna owe me, but I'm not going to NightCaps. I was going to read, but now I think I'll start plotting my romance. *Hm.* What should I call it? *Sci-fi Sexiness?*" She couldn't wait to tell Kiki about the bet. She loved the genre as much as Janie did, and she'd get a kick out of Janie actually trying to write a sexy story.

"That doesn't even sound romantic," Boyd said. "I'm going to win the bet, and when I do, you have to attend Comic Con with me. You'll make a hot Catwoman."

Janie laughed. "Yeah, that's *so* not going to happen. I'm writing this book and you're going to spend an entire day meeting romance authors and male cover models."

Boyd hooked his arm in hers as she touched the tip of her cane to the ground.

"You know what that cane does to me," he said in a seductively low voice.

"I know what it's going to do *to* you if you don't stop teasing me."

As they left the office, the crisp night air rolled over Janie's skin. The sounds of people walking by, cars moving along the road, and horns honking were familiar and comforting. The smell of exhaust tangled with what Janie had come to know as the dark scents of the city. Tension was thicker at night in New York City, as if everyone was shrouded with awareness. Janie felt that awareness prickling her skin.

"Want me to flag down a cab?" Boyd asked.

"No thanks. I hate riding in cabs here. The drivers petrify me. I like the subway better." She'd ridden in cabs with Kiki when they'd first moved to the city after college, and the constant stopping and starting and traveling alone when someone else was in complete control of her end destination made her feel unsafe. Navigating the city alone presented enough of a challenge. She didn't need to end up in some back alley with a cab-driving killer.

"The subway? To each their own, I guess."

Janie's phone rang as they made their way down the sidewalk.

She stopped to dig it out of her bag. "Sorry. We can keep walking as long as you can guide me. It's a little distracting to use my cane and talk on the phone."

Boyd placed a hand on her arm. "Sneaky way to get me to touch you."

Janie shook her head and answered the phone, immediately greeted by Kiki's excited voice.

"Hey, just wanted you to know that since you blew off coming home with me this weekend, I'm not going to tell you about the date I had last night." Kiki had been her best friend since the third grade, when Kiki had put a boy in his place for teasing Janie about using a specially lighted magnifying device to read large-print books. Not that Janie needed protecting. Even back then she'd known some people were just too self-centered to care about other people's lives. Not Kiki, though. As soon as she'd finished with the bully, she'd wanted to know everything about Janie's eye condition: Cone-Rod Dystrophy, a degenerative eye disease. The disease had varying degrees of severity, from mild to complete loss of vision. So far Janie was lucky. She still had some light perception. If there were very bright lights, large planes of bright colors, or if the contrast was just right, and she looked out of her peripheral vision and got up super close, she could still sometimes make out shapes.

"Was it your headboard I heard banging the wall at three in the morning?" She loved teasing Kiki about her sexual proclivities.

"I wish. Anyway, when I come back, we're having a girls' night for sure," Kiki said. "I need to touch up your roots, so we'll do margaritas and hair dye. A great combination." Ever since they were little, Kiki had insisted on helping Janie with all things girly, which included not only hair and makeup, but also clothing and manicures and anything else Kiki put into the *girls must do* category. Kiki was the only person who had ever *not* been afraid to jump into those personal aspects of Janie's life, and Janie loved her even more for it because Kiki accepted and pushed and made sure that Janie missed out on nothing.

"Last time we did drinks and dye you blonded me out, which is why I *have* roots."

"You're a hot blonde," Kiki said.

"You also said I was a hot brunette. I've got to run. Have fun." She ended the call.

Boyd chuckled and said, "You'd be hot no matter what color your hair was. Careful stepping off the curb."

Janie was used to his flirty comments and knew better than to take them seriously. He doled them out in the office like she dotted her i's and crossed her t's, adding a touch of humor to their otherwise stoic workplace.

"Curb, careful," he said as she stepped back onto the sidewalk.

She liked that he knew enough to warn her to the change in her footing. Not everyone did, which was why she continued to use her cane, especially if guided by someone she didn't know very well. She knew they were nearing the subway and shifted her bag to her other shoulder, dropping her phone in the process.

"I've got it." Boyd stopped to pick it up. "So, you're really going to try to write that novel?"

"Darn right I am." She resituated her cane and bag, and they continued walking.

"You sure you want to take the subway?" Boyd asked again. "I'll even pay for a cab if you're worried about the money."

"It's not the money. It's the freakishly fast driving and then slamming on the brakes thing that New York cabbies do. I'm fine, really. Have fun on your date. I'll see you the next time you're at TEC."

Janie made her way down the steps to the subway, mentally playing with ideas for her romance story. At twenty-seven, she had only a few sexual experiences to draw from, although they'd never fully lived up to the sexual exploits of the heroes and heroines in the novels she'd read. She also knew absolutely nothing about sci-fi, or for that matter, kinky sex, other than what she'd read about. She might not have experience, but she was a master at research.

The subway platform was eerily quiet. She tried to focus on the bet instead of the fact that every *tap* of her cane echoed in what she assumed was an empty station. She'd boarded trains alone plenty of times, but as much as other people feared strangers, in the subway, she relied on auditory cues from them. Tingles of anxiety prickled through her chest as the heels of her shoes echoed chillingly.

She tapped her way to the bumpy strip along the edge of the platform, which was designed to let people who were visually impaired know they were nearing the edge. Her bag slid down her arm. She twisted sideways, trying to catch it. Her toe caught on a bump, sending her sprawling forward. In the space of a breath, her cane dropped through the air, and suddenly she was falling. Fear gripped her seconds before she landed on her right side with a painful *thud*. She sucked in air as pain spiraled through her. Something sharp dug into her cheek. *Rocks?* The pungent smell of grease and gasoline permeated the cold, dank air, and she realized she'd fallen off the platform.

Her heart thundered in her chest, battling with the blood rushing through her ears as she frantically searched for her cane, listening for a train. Tears streamed from her eyes as fear consumed her. *Get up. Get away from the tracks. Move. Move. Move.* Finding her cane, she clutched it to her aching chest and pushed up to her knees. A blood-curdling pain shot through her ankle. Fighting light-headedness, she clenched her teeth together and forced herself upright, bending her right knee to keep from putting pressure on her ankle. She gripped the cold, hard edge of the platform and tried to pull herself up.

"Help!" Her voice echoed in the empty station, magnifying her fear.

Her ankle rolled on the rocks, sending her tumbling down to the ground again. *Get up. Get up.* Pushing past the pain, she rose again, determined to get to safety. Her fingers moved over the platform's bumpy ridges that had tripped her up. Her fingertips grazed the smoother concrete just beyond. She used her left, uninjured foot for leverage as she pulled, pushed, and climbed her way onto the platform. Vibrations rumbled beneath her, and the sound of the train squealed in the distance. On the platform, she rolled onto her back, gasping for air and clutching her cane to her chest. The concrete vibrated as the train approached. Sobs wrenched from her lungs, and miraculously, she felt herself smile, because *goddamn it*, she wasn't going to get run over by the stupid train.

To continue reading, buy **TOUCHED BY LOVE**

STRAWBERRY SPICE JAM RECIPE

1 cup water

3 habanero peppers

1 1.75-oz package powdered pectin

1 teaspoon lemon juice

1 750-ml bottle of strawberry wine

5 1/2 cups sugar

Add 1 cup of water to a large saucepan and bring to a boil. Cut the tops of the habanero peppers, leaving them whole, and add them to the boiling water. Stir in the powdered pectin and lemon juice and bring to a boil. Add the wine and return to a boil. Slowly add the sugar one cup at a time while stirring (stainless-steel spoon works best). Bring to a boil for one minute. If you lift your spoon up and let the liquid drip, you should see it thicken as it drips. Remove the habaneros, along with any seeds, from the jelly. Remove any foam from the surface and add to the jars.

This recipe makes seven to eight 8-ounce jars of jelly.

Available at www.AlsBackwoodsBerrie.com, Amazon, and other retailers.

MORE BOOKS BY MELISSA FOSTER

<u>**LOVE IN BLOOM SERIES**</u>

SNOW SISTERS

Sisters in Love

Sisters in Bloom

Sisters in White

THE BRADENS at Weston

Lovers at Heart, Reimagined

Destined for Love

Friendship on Fire

Sea of Love

Bursting with Love

Hearts at Play

THE BRADENS at Trusty

Taken by Love

Fated for Love

Romancing My Love

Flirting with Love

Dreaming of Love

Crashing into Love

THE BRADENS at Peaceful Harbor

Healed by Love

Surrender My Love

River of Love

Crushing on Love

Whisper of Love
Thrill of Love

THE BRADENS & MONTGOMERYS at Pleasant Hill – Oak Falls

Embracing Her Heart
Anything For Love
Trails of Love
Wild, Crazy Hearts
Making You Mine
Searching For Love

THE BRADEN NOVELLAS

Promise My Love
Our New Love
Daring Her Love
Story of Love
Love at Last
A Very Braden Christmas

THE REMINGTONS

Game of Love
Stroke of Love
Flames of Love
Slope of Love
Read, Write, Love
Touched by Love

SEASIDE SUMMERS

Seaside Dreams

Seaside Hearts

Seaside Sunsets

Seaside Secrets

Seaside Nights

Seaside Embrace

Seaside Lovers

Seaside Whispers

Seaside Serenade

BAYSIDE SUMMERS

Bayside Desires

Bayside Passions

Bayside Heat

Bayside Escape

Bayside Romance

Bayside Fantasies

THE RYDERS

Seized by Love

Claimed by Love

Chased by Love

Rescued by Love

Swept Into Love

THE WHISKEYS: DARK KNIGHTS AT PEACEFUL HARBOR
Tru Blue
Truly, Madly, Whiskey
Driving Whiskey Wild
Wicked Whiskey Love
Mad About Moon
Taming My Whiskey
The Gritty Truth

SUGAR LAKE
The Real Thing
Only for You
Love Like Ours
Finding My Girl

HARMONY POINTE
Call Her Mine
This is Love
She Loves Me

THE WICKEDS: DARK KNIGHTS AT BAYSIDE
A Little Bit Wicked
Wicked Aftermath

WILD BOYS AFTER DARK (Billionaires After Dark)
Logan
Heath
Jackson
Cooper

BAD BOYS AFTER DARK (Billionaires After Dark)
Mick
Dylan
Carson
Brett

<u>HARBORSIDE NIGHTS SERIES</u>
Includes characters from the Love in Bloom series
Catching Cassidy
Discovering Delilah
Tempting Tristan

More Books by Melissa
Chasing Amanda (mystery/suspense)
Come Back to Me (mystery/suspense)
Have No Shame (historical fiction/romance)
Love, Lies & Mystery (3-book bundle)
Megan's Way (literary fiction)
Traces of Kara (psychological thriller)
Where Petals Fall (suspense)

ACKNOWLEDGMENTS

One of my greatest joys is writing about Cape Cod, and when I told my street team that the Seaside Summers series might end after Matt Lacroux's book, I had to run into a closet and hide from the backlash. So, my dear readers, you have my awesome street team to thank for our next Seaside Summers spinoff, Bayside Boys. (That is a working series title and may change.) There's nothing more exciting for me than hearing from my fans and knowing you love my stories as much as I enjoy writing them. Please keep your emails and your posts on social media coming. If you haven't joined my street team, please do! We have loads of fun, chat about books, and members get special sneak peeks of upcoming publications. www.facebook.com/groups/MelissaFosterFans

A special thank-you goes to Nina Lane, Elise Sax, and Kathie Shoop for our brainstorming sessions.

My work shines because my editorial team is incredibly talented. Thank you, Kristen, Penina, Jenna, Juliette, Marlene, and Lynn, for all you do for me and for our readers.

And to my family, thank you for your endless love and support.

www.MelissaFoster.com

Melissa Foster is the *New York Times*, *Wall Street Journal*, and *USA Today* bestselling and award-winning author of more than 100 novels. Her books have been recommended by *USA Today*'s book blog, *Hagerstown* magazine, *The Patriot*, and several other print venues.

Melissa enjoys discussing her books with book clubs and reader groups and welcomes an invitation to your event. Melissa's books are available through most online retailers in paperback, digital, and audio formats.

Shop Melissa's store for exclusive discounts, bundles, and more. shop.melissafoster.com

Melissa also writes sweet romance under the pen name Addison Cole.